NATION OF THE SUN

By HR Moore

Titles by HR Moore:

The Relic Trilogy:
Queen of Empire
Temple of Sand
Court of Crystal

In the Gleaming Light

The Ancient Souls Series:
Nation of the Sun

http://www.hrmoore.com

PART 1

It's a touch, the gentlest of touches. Always. The thing that finally wakes me, reminds me, pulls down the veil so I can remember. It's the strangest thing, remembering. Past lives, past feuds, past loves, past me. It's double edged. I come alive at the knowledge, the power, the secrets.

But the other part, the part that knows of sacrifice, danger, betrayal, would claw and fight and kill its way back to the blissful, ignorant darkness. It would lie peacefully in the restorative slumber of oblivion, covering its eyes, ears, nose, mouth, soul. It would hide, and it would be right to do so.

Chapter 1

Raina had always been stubborn. Willful. Downright annoying. Not that any of that had stopped him from loving her. Like that word, love, bandied around so freely in these modern times, could even begin to convey the deep history that beat between them. Like a slinky stretched thin, just when he thought it would snap, a pulse would come barreling down the line, smashing into him, battering his heart.

How he longed for that painful euphoria now, the link between them stretched toward breaking. It had been stretching for a hundred years, and Caspar was terrified that this time it would finally snap, each side hurtling away from the other.

Damn her to hell.

Caspar had been trying to find her for almost all of the three decades he'd spent in this body. He, unlike Raina, remembered everything, almost as soon as he was born; that was just the kind of demon he was. It had made for some awkward moments in past lives, and he'd been the subject of several more exorcisms than any child should have to endure. He'd learned to keep his mouth shut after the first few reincarnations, and then, after four or five lives, he'd finally been found by a hunter. At last, it had all made sense.

Caspar walked down a grey London street, the scent of summer rain in the air, flicking his fingers nervously as he approached a Chelsea townhouse. Nervousness was an estranged emotion, and he relished it; it reminded him he was alive.

He strode up the steps to the front door, ringing the bell encircled in an elaborate metal sconce. People didn't worry about those kinds of details any longer. It was all small, ugly, white plastic boxes with clicky buttons and gaudy lights. His fingers lingered, drawing strength from the solid, cool metal.

The door swung open and a short, middle-aged woman with a blond bob and kind eyes smiled up at him. A trickle of guilt pooled in his gut.

'Can I help you?' she asked, her English accent impeccable.

'Yes, please,' replied Caspar, in a matching tone. 'If it's not too much trouble, I'd like to request a few moments with the bride.'

'Are you a friend?' she asked, her face brightening at the prospect, body language opening.

'Ah, not exactly … but I need to speak with her about an ongoing investigation.' Caspar pulled out his government ID and held it up. 'There's absolutely nothing to worry about, and I do apologize for the terrible timing, but I'm afraid I need to speak with her quite urgently.'

The woman faltered, not sure what to do. 'I … um … come in. You can wait in the sitting room.'

She showed him into a room where a pair of comfortable looking cream sofas faced each other over a glass coffee table.

'I'll be back in a moment,' she said.

She walked through the arch that connected the sitting room to an office, which led to a dining area around the corner. Caspar stepped forward, following her progress as she approached the loud rehearsal dinner in full swing.

She stopped as the man at the head of the table stood, to raucous, approving cheers, taking the hand of the woman to his right.

Caspar tried to get a look at her, but the man's bulk was in the way. He caught a glimpse of her slender, tanned arm, the curve of her shoulder, her long, silky dark hair, as the man turned to address the table.

Caspar's pulse spiked, his mouth went dry, every sense came alive. He couldn't hear the words, but the man was making a toast, looking lovingly down at his bride. *Not his bride*, Caspar's mind whispered. *Mine.*

Cheering erupted from the table as the man pulled the woman to her feet and drew her to him, the flowing ivory silk of her dress rippling around her. The man lowered his lips to hers and jealousy thrashed across Caspar's insides. The man pulled back, shifting, and Caspar got his first proper view.

The look on her face was a physical punch in his gut. Caspar staggered back a pace, his breathing labored. The bride looked adoringly up at her future husband, her whole being focused on him as she smiled, caressing his cheek with long, alluring fingers. Her diamond engagement ring glinted as it caught the light.

The man lowered his forehead to hers and kissed her again, catcalls and whistles filling the air. She pulled back, the man dropping his hand to her waist, then to her backside when she moved to sit down.

Caspar had to look away, lest he forget to keep the leash attached to his temper.

The woman who'd let Caspar in waited for the table's attention to shift away before she approached the bride, whispering in her ear. The bride stood, kissed

6

her fiancé's cheek, then sauntered towards the sitting room.

Caspar sat on the back of a sofa, adopting a casual, nonchalant air, glad he'd worn an expensive suit. It was one of the things that still mystified him, even after all this time, that clothes could offer such powerful fortification.

She came alone, her long, dark, perfectly blown-out hair wafting around her face, earrings swaying in time with her steps. Her cream dress eddied around her, leaving little of her slim, tanned legs to the imagination. Indeed, there was little that the thin silk didn't show off.

She held out her hand, confusion written across her features. Caspar pushed himself to his feet, a step too close for comfort, ensuring she could smell his cologne. He took her hand, looking into her eyes.

She faltered before meeting his gaze, holding it with ancient intensity. Caspar searched for the telltale signs, sure now she was who he wanted her to be, hoping for some trace of awakening.

She shook his hand, their eyes still locked. She seemed to be searching him too, looking into his very soul. Caspar shuddered. Her eyes told him she was sleeping, but she seemed so much like herself.

'Sol uigiliarum,' he said, casually, as though saying *the sun awakes* in Latin were an everyday occurrence.

'Et deditionem astra,' she immediately replied. *And the stars surrender.*

Caspar's composure cracked. He almost grabbed her hands, almost pulled them to his lips, almost embraced her. Confusion spread across her face and Caspar faltered.

'What's this about?' she asked, taking a step back, breaking their eye contact. She walked to the fireplace, pausing before turning back to face him. 'Penny said it was urgent?'

Caspar pulled himself together: caution was the best approach. 'Miss Conti, I work for the government, and we're in need of your help.'

She laughed. 'I'm a food critic! What could the government possibly want from me?' She perched on the padded fire surround, appraising every inch of him.

'All I can tell you is that it's a matter of national security.'

She gave him a disbelieving look. 'I'd love to assist, but I'm getting married tomorrow and have a lot to do.'

'You know it's supposed to rain tomorrow?' said Caspar.

'Rain on your wedding day's lucky.'

'Is it? My wife was always adamant of the opposite.'

Did her eyes flash?

'Is that everything?' she said, but didn't stand. Her gaze didn't leave him for a second.

'The situation is urgent. I can compel you to come, if that's required, but I'd really rather not.'

'After the wedding, Dean and I are spending two weeks at Lake Como. I'll be available to help when I return. I can't see how anything relating to high-end restaurants could be so time sensitive.'

'Miss Conti, please don't make me arrest you.'

Amari pushed to her feet. 'Why me? There are plenty of food critics … how did you even find me?'

Caspar's heart gave a sharp thud. Was she toying with him? *How did you find me?*

'You're not so hard to track down,' he said, studying her face for any hint of what he hoped.

'Everything okay in here, Amari?' The deep, assured, American voice of Amari's fiancé cut through the air as he strolled into the room, crystal tumbler in hand.

Amari walked to her fiancé, his arm settling around her.

'This is Dean Sanderson,' she said, reaching up to peck him on the lips. 'He's one of America's top human rights lawyers. If you're planning to try and force me go with you, I suggest you speak to him.'

Caspar huffed out a frustrated breath, pulled out his phone, and took a step towards them. He snapped a photo of Amari before she could object. 'Have it your way,' he said, leaving a business card on a table as he left. 'I'll be in touch.'

The sound of laughter accompanied his retreat, slithering up his spine like a serpent. The name Amari suited her, but he would get Raina back, if it was the last thing he did.

Chapter 2

Caspar returned to the City of London—to Cloister Cottage—the place he and his fellow demons had called home for hundreds of years. He slipped between two modern monstrosities, turning onto a small, cobbled side street, then ducked through an ancient wooden door into the church-like hall that felt like home.

Talli, a short, wispy, blonde-haired White woman (in this life, anyway), was brewing a herbal concoction in something that looked a lot like a cauldron. She was in the middle of the space, muttering ancient words, wafting steam towards her.

Four copper vessels sat at the four compass points, each a few paces from the cauldron. They contained the elements: earth, air, fire, and water, each playing its part in the ceremony.

Caspar was in such a dark mood he was tempted to step right into the sacred space. No doubt Talli had painstakingly prepared the area, cutting the air, smudging with sage, and she'd probably salted too. But before he'd fully decided not to, a hand closed around his upper arm.

'Don't you dare,' whispered Christa, a tall Black woman with a curly pixie cut.

Christa had only recently awakened, and Caspar was still getting used to her as a woman. Christa was one of the rare demons who regularly switched sexes between lives.

'Talli's been at this all day. She's almost finished, and if you ruin it now, you'll spoil everyone's night.'

Christa held a small bundle of sage into the fire that danced in the copper bowl, blew out the flames, then waved the resulting smoke over both Caspar and herself. 'Watch if you must, but don't you dare wreck this.'

Christa smudged herself some more, handed the herbs to Caspar, then stepped into the circle. Talli had finished the brew, ready to perform the cleansing ritual ahead of Midsummer.

Talli and Christa stood side by side, fire to their backs, and curtsied to the cauldron. They turned as one to face each other and curtsied again. Then they linked hands, stepping in unison to close the space between them, bringing their lips together, looking ancient in their floor-length white tunics and leaf headbands.

Caspar walked away. There was no telling how far they'd take this stage of the ritual, and the last thing he needed was to be around an ecstatically happy, recently reunited couple, when he felt like punching something.

Caspar slipped out of the hall into the room next door. It too was old and big, but it was also cozy, housing the kitchen and dining area. It had an Aga oven, an inglenook fireplace, and a banquet table. Bunches of dried herbs hung from a drying rack above a granite-topped island, and endless jars of preserved fruits and vegetables, spices and condiments adorned the many open shelves. Two large, shaggy dogs curled up in front of the oven.

Next to the inglenook stood an old wooden door that led to the rest of the building. At the other end, by the Aga, was a glass-paneled door and row of windows, leading out into a sunroom filled with plants. It had the feel of a kitchen from times gone by, but meticulously updated with all the necessities of modern life. The coffee machine was particularly impressive.

An old White woman with short, white hair and arthritis-damaged hands stood at the Aga, waiting for the kettle to boil. She absently petted one of the dogs, looking up when Caspar entered.

'Don't tell me,' she said, holding up a hand. 'You screwed it up.'

'I need you to look at this photo,' said Caspar, not rising to her bait. 'I think she might already be awake … some of the things she said …'

'Unlikely, Caspar, but I'll take a look,' she said, accepting his phone.

She zoomed in, carefully studying Amari's green eyes. 'It's hard to tell for certain—the quality's bad—but it looks to me as though she's still asleep.'

'But, her eyes …'

'I know she's got some specks of metal, but that's normal for demons once they reach a certain vintage. And Raina's very old.'

'But she mocked me, joked about how hard it had been to find her.'

'Coincidence?'

'She's marrying a human rights lawyer.'

Rose laughed. 'Your government trick didn't work then?'

'Would I be standing here alone if it had?'

'Going to try and stop the wedding?'

'It's tomorrow.'

Rose laughed again. It was almost a cackle.

'What's happening tomorrow?' asked a boisterous voice from behind them.

Two men entered the room, lowering themselves into seats at the table.

'Ah, the captains of industry,' said Caspar. 'Just who we need.'

'Hey, we're doing a valuable job, bankrolling your lifestyle,' said Jon, the younger of the two well-dressed men, with a smirk. He was well-built, and looked like a stereotypical city trader with his slicked-back sandy blond hair.

'Firstly,' said Caspar, 'don't flatter yourself. We have enough wealth to last us until well into the next millennium, mostly because of my and Raina's previous incarnations.'

'Come on,' laughed Elliot, a tall, broad man in his forties, grey peppering his dark hair. 'We all know it was Raina alone who made us rich.'

Caspar shot him a dirty look. 'And secondly, you're young; you'll care less about money in time.'

'What's got into Granddad?' asked Jon, sending Rose a meaningful look.

'He found Raina,' said Rose. 'She threw him out on his ear. She's marrying a high-flying human rights lawyer in the morning.'

'Ouch,' said Jon. 'Going to stop it?'

'I was just asking,' said Rose, 'before you two interrupted.'

'Well?' said Jon, looking expectantly at Caspar. 'What've you got up your sleeve this time?'

Caspar took a deep breath. 'I don't know ... I'm not sure I should meddle in her wedding.'

'What? After the last time went so well?' Jon joked.

'The last three times,' corrected Elliot.

'Yes, thank you; the last three times could have gone better.'

This was an understatement. Raina had a terrible habit of marrying other people before she awoke.

Caspar had staged several interventions during their many previous lives. None had gone well.

'I'm going to try a new approach.'

'Which is?' asked Talli, entering the room with Christa, their faces red, hair tousled.

Caspar went to the stove and removed the now-whistling kettle, shooing Rose and the dogs out of the way. He threw tea bags into an enormous, ugly, industrial-looking silver tea pot and sloshed the water on top.

'Scones?' asked Christa, looking expectantly at Elliot.

'In the tin. Made a new batch this morning,' he said.

'Get the nice jam,' said Rose, to no one in particular, 'and there's clotted cream in the fridge.'

Jon jumped to obey. Christa got the scones, Talli got plates and cutlery, Elliot got mugs and milk. Rose watched, then joined them, taking her place at the head of the table.

'The plan?' asked Talli, slathering cream on her scone.

'I didn't say I had a plan,' said Caspar. 'I just know I need to do it differently to all the times before.'

'But she woke up that one time, when you rode your horse into the church,' said Christa. 'Maybe that would work again …'

'The part after the waking didn't go so well,' said Jon.

'She always was a stubborn one,' said Rose. 'Difficult to wake up.'

'Obstinate,' chipped in Talli.

'Knows how to hold a grudge,' added Jon.

'Maybe someone else should wake her this time,' said Christa. 'It's better when she likes Caspar.'

'She won't like me, even if I'm not the one to wake her,' said Caspar. 'She still hates me.'

'Can't really blame her,' said Jon.

Caspar scowled.

'I'm just saying, it was bad … maybe *I* could be her shoulder to cry on …'

Caspar balled his fists. He hadn't lost his temper in over a hundred years, but given this was his third miserable incarnation in a row, he was beginning to fray around the edges.

Rose put her hand on Caspar's arm. 'Maybe Jon's onto something,' she said. 'Raina wants to be angry with you. She wants to punish you, and the only way she can do that is if she's near you.

'Let one of the others try to wake her this time. Stay away for a while. Let us focus her on more important things, then come back, move slowly, and regain her trust.'

Caspar didn't like it, but he knew they were right… Lifetimes had taught him if you were going to capitulate, you might as well do it early. 'Fine,' he said, 'but don't ruin her wedding. Let her have her honeymoon, and start at Midsummer.'

'Ooh, let's try and wake her at Midsummer,' said Talli. 'It would be auspicious.'

'You'll have to fly to Lake Como and tail her,' said Caspar.

'I've had worse assignments,' said Talli, flashing a smile. 'And Christa can come too.'

'Subtle,' said Jon.

'Let her have her honeymoon,' said Caspar, 'and after that, do whatever's required.'

Chapter 3

Amari woke in a decadent yet gloomy hotel room; stylish décor could only go so far in combating dreary weather. She pushed back the covers and padded across the plush carpet to one of three long windows. She drew the curtains and surveyed the rain-splattered street below.

It was still early, but she hadn't been able to sleep. Something about Mr. Caspar Jackson was nagging at her. He'd felt ... familiar in some way, like déjà vu. Some primal part of her had wanted to claim him as her own, had told her to kiss him, grab handfuls of his hair, rip off his clothes ...

She'd thought her feelings could be explained by the emotion of the wedding and the alcohol from dinner, but even now—alcohol long gone—she couldn't shake the feeling that his arms would feel like home. Something deep in her mind was firmly fixed on the opinion.

He wasn't even her usual type. He was six foot, the same height she'd been in her heels, with dark skin and brown eyes. He was muscular, but not stacked. She liked it when a man could make her feel small, light, dainty; the way Dean made her feel. Caspar was attractive—there was no disputing that—but what on earth was causing this level of lust?

The way he'd held her gaze, searched deep within her, looked into her soul. Even thinking about it made her hair stand on end. And his words. Were they Latin? She hadn't realized she knew the response to any Latin phrase … and his comment about the weather. It was irrational, but he was right, the raindrops were like little missiles sent to blow up her wedding. It made her consider that the universe didn't want her to marry Dean …

She was crazy, she knew this. Dean was perfect. They were perfect together. He made her laugh, his mind like a razor, always parrying with hers. His family were wonderful, their parents all played tennis together, and he was a wildly successful lawyer. She loved him. She really did.

Probably just wedding day nerves.

But Caspar … Caspar had made her feel the way old things made her feel. Comfortable. Happy. Safe. Right. Like he could literally chase away the wrongness that had always plagued her …

A loud knock sounded through the room. She took a breath. *It's just wedding day nerves,* she told herself forcefully, picking up her silk satin dressing gown and throwing it over her negligee. She tied it tightly, then opened the door.

'Hi! I'm Talli,' said a stranger, forcing Amari to step out of the way as she wheeled a suitcase across the threshold. 'And this is Christa.'

'How are we feeling?' asked Christa, with excessive hand movements. She swept into the room behind Talli.

'I … uh … think you might have the wrong room,' said Amari, although the déjà vu was back, this time so strong it made her woozy.

'Maria, your hairdresser, and Sandy, your makeup artist, had a last-minute celebrity *emergency*,' said Christa. 'But don't worry, we're even more sought after than they are.'

'True,' said Talli, opening her case and placing suspicious bottle after suspicious bottle onto the dining table. 'We won't even work with celebrities anymore.'

'They're such divas,' said Christa.

'And they always want you to drop everything and fly around the world at a moment's notice,' added Talli. 'I'm too old for that bullshit.'

'You don't look a day over thirty,' said Amari, her mind somehow deciding this was the most important place to start.

'Thank you, but I'm much older than that. It's these products; they keep me young.'

'Speaking of which,' said Christa, pulling a few more bottles from Talli's bag and shuffling Amari towards the bathroom, 'we need to get going if you want to be ready in time.'

Talli and Christa weren't trying to stop the wedding, per se. They were merely encouraging Raina to the surface. And to do so, they left no stone unturned, from scented candles in the bathroom, to homemade hair products that smelled of rosemary, because that was Raina's favorite herb.

They massaged her hands and feet, stimulating all the right spots. They did her hair as she'd had it for two of her previous weddings; Amari had protested a little at this, but had quieted down the minute she saw the results in the mirror. They applied the perfume they'd made for her. They even had her eat an oat and nut mix she'd once loved for breakfast, accompanied by a special blend of Lapsang Souchong and Earl Grey tea.

For their final touch, Talli retrieved an ornate metal hair pin from her bag and gave it to Amari. It had belonged to Raina in a previous life, but they told her it was just something old for luck. Talli placed it near the front, so Amari would be able to see it every time she checked her reflection in the mirror.

Talli and Christa stood back and admired their handiwork, smiling wistfully at their creation. They looked meaningfully at each other, wishing the marriage was to Caspar, but congratulating themselves nonetheless.

Amari's sense of rightness, belonging, and familiarity gained in strength as the two women worked. Amari felt comfortable, almost like she knew them. She supposed it was just … like that with some people. She'd almost cried when they'd produced the pin. She had no idea what came over her, whether it was pre-wedding nerves, or that she loved old things, or that it too felt oddly familiar.

By the time her mother, Grace, arrived, her face worryingly grave, Talli and Christa were preparing to leave.

'You look beautiful. Truly beautiful,' said Grace, staring at Amari's face.

'Um, thanks?' said Amari, taking a step back and ushering her mother into the room. 'Is everything okay?'

'Yes,' said Grace. 'Although, there's been a development with Dean's latest case, and I'm afraid you're not going to like it.'

'Oh God,' said Amari. She'd known something was going to happen. Between the rain, her stylists not being able to make it, and the *off* feeling … it was like the universe didn't want her to get married today.

'It's not that bad,' said her mother, guiding Amari to a chair. 'You'll just have to delay your honeymoon for a few weeks. Dean has to fly back to the States to deal with something that can't wait.'

Yep, the universe hated her. 'What am I supposed to do? Sit around and wait for his return?'

Grace looked flustered. 'It's not like *that*. I suppose you could go to the states with him. Or you could fly to Lake Como as planned, and take a longer holiday. That would be nice,' she said, searching desperately for a silver lining.

Not likely. Holidaying among loved-up honeymooners while her husband was absent didn't sound like much fun to Amari. She caught sight of the card sitting on her bedside table.

'It's fine. If Dean's going to spend our honeymoon working, then so am I. Mum, I'll see you down in your room. Are the bridesmaids there?'

Grace nodded, but looked as though she might protest.

'I'll only be a minute. Thank you Talli, Christa, you've done a great job. I love it.'

Talli and Christa shared a beaming smile, spritzed Amari one more time, then practically skipped from the room.

Caspar waited in the hotel's lobby. The concierge—noting his agitated body language—glanced nervously at him a few times a minute. He paced back and forth, balling and unballing his fists, furious that his friends had conspired to ruin Amari's wedding day, when he'd specifically told them not to.

It was Jon who'd let it slip, pouring some of the surplus oat and fruit mix Talli had made into a bowl, and asking Elliot if he thought some boring old oats could wake her. Caspar had entered the kitchen at that moment, and his blood had run cold.

'Oops,' Jon had said, flippant as ever.

Elliot had rolled his eyes. 'It's not what you think.'

But Caspar hadn't stuck around to hear any more. He'd raced to the hotel, trying desperately to come up with a plan. But he couldn't think of anything that wouldn't make him look like a stalker. So instead, he hovered in the entrance, waiting for inspiration to strike.

Talli and Christa sauntered across the wide expanse of the lobby, whispering excitedly like schoolgirls.

'What the hell are you two playing at?' he hissed, as they capered down the steps towards the door.

He pulled them outside, because the concierge's fingers were hovering over the phone, probably seconds away from calling security. He dragged them down the steps on the outside and away from the entrance. The ground was littered with rose petals, presumably from the arrangements for the wedding.

'You can thank us later,' said Christa.

'What did you do?' said Caspar.

'Her hair and make-up,' said Talli.

'We did an excellent job,' added Christa, as Talli pulled out an oddly shaped blue glass bottle and spritzed Caspar.

'What? Oh my Gods,' he said, closing his eyes against the memory.

'Made especially for you for wedding number four, if I correctly recall,' said Talli.

'What did you use on Amari?' he asked.

'You'll just have to wait and see,' sang Christa. 'As I said, you can thank us later.'

'Did she wake up?' he asked, desperation in his tone.

Talli put her hand on his arm, her demeanor suddenly calm, compassionate. 'Not yet, but her fiancé postponed the honeymoon, because he has to go back to the States.'

'I'd expect a call any minute,' said Christa, smiling conspiratorially. 'Good luck!'

'Wait, what?' Caspar's phone vibrated in his pocket. He snatched it up. 'Hello?'

Chapter 4

Amari hung up her phone, then knocked on the door of her mother's room. She braced herself for the frantic chatter emanating from the other side. The door swung open, and her future mother-in-law's face crumpled. 'You look so beautiful,' she said, trying to hold back tears.

Amari entered the room and took in the scene. Her cousin, Leila, lounged back on the elaborate four-poster bed, sipping a glass of champagne, her hair and makeup already done. Amari and Dean's mothers were being beautified by hairdressers and makeup artists near the windows. Dean's mum returned to her seat, the makeup artist chastising her over the tears. Dean's teenaged sister, Jade, sat in a chair near the fireplace, earbud in, typing frantically on her phone. She barely even looked up as Amari entered.

'You look nice,' said Jade, her eyes already back on the screen.

A sense of wrongness crept through Amari's veins.

'You okay?' asked her cousin, getting up and handing Amari a glass of champagne. She was an inch shorter than Amari, with dazzling, naturally blonde hair and blue eyes. 'Last-minute nerves?'

Heads swung to look at her, and even Jade flicked her eyes up for a second.

'No, of course not,' she lied.

Everything about today felt wrong. Only the call with Caspar, and the hair and make-up artists, had felt anything other.

'Just disappointed about the honeymoon.'

'I know, total nightmare,' said Leila, topping up her glass. 'At least he's starting as he means to go on.'

'Hey! Don't slag off my brother,' said Jade, her angry grey eyes trained on Leila.

Leila dismissed her. 'Seriously though, Amari. This is going to be your life; his work will always come first.'

'It's not like that,' said Amari, quietly, not wanting to have this conversation at all, but especially not in front of Dean's mother and sister.

A knock on the door saved her, and Amari rushed to open it. 'Callie!' said Amari, wrapping her arms around her neighbor's five-year-old granddaughter.

'I'll see you downstairs,' said Callie's grandmother. 'Good luck darling, and do exactly what you're told. Okay?'

She hugged Callie and the girl promised to be good.

Amari felt a strange affinity to Callie. It was the weirdest thing. She usually found kids repulsive, avoiding them at all costs, but Callie was different. She had this soothing quality.

'You look wonderful,' said Amari, turning the girl in a circle under her arm.

Callie giggled, delighted. 'You look pretty,' she said, 'but you need to put your dress on.'

Amari laughed, clapping her hands together. 'My goodness, you're right! I'm so glad you're here! I knew something was missing.'

Amari took a step towards the closet where her dress was hanging, but Callie stopped her with a hand on her arm. 'What's that?' Callie asked, pointing to Amari's hair.

'My hair?' said Amari, confused.

'The thing in your hair.'

'Oh!' said Amari, remembering the old pin. 'That was a gift from two very kind ladies. They said it was something old for luck.'

Jade's eyes flicked up from her phone, scrutinizing Amari's hair.

'Don't worry,' Leila said to Jade, 'it's not more exciting than Instagram.'

'TikTok,' said Jade, her eyes lingering on Amari's updo.

'I love it,' said Callie, pulling Amari down so she could get a better look. 'It's so pretty.'

'You can have it after the wedding,' said Amari, worried Callie would try and pull it out right then and there.

Callie's face lit up and she giggled again. 'Thank you.'

'You're welcome. Now, I should put my dress on, don't you think?'

Callie nodded her agreement, her face suddenly serious. 'You can't be late for your wedding.'

'Luckily, we don't have far to go,' said Amari. 'Why don't you take a seat by Jade while I put this on.'

Callie went still. 'No,' she said, with a forcefulness Amari hadn't seen from her before.

'Come sit by me,' said Leila, shuffling over on the bed.

Callie skipped to the bed and climbed up. She took Leila's hand, shot a wary glance at Jade, then watched closely as the stylists helped Amari into her dress.

After the finishing touches had been applied to everyone, and a photographer had held them hostage for an hour, finally it was time.

The mothers left first, each of them doing their best to keep their tears at bay. They gushed about how wonderful Amari looked, and how happy she and Dean were going to make each other.

Amari smiled, trying to will the smile into her eyes. She was glad when they departed.

Amari stood at the window, looking at the raindrops that jumped as they hit the puddles. *Not even a rainbow … or lightning. Lightning would provide dynamism at least …*

'Ready?' asked Leila, appearing at her shoulder.

'Ready,' said Amari, although she knew she didn't sound sure. 'You guys looks amazing,' she said, taking in her two bridesmaids and flower girl.

They wore dainty flower crowns and flowing white dresses, cinched in at the waist with gold ties. Leila was a voluptuous goddess, Jade a younger, ganglier version; a gazelle still learning how to use her body.

'So do you,' said Leila. 'There aren't many people who could pull that dress off, you know.'

Amari's dress was a halter-necked sheath of white silk. It was cut low at the back, skirting tight over her behind before billowing to the floor. It somehow showed off her waist, creating an alluring silhouette, yet didn't cling, allowing her to move freely.

'Kind of provocative if you ask me,' said Jade, who had sulkily put away her phone.

'Have you met Amari?' joked Leila.

'I think it's beautiful,' said Callie, taking Amari's hand.

A wave of warmth radiated through her. 'Thank you, Callie. You look beautiful too.'

'Come on, we're already fashionably late,' said Leila, shepherding them out of the room and into the ornate elevator. 'We don't want to give Dean a heart attack.'

Amari's heart sank. Something inside was screaming at her not to do this. It was like there was something just out of reach, something she didn't understand. Whatever it was, it was yelling at her to run away … to … oh my God … to find Caspar. She had to be insane. Legitimately, certifiably insane. She'd met Caspar one single time. They'd had two conversations; she didn't know anything about him.

She breathed deeply, shaking it off. *Evidently wedding day nerves are a real thing.*

'Amari? Are you okay?' asked Leila.

Amari looked up to find the doors open, the hotel's wide lobby stretching out before her. 'Uh, sorry, yes. Just taking a moment.'

Jade strode out into the lobby, huffing at the delay. Callie still had hold of Amari's hand.

'Amari, you know you don't have to do this, right?' said Leila, her voice low. 'If you're having second thoughts …'

'I'm not,' Amari snapped, her tone harsher than she'd intended. 'Wait, can you smell jasmine?'

Leila looked at her like she might be losing her mind.

'I'm fine, Leila, really, I just need a minute alone to … savor the moment.'

'Savor the moment?'

'To be present and in the moment and all that other bullshitty stuff people tell you to do on your wedding day. If I go in there now, I'm not going to remember a single thing. I need to get … centered, or something.'

Leila raised an eyebrow. 'Centered? Amari, are you okay? I mean, I know the wedding magazines go on about this stuff a lot, but it's not very *you*.'

'I'll be back before you know it,' said Amari. 'Callie, stay here with Leila. I'll only be a minute.'

'Okay,' said Callie, taking Leila's hand. 'Are we going to get cake soon?'

Amari laughed. 'Soon, I promise.'

After Talli and Christa departed, Caspar went back inside the hotel. He slipped past the concierge, walked boldly towards the function room, heard the loud buzz coming from rows of seated wedding guests, realized he was being an idiot, and turned around.

His feet navigated to a secluded corridor where he paced distractedly, trying to decide what to do. Should he go to Amari's room? Should he intercept her before entering the function room? If he did either of those things, what would he say? At least the smell of his cologne was comforting, although, knowing his luck, even if he did see her, it wouldn't do any good. Why did Raina have to be so God-damned stubborn?

Urgh, this was madness. She'd just called to say she could start work tomorrow; why was he here, jeopardizing that? *Because every fiber of your being wants to stop this, that's why.*

It would be too late now anyway; the wedding was almost certainly underway. Short of standing up in front of a hundred hostile guests and asking her to leave with him, there was nothing he could do.

He headed for the exit. But as he reached the corner of the corridor, a vison in white silk appeared, almost colliding with him. Caspar got his hands up just

28

in time, catching Amari's arms, absorbing the impact of their collision.

She looked into his eyes, almost level with him in her heels, saying, 'Sorry,' reflexively, before recognition turned to confusion, then rage.

'You? What are you doing here?'

'I … um … you … you look …' Her perfume hit him. '… you smell like spring on the French Riviera.'

She faltered at that. She breathed deeply, about to step back, but instead, her eyes fluttered closed. 'The English countryside in late summer,' she murmured.

'Maltings,' he said, his voice low. He loved Talli and Christa more than ever before.

Amari reached up and placed a hand on Caspar's chest. She grabbed hold, pulling herself a step closer, breathing him in.

Caspar's heart stopped, his whole being waiting, hoping, wishing, praying. He would have made a deal with any number of devils in that moment, if only she would awaken. He longed to wrap his arms around her, to look into her eyes and see the flecks of gold that would mean she'd returned to him. But he was too scared to move.

'Raina?' he whispered, moving his head so their cheeks touched.

She shivered, her other hand joining the first on his chest. She leaned into his touch, resting her cheek against his, a small hum escaping her lips as she exhaled.

'Raina?' It was a struggle to keep his voice even, to stop himself from grabbing her face between his hands and search her eyes.

'Susssh,' she murmured, nudging his cheek with hers, the move small and intimate.

He heeded her, saying nothing, doing nothing. He stood there, breathing her in, reveling in the feel of her against him, intoxicated by the scents of their past lives.

'Amari?' said a voice from behind them. A woman in a white dress approached, hands on her hips, clearly about to demand what the hell was going on.

Amari pulled back, lazily opening her eyes, looking into his. 'There's something about you,' she said quietly, so the woman couldn't hear.

Caspar couldn't find the words to respond. He'd failed to wake her. He was terrified of letting her walk away, terrified of her marrying another man, terrified of losing her. But there was nothing he could do, short of kidnapping her. He studied her eyes, trying to convey the depth of his feelings, trying to wake her by sheer force of will.

Later, he would wonder if he should have thrown caution to the wind, should have kissed her. Maybe he should have thrown himself onto his knees and chanted lost incantations, aiming for a place deep within her brain. Maybe he should have declared his eternal love for her. Maybe he should have whisked her up into his arms and made a run for the exit.

'Amari,' said the woman, not unkindly, 'people are starting to wonder where you are. You're fifteen minutes late. Are you … um … coming?'

Amari reached a hand up to Caspar's face and ran her thumb across his cheek. 'Thank you, Caspar. That was exactly what I needed.'

Chapter 5

People kept approaching her, saying the most inane things. Was she having a good time? Didn't the flower decorations look lovely? Wasn't the food delicious? Didn't they make the most wonderful couple?

Amari could barely remember a single moment. She'd floated into the wedding, down the aisle, through the vows. When Dean had kissed her, it had felt … foggy. There had been no special sensation or emotion at their joining. Indeed, the kiss had been less remarkable than any other they'd ever shared.

Dean had led her back up the aisle. He'd whispered in her ear about how much he wanted to slide his hands into the back of her dress. Usually, those words would have sent a thrill up her spine, set her on fire, especially with an audience watching their every move. But she was floating, numb. So she ignored him, barely registering where she was, who she talked to, the passage of time …

Dean hadn't noticed she wasn't really present, or at least, that's how it seemed. There had been shards of clarity throughout the day, moments of pure focus: the jasmine scent in the lobby, Callie dancing with Leila, the color of the roses in the flower arrangements, the music accompanying her down the aisle, the poem someone had placed in her order of service. But since she'd walked away from Caspar, she'd been hazy.

Her mind kept jumping back to him. The French Riviera. Maltings. His eyes. It was all so familiar, but like a memory just out of reach, she couldn't piece it all together. Did she know him? He'd said the word *Raina* twice. Was she supposed to know what that meant?

Dean came up beside her and took her hand in his, leaning in to kiss her cheek. 'Ready to go, Mrs. Sanderson?' His voice was gravelly, husky, and she finally felt the fog abate, burned away by a searing prickle of desire.

'Hmmm,' she sighed, relief flooding her. The haze was probably some weird wedding day thing. It was over. She raised a hand to Dean's muscular neck, pulling him down so she could kiss him. 'Lead the way.'

They slipped away, Dean hoisting her against the elevator's handrail even before the doors had fully closed. She pulled up her dress, wrapping her legs around him, his fingers climbing her inner thighs as their mouths devoured each other.

They pushed into the honeymoon suite, neither of them so much as glancing at their surroundings. Dean's hands roamed down her bare back, slipping inside the fabric covering her backside.

'I've been dreaming of doing this all day,' he rasped, pressing her body against his. 'As soon as I saw your back … Jesus, this dress.'

'I knew you'd like it,' she said, smiling into his mouth as his hands massaged her.

He moved them towards the bed, one slow, connected pace at a time, but her dress hampered his movements. He halted their progress, hands moving to the fastening at the base of her neck. He undid the clasp, letting the top section fall to her waist, her small, round breasts exposed. He growled, but she placed a hand on his chest before he could close the gap between them. She watched him closely as she slipped the dress to the floor.

He loosed a breath at the sight of her suspenders, skimpy underwear, and towering stiletto heels. His eyes went black and his hands roamed over her, tracing her silhouette, lingering on her nipples, rolling them in his fingers. He pushed her to the end of the bed, where a padded bench butted up against the mattress. He turned them as he sat, so she came down on top, straddling him.

She slid his jacket off his shoulders, down his arms, then took his face in her hands, kissing him, her body moving against him of its own accord.

His hands went to her hips, pressing her into him as she kissed and sucked her way down his neck, licking the hollow at the open neck of his shirt. He shivered, then rolled her over, pushing her back to rest on the bed. He bowed over her, sucking a nipple into his mouth.

She arched her back, pressing her head into the mattress, moaning at the unexpectedly intense pleasure.

Dean chuckled. 'Like that?' he said, moving to the other side. 'How about this?' He ran his fingers up her inner thigh.

She writhed underneath him, but then, as his fingers reached the apex of her thighs, a sudden, sharp, debilitating crack of pain shot through her head, a terrible sense of wrongness filling her.

Every cell in her body screamed at her to get away. She cried out, pushing Dean off as a million tiny daggers stabbed at her mind.

'Amari?' said Dean. 'What's wrong? What did I do?' He pulled back, removing his weight, helping her sit.

She doubled over, clutching her head.

'Amari, talk to me!'

Dean's tone was frantic, but in that moment, Amari didn't know how to speak, couldn't remember words, didn't know her mouth could form intelligible sounds. Apart from one. She knew she could scream.

Chapter 6

When Amari woke, the sun was high in the sky, streaming in through the windows. All she knew was that she was in the honeymoon suite, and her head felt like a cymbal being hit with a hammer. Big, belting shots of pain seared through her, followed by lesser shocks of reducing intensity, but then, with no seeming regularity, the hammer would come down, walloping her once more.

She was alone, but could hear angry voices outside the door. She wanted to get up and see who was there, what they were arguing about, but every time she prepared to pull back the covers, another hammer blow hit.

She closed her eyes and focused on breathing, on remembering what she could from the night before. Everything had been fine—better than fine ... until it hadn't.

Dean had freaked out and called a doctor, then had pulled one of his big white t-shirts over her head, removed her shoes, and put her under the covers.

Agonizing pain had radiated out from everywhere their skin touched, so she hadn't let him touch her, or even sit near her after that. He'd kept trying to move closer, saying he just wanted to hold her hand, wanted to help, but he felt wrong, alien, dangerous. Every part of her found him repulsive.

The doctor had arrived, and Dean had told him—in embarrassing detail—what had happened.

He'd given her a sedative. That was the last thing she could remember, aside from waking once to a burning pain on her arm and forehead. She vaguely recalled Dean's face hovering above her as she screamed.

There was no sign of him now. No clothes, no case, no watch or cufflinks. His client was evidently more important than his wife … but then again, his absence provided a strange relief. It had never been like that before …

The door to her room opened, and Leila slipped in. She closed the door behind her, scowling at whoever was on the other side. 'You're awake. Finally,' she said, coming to sit on the edge of the bed.

'I wish I wasn't, given the pounding in my head.' Although she was glad to find Leila didn't have the same abhorrent effect on her as Dean.

'What happened?' asked Leila, scrutinizing her with both suspicion and concern. Amari marveled at the combination.

'Honestly, I have no idea. One minute we were enjoying our honeymoon suite, the next, it felt like there was something inside my head, clawing to get out. It was worse when Dean was near.'

'How are you feeling now?'

'Like I've got the worst hangover of my life.'

Leila smiled. 'You and everyone else. The bar was hit hard last night …'

'Did Dean go to work?'

Leila's face dropped. 'Yeah. Arsehole.'

'Leila!'

'Sorry, but when your wife has a fit, you don't get on a plane and fly away.'

Had she had a fit? Was that what it was? 'I wouldn't let him touch me, or be close to me. It was worse when he was near.'

'That's kinda crazy. You know that, right?'

'I know. Maybe I'm losing it.'

'You have always been a bit questionable in the head …'

'If I were feeling less delicate, I would shove you off this bed.'

'I'd like to see you try.'

'Who were you arguing with outside? Mum?'

Leila laughed. 'No. Neither of your parents are up yet. They danced until dawn.'

Amari started to laugh, but had to stop when another bout of pain hit. She waited for it to pass.

Leila sympathetically patted her leg through the duvet.

'I'm glad someone had a good night,' said Amari. 'Who's outside, then?'

Leila took a deep breath. 'That guy you were with just before the wedding. What's his name?'

Amari's blood sang. 'Caspar? Let him in.'

'What?' Leila's tone was stern. 'You rejected your husband, but want to see *him*? The two of you looked pretty cozy when I interrupted yesterday.'

Amari pulled a face. 'Don't be dramatic; I've only met him twice. He works for the government and there's a project he wants me to help with. I need something to distract me until Dean gets back.'

'You're going to work? You can't! You need tests, and rest, and … and … time to work through whatever's going on.'

'No, I need a distraction, and he can provide one. Are you going to get him, or are you going to make me do it?' She made to pull back the covers and found, to her surprise, no accompanying stab of pain.

'Okay, okay,' said Leila, pushing Amari back down. 'I'll get him. But promise you'll agree to some tests.'

Amari nodded. 'Fine.'

Leila huffed. 'You never were a good liar,' she said, walking to the door. 'This is going to get messy; I can feel it. Don't come crying to me when it all blows up in your face.'

Leila opened the door, gestured for Caspar to enter, and then left, closing the door forcefully behind her.

Caspar didn't seem to notice, his eyes locked on Amari. 'Are you okay?' he asked, picking up a dining chair and moving it to her bedside. He perched nervously on the edge of the seat, like a wary bird ready to take flight.

'I don't know,' she said, noting her headache had entirely abated since he'd entered the room. Was that a coincidence? 'What are you doing here?'

'After our phone call yesterday, I was hoping you'd be happy to start work today, so I came to ask you.'

'You could've called for that.'

'I heard Leila talking to the receptionist. She said you were ill. She wanted to extend your stay so you wouldn't have to move. I asked Leila what happened, but she wouldn't tell me, so here I am.'

'Again, you didn't have to come in person. You could've called.'

'Our work is extremely important; it's better to do things in person.'

'You haven't told me what you need me to do yet.'

Caspar smiled. 'Will you be fit to work today, Miss Conti?'

'I am,' she said, throwing back the covers, revealing her stockings and suspenders, the t-shirt having ridden up around her waist.

Caspar inhaled sharply and Amari stifled a laugh. 'Sorry,' she said, pulling the t-shirt down as she stood.

'I'll wait for you outside,' said Caspar, standing, which put him squarely in her personal space.

Amari laughed again, astounded to find that her head felt clear—refreshed even. 'Don't worry, I'll change in the bathroom. You can wait here. But it's Mrs. Sanderson now, remember?'

Amari put a hand on his shoulder as she squeezed past. Caspar's hand came up in a flash to hold hers.

'Amari,' he said, their faces inches apart, 'are you sure you're okay?'

Amari's eyes flicked to Caspar's lips, then back to his eyes. 'Honestly? I have absolutely no idea.'

Caspar led Amari into an old townhouse in Kensington. The building had no identifying markers on the outside and the receptionist was somber, giving nothing away. They entered an office on the ground floor, and Amari nearly gasped at the mess. This was not at all what she'd been expecting: bookshelves piled high, chairs covered with papers, lamps propped up at odd angles.

Caspar laughed at her expression, removing a pile of papers from a wood and leather chair, and gesturing for her to sit. 'I like to think it's organized chaos,' he said, moving round to the other side of a large, mahogany desk. 'As a general rule, my friends think otherwise.'

'First impressions put me firmly on the side of your friends,' said Amari.

'That doesn't surprise me at all,' said Caspar.

He pulled out a small gold key and strode towards a wooden floor-to-ceiling cabinet at the back of the room. It contained hundreds of little drawers, and Amari had the distinct feeling she'd walked into a sweet shop. He unlocked two drawers and retrieved an artifact from each: a gold ring, and something that looked like a tiara.

Amari sucked in a breath, frowning as he put the tiara on the desk. No, not a tiara—that's what you called sparkly showy things—this was a Celtic headpiece, made only of metal and designed to sit low on a person's brow.

Something about the jewelry sent a shiver down her spine. She couldn't pull her focus from it, barely noticing that Caspar had perched on the desk's edge, and was picking up her right hand. She forced her eyes up, watching as Caspar slid the ring over the knuckle of her index finger.

She should have protested, but the movement felt so natural, soothing even, that she did nothing but watch. Caspar ran his thumb across the plain, hammered gold band, then stilled, holding her fingers, waiting for her to make the next move.

'I ... ah ...' Amari pulled her hand back. This was all so bizarre. Yesterday she'd married the love of her life. Today, when she should be on her honeymoon, another man caressed her hand. And she felt more at home here, in this mess, than she'd felt anywhere. She was fonder of the plain gold band sitting on her index finger than she was of the large glittering rings adorning her left hand. Fond ... that's how she felt. How could she be fond of something she'd only just set eyes on?

Amari frowned again. 'I feel like I've seen this before, and the headpiece too. Have they been on display?'

Caspar smirked. 'Not recently.'

'It's so strange …'

'Try the headpiece on; it'll suit you.'

'I can't! How old is it? It should be in a museum.'

'Come now, not everything with a bit of age should be entombed behind glass.'

Amari gave him a look, but something deep within her yearned to try it on.

'Who owns it?' she said. 'Won't they mind?'

'A private collector, and I can guarantee she won't mind. In fact, she'd be disappointed if you didn't.'

What kind of crazy show was he running? No collector she'd ever met would be so casual with their possessions.

'Ready?' said Caspar, picking up the headpiece.

She sighed. 'Well, if you insist …'

Caspar smiled, clearly delighted. A thrill ran through her, a knot of excitement balling in her chest. What in the world had got into her? Seduced by a pretty piece of jewelry? She found herself rubbing the ring, the movement feeling habitual. Had she ever worn a ring on her index finger? Not that she could recall …

Caspar lowered the headpiece, the cool metal settling on her brow, caressing her forehead. He looked into her eyes, made a small adjustment, then stepped back, holding her gaze. Was she imagining it, or did he look … hopeful? She closed her eyes, savoring the weight of the metal, getting used to the feel of it.

'Here, take a look,' said Caspar, offering her a handheld mirror.

'Where did that come from?' she laughed.

'As I said: organized chaos.'

She took the mirror, still chuckling as she held it up, but when she saw her reflection, emotion gripped her, her body locked in place. She closed her eyes, trying to clear the strangeness, but images began to play: a bonfire, a celebration, people dancing.

Part of her wanted to open her eyes, tear off the jewelry, run away. She had no idea who Caspar was, and this was bizarre. He could be a serial killer, and she'd gone with him—based on a feeling—without even a second thought. But then, just as she'd resolved to open her eyes, a man, wearing only loose, three-quarter-length trousers, with leaves in his hair, walked straight towards her, holding a gleaming metal headpiece.

The way he looked at her … she was everything; the brightest star in the sky, his reason to be. The way his face lit up as he came close, settled the headpiece on her head … 'You're beautiful,' he breathed, taking her face in his hands and kissing her, like he might never kiss again.

Amari felt that kiss, leaned into it, kissed him back. Blood pounded in her ears, desire pooled in her core, and her breathing shallowed. She melted into him, swaying with him in time to the music. Their mouths demanded everything, going deeper, harder, until she begged him to lower her to the ground, or push her against a tree. And he would have, was going to, was doing it, until Caspar snatched the jewelry from her head and bundled her down onto the hard, wooden floor of his office.

'Caspar! What are you doing?' she cried.

He grabbed her head and made her look at him. His voice was low when he said, 'Quiet. Now. We're in danger.'

Amari's eyes went wide. 'What? Caspar, what the fuck is happening?'

Caspar shushed her with eyes so deadly that she swallowed her protest.

'We're going to run ... there's a back door. Hold my hand and don't look back. I'll explain when we're safe.'

He looked at her, his eyes uncompromising, and she nodded her assent.

'Now,' he hissed.

He pulled her up and hurtled towards the door.

Jon tore into the kitchen. 'Have you heard?' he gasped. 'There's been an attack on Caspar's office.'

'I heard,' said Rose, barely deigning to look up, petting one of the dogs.

'Talli told me Caspar was taking Amari there.'

'What?' Rose's head snapped up. 'He's got her? Is she awake?'

'Not when they left the hotel this morning, but she could be by now.'

'Damn it. Why's her timing always so terrible? It's like she plans it, just to raise my blood pressure.'

'Developments with the Templars?' asked Jon.

'Unfortunately, yes.'

'Can't we just register her now?'

'No.'

'There's never even been a single exception?'

Rose huffed. 'There was. Once. It didn't end well.'

'Oh.'

The kitchen door crashed open, revealing Caspar, dragging a furious-looking Amari behind him.

'Lock everything down,' Caspar gasped.

'Were you followed?' asked Rose, gesturing to Jon to do as Caspar said. She sat casually in her seat, but her features were serious, calculating.

'No. I used the tunnels. We lost them.'

'Who was it?' asked Rose.

'I have no idea, and I didn't have time to grab their dagger.'

'Their *dagger*?' said Amari, rounding on Caspar. 'There was a dagger?'

'Yes. But it was more important to get out alive than retrieve it.'

'I …' said Amari, with a shake of her head. 'What the hell is going on?'

'Jon,' said Rose, 'call Meredith and Gemma. Tell them to go to Caspar's office and track from there.'

Jon pulled out his phone and followed Rose's command.

'Any clues at all?' asked Rose, looking expectantly at Caspar. 'Slayer?'

'Honestly, it's hard to say. I …'

'… I'm sorry, what? A Slayer? With daggers? I've had enough of this insanity. I'm leaving. Never contact me again.'

Rose rolled her eyes.

'Amari, give me a chance to explain,' said Caspar.

'It would be unwise for you to leave before we know who's after you,' said Rose, her tone hard as iron. 'Unless you want to end up captured, or with a knife in your back.'

Amari paled.

'Five minutes, that's all I ask,' said Caspar, motioning to the door at the back of the room.

'Fine,' she growled.

Amari followed Caspar up a short set of spiral stone stairs. They were shallow and worn with time, pagan symbols adorning the walls. She found herself admiring them, despite her mood.

The stairs led to a low-ceilinged stone hallway, with windows running down one side of its short length. The windows were made of small, thin glass panes, and someone had placed simple flower arrangements on several of the sills. They contained old English roses and smelled divine, basking in the sunlight. Amari walked slowly, trying to take in every detail of her surprising surroundings.

Caspar opened the wooden door at the end of the corridor, revealing another corridor beyond, with a steep set of wooden stairs to the left, just after the door.

Caspar climbed the stairs. Amari followed, wondering if she was willingly walking into something terrible.

They emerged onto a landing, doors leading off on three sides, windows letting in light straight in front of them. Caspar turned right, pushing through one final wooden door, which he closed behind them.

Amari took in the plush yet cozy room with its fourposter bed, freestanding wardrobe, dressing table, chest of drawers, nightstands, and small seating area. The seating area contained two button-backed velvet chairs, a stumpy wooden table between them. The window had a cushioned sill, which looked out over a courtyard two stories below.

The carpet was cream and thick, the curtains heavy and embroidered with pink hollyhocks. It was beautiful, and homely. Amari sank into a button-back, almost forgetting Caspar entirely. It was only when he started to talk that her focus snapped back into place.

'I'm so sorry. I didn't think this morning would end up like this,' he said, lowering himself onto the other chair.

Amari frowned. 'I should damn well hope not.'

'I'm going to explain it all, but you're going to think it's crazy, that I'm crazy. So before you run away—into danger—please take a moment to consider what I say, and keep an open mind.'

Amari looked at him with concern. What had she got herself into?

'When you had the headpiece on,' said Caspar, pulling it out of his pocket, 'what happened?'

Amari's eyes scrutinized the metal, remembering the strange dream, the man who'd kissed her, the way her mind and body had reacted. She'd had no time to think about it since Caspar had snatched the headpiece from her brow.

'I had a dream,' she said, tentatively. 'I know it sounds stupid.'

Caspar leaned forward. 'What was the dream about?'

'There was a celebration. People were dancing around a bonfire. There were flower crowns and people wearing white tunics. There was a man. He had the headpiece. He put it on me, then kissed me.'

'And then?' asked Caspar.

Amari's cheeks heated. 'And then you pulled off the headpiece and threw me to the floor.'

Caspar looked angry.

'What?' said Amari.

'The idiot with the dagger couldn't have picked a worse time.'

'What do you mean?'

'That wasn't a dream, Amari. It was a memory.'

Amari laughed. 'I don't have any memories like that. It was ancient; people were arriving on horseback.

And don't tell me the headpiece can carry memories, or I'll have to call you a psychiatrist.'

'Inanimate objects don't have memories,' said Caspar carefully, 'people do. And people who've been reincarnated have a lot of them.'

Amari laughed loudly. 'This is a joke, right? Because if you're serious, I'm leaving. Right now.'

'I told you, it sounds crazy, but think about how the headpiece and the ring *feel* to you,' he said, pointing to the ring still on her index finger. He placed the headpiece in her hand. 'How does this place feel? How … how did I feel, yesterday, before the wedding?'

Her brain was too full of questions, and sensations, and doubts, and ridiculous, outlandish thoughts. He'd touched a nerve. These things felt like nothing else; they felt right … familiar.

She knew she should give the jewelry back, get up, and walk away, but she couldn't bring herself to do it. The ring especially was too *important* to her. It was only a thin, battered band of gold, but the idea of taking it off, handing it over, being made to part with it … made her want to claw someone's eyes out.

'How do I feel?' he repeated, kneeling beside her, taking hold of her hand, looking deep into her eyes. Those eyes … they were … they were the eyes from the dream.

She snatched her hand back and stood, whirling away. He'd been different, in the dream, in every way: height, weight, skin color, hair color … everything. But his eyes, they were the same.

Amari's heart pounded. Her brain went silent, numb. This didn't make any sense. Had she been drugged? Was she ill? Maybe she was still sedated, and was dreaming. Maybe her headache, rejecting Dean, had all been caused by Caspar.

'What did you do to me?' she said, rounding on him. 'Did you drug me?'

'What? No! Why would you think that?'

'After I saw you yesterday, it was like my brain was full of smoke. Like I was there at the wedding, but not *really* there, until all of a sudden, I snapped out of it. Then twenty minutes later, I had some kind of psychotic break, and Dean had to call a doctor.'

'I didn't drug you.'

Caspar paused, looked away, took a deep breath. He was fighting some internal battle.

'Your subconscious recognizes me. You recognized the smell of my cologne, my eyes, the way I speak. Your brain's trying to suppress the memories, and it's causing conflict.'

'You rejected Dean because—and please don't flip out when I say this—but you're rejecting Dean because he's not me.'

Amari barked out a laugh, then clamped her lips shut.

'We've been together for countless lifetimes, hundreds of years. After seeing me, your relationship with Dean could never be the same.'

'Have you got any idea how deluded, or … arrogant, that sounds?'

'Yes. It's mad. I sound like I should be committed, but that doesn't mean I'm not telling you the truth. How did Rose and Jon feel to you? You've known Rose for longer even than you've known me. And Jon is young, but you've known him a few lifetimes.'

Every rational part of Amari screamed at her to run. She'd stumbled into a cult, or a mental institution with no obvious medical professionals. Maybe that's who the person with the dagger was: someone to take them back to their rooms …

Come to think of it, she hadn't actually *seen* the dagger. Maybe he'd made the whole thing up … But every emotional part of her compelled her to stay, to hear him out, to keep hold of the ring for as long as she could. Maybe she could buy it: it had so much sentimental value.

Oh Jesus. She *was* mentally ill. Maybe Dean had had her committed, and she was a patient here too.

Amari sat back in her chair and rubbed her face with her hands. Caspar was right; everything about this place, these people, felt familiar and safe. Much as she wanted to, she couldn't rule out the possibility that he was telling the truth.

'Who was chasing us?' she asked, trying to stick to the facts.

Caspar leaned forward in his chair. 'I don't know, but there are three possibilities: Slayers, hunters, or someone affiliated to another demon nation.'

'In English?'

Caspar stood and walked to the window. He looked out, pausing for such a long time Amari wondered if he was going to answer. He eventually turned and sat on the window seat, meeting Amari's gaze.

'Those who reincarnate are known as demons. We fall into two groups: people like us, who are affiliated with a demon nation, and hunters, who work individually, or in small, independent groups.

'Hunters look for sleeping demons like you. Once they've found a lead, they sell the information to the highest bidder. Slayers, on the other hand, don't

49

reincarnate. They belong to an ancient group of humans who want to wipe out the demon race.'

'Wow,' said Amari.

'I know; it sounds farfetched.'

'And earlier, it could've been a hunter looking for me?' *Did I really just ask that?*

'That's one possibility. That's how I found you in the first place. A hunter we've had a relationship with for generations found you, recognized your eyes, and knew I'd be looking for you.'

'You paid one of those maniacs to track me down?'

'In fairness, they found you first, and then I paid.'

'What do you mean, they recognized my eyes?'

'Demons have unique eyes, just like anyone else, but ours contain markers that make us identifiable as demons. Hunters are blessed with the gift of being able to read eyes more easily than others. Not everyone with the gift chooses to become a hunter, but it's a lucrative occupation.'

Amari pushed herself up and walked to the dressing table. She sat on the stool and leaned towards the mirror, scrutinizing her eyes. They looked normal to her.

'So, some other demon could be trying to find me?'

'It's possible.'

'Why?'

'Amari,' he said, opening his hands, palms up, 'you've lived for over a thousand years. During that time, you've had your fair share of alliances-gone-wrong, and feuds, and more than a few lovers.'

'Oh. But it might've been a Slayer?' she asked, almost hopefully. The prospect seemed better than a jealous ex-lover.

'It's possible. In which case, it's more likely that I was the target, given that you're yet to awake.'

He stood and began to pace.

'Unless the hunter I paid also sold your lead to the Slayers. But that's unlikely; Slayers want to kill the hunters too.'

'Jesus Christ.' Amari stood, running her hands through her hair. She shook her head, trying to clear it. 'This is … it's … so much.'

'I'm sorry. I wish I knew a way to wake you, then all of this would be unnecessary.'

He leaned over a button-back, his hands gripping the fabric so hard his knuckles turned white.

Amari walked to the window. She looked down at the courtyard, and watched the birds flit among the shrubbery.

'How does a demon wake up? What makes it happen?' Her tone was skeptical, but she wanted the answer.

'Exposure to artifacts from the past is a good place to start.'

'Things like the jewelry?' she asked.

'Yes, as well as books, pictures, places, smells. And spending time with other demons: eating meals, observing rituals, attending events. Midsummer's approaching. It's the celebration you saw in the memory. We're going to Maltings.'

'Maltings?' she turned her head to look at him. 'You said that word yesterday.'

'Yes. You said I smelled like the English countryside in late summer. I smelled like the garden at Maltings, our country house.'

'*Our* country house?'

'Um, yes. It was mine first. You yelled at me for buying it without you. But then you said, *what's mine is yours,* and made me sign half of it over to you. Not that it matters; everything we own really belongs to our nation. We pool all resources.'

51

'What is a nation, exactly?' Amari's mind raced at all the information, and she ran an agitated hand through her hair.

'Maybe we should take a break. I can bring you some tea? Or you can come down to the kitchen and talk to the others?'

'I'm not ready for that,' she said, adamantly, wondering if he was dodging her question ... 'I think I'd like some time alone.'

'Of course; I'll give you some space. There are plenty more objects from your past in this room; feel free to rummage around. The bathroom's across the landing, and I'll come back in a bit with lunch.'

He stopped in the doorway. 'Amari, if you're thinking about making a break for it, just remember, there's someone out there who might want to hurt you. Of course, you're free to leave whenever you want—we're not holding you hostage—but it would be helpful if you told us you were going, so we can send someone to protect you.'

Amari thought about telling him where he could stick it, but there was no point in arguing. As long as there was someone out there who might want to hurt her, she was staying put. And anyway, as odd as all this was, this place was irresistible. It was impossible to fathom, but some deep part of her told her she was home.

As soon as Caspar's footsteps faded, Amari pulled her phone out of her jacket. Dean had sent her a string of messages: He was sorry he had to leave. He was at the airport. He missed her. How was she feeling? He was getting on his flight. He loved her. He'd call as soon as he landed.

Amari checked her watch. He'd be on the flight for another couple of hours. The thought filled her with relief; what in the world was she going to tell him? This whole thing was crazy. Batshit crazy. But she couldn't deny the way she felt about the ring on her finger, or the comfort and familiarity this room brought, or that she was drawn to Caspar, or the dream ... memory ... whatever it had been. She put her phone down.

She walked around the room, looking closely at the paintings and furniture. They felt familiar, but she wasn't particularly drawn to them.

She opened the wardrobe and found it stocked with clothes, most of them dated and wholly impractical. A heavy, beaded, twenties-style flapper dress caught her eye. She reached out and touched it. The smell of cigars filled her nostrils. Music, laughter, and chatter filled her ears. Someone placed their hand on her back as she sipped a cocktail. She jumped back, releasing the dress, and with it the flashes of sensation.

She sat on the bed and took some deep breaths. Was she on some drug-fueled trip? She lay down and closed her eyes, her hands going to her forehead. Maybe she should nap. Maybe she'd wake up back in her hotel room. Maybe she'd wake up and find her wedding hadn't yet happened.

There was something wrong with her; that was the only logical explanation. She should leave here and check herself into a psychiatric hospital.

How did one go about committing oneself in practical terms? Presumably, on the NHS, it would take some time. She'd have to get Dean to pay for a private facility, assuming he didn't annul the wedding ... She'd have to be evasive with the details; he probably wouldn't understand. No, strike that, she was absolutely sure he wouldn't understand.

Amari had always been the strong, dependable, totally rational type. Dean wouldn't like a mentally ill wife. Which, now she thought about it, said something about him. And he'd flown to the other side of the Atlantic when his wife was under the care of a doctor, being treated for an unknown illness. Assuming they had, in fact, got married, and she hadn't hallucinated the whole thing.

Dean's best man used to get high all the time. Maybe he'd slipped something into her drink at the rehearsal dinner. That's when this had all started, after all.

She rubbed her face, as though the action could wash away the grimy layer of uncertainty.

She opened her eyes, taking in the stars carved into the wooden ceiling of the four-poster. They were beautiful, and peaceful, and comforting. She closed her eyes, another dream pouring into her mind. She was torn, wanting to fling her eyes open and reject all of this, but also wanting to indulge the voracious craving that urged her to find out more.

Cravings always win, especially the voracious variety ...

She was lying on a beach, elated, euphoric even, the soothing sound of lapping waves filling her ears. Her pink evening dress provided little defense against the chill, but she wouldn't let that put a damper on her mood.

She was waiting for something. For someone. For him. And despite herself, Amari couldn't help but let these emotions fill her too. She was buzzing with excitement by the time a man's face appeared above her.

He wore a perfect tuxedo, looking every inch the achingly irresistible gentleman, dark hair swept to one side, a knowing smile on his lips. But his eyes. They weren't Caspar's deep brown eyes. These were grey, like the sky before a storm.

'Raina,' he said, in a tempting American drawl—he sounded a lot like Dean. 'I've been trying to get away all night, but they wouldn't stop talking about the alliance.' He dropped down next to her, stroking a stay lock of hair off her face.

'Urgh, don't say another word about it.' To Amari's surprise, Raina's accent was American too. 'I've had my fill of politics. Now kiss me, before I find someone else who will.'

He did as he was told, this kiss worlds apart from the one in the earlier memory. Raina's desire was laced with guilt, and it made her hold something back, to only go so far, to push him away before he could rip off her dress.

'Someone will see us,' she laughed, cuddling into him, stealing his warmth, stroking her hand across his chest.

'God, I love you, Raina. You know that, right?'

'I know,' she said, her tone light.

'No,' he said, sitting up, making her look at him. 'I really love you. I want us to be together. I want to spend lifetimes with you.'

Panic ripped through her, although she kept her features trained. She stroked his face, ran a thumb across his lips.

'Jamie, sweetie, you know I love you too.'

She kissed him. He seemed convinced, but Raina's guts churned at the lie.

Chapter 7

'You just left her upstairs?' asked Jon, incredulous. 'She's probably bolted. She must think we're insane.'

'Perhaps,' said Caspar, cradling his tea, 'but enough's come back to her to make her at least consider what I said.'

Rose, Elliot, and Meredith entered the kitchen. Meredith, the Pagans' head of security, was long-haired and muscular. She looked like she should be on the set of Black Panther, albeit a Native American version. She raised her eyes as she took in the scene.

'Caspar feeling sorry for himself in yet another lifetime?' she said.

'Shut up,' said Caspar, throwing her a dirty look. 'When you've found your one true love, tell me how easy it is then.'

'No such thing,' said Meredith, sitting on the floor by the Aga with the dogs. They moved to lie closer, nudging her until she petted them.

'Casual flings more your style?' said Jon, suggestively.

Meredith rolled her eyes. She accepted a biscuit from the tin Elliot held out. 'Thanks. I already had a couple this morning. They're delicious.'

'It's the ginger and berry mix,' said Elliot. 'I've been perfecting the balance for a hundred years. Think I might finally be close.'

'I'd say you're there. They're perfection as they are,' said Meredith, motioning for Elliot to pass her another.

Rose and Gemma—Meredith's sidekick—sat at the table, helping themselves to biscuits too. Gemma was about the same height as Meredith, and muscular, but with white skin, a soft, heart-shaped face, and long auburn hair.

'Are we going to talk about biscuits all day, or are you going to tell us what you found?' asked Caspar. 'You know, given that someone tried to kill me earlier.'

Meredith rolled her eyes again. 'Trackers require sustenance too. And I didn't find much to go on, I'm afraid. CCTV footage showed a figure entering the building, knocking out the receptionist, and entering your office.

'They threw the dagger and then ducked back out of the room. I think they threw it at you, Caspar, although it's hard to tell. The footage isn't great. I've been telling you for years to let me upgrade your equipment.'

'Thanks. Helpful,' said Caspar. 'Go on.'

'You left through the back door and the figure followed. They didn't search your office. That's where the CCTV ends. I'm working on pulling more, but it takes time, because we need assistance from the police.'

'Have we got anyone on the inside?' asked Jon.

'Yes,' said Rose, 'but it still takes time.'

'Do you think it's the Templars?' asked Jon. 'Given everything that's going on, and given it's Raina?'

'It's possible,' said Rose, 'but impossible to say for sure. Meredith's team will keep tracking, and Meredith and Gemma will stay around for our general protection. We've called in a couple of cells to help keep this place secure too. But if it is the Templars, make no mistake, it's an act of war.'

Amari ventured back down to the kitchen. Her stomach had started to growl, and she was curious about the others. Not to mention she felt like a caged animal, hidden away upstairs.

'I am not,' said Jon.

'You so are,' said Elliot.

'I'm not. Caspar, come on, back me up,' said Jon.

'Honestly, I think you might be. Not that I blame you,' said Caspar.

'I am not in love with Meredith,' shouted Jon. 'She just has a certain … allure.'

'Head over heels,' laughed Elliot.

'Yep,' said Caspar, 'totally smitten.'

Amari watched the exchange with fascination. 'Who's Meredith?' she asked.

'Urgh, don't you start,' said Jon, storming out of the room.

Amari couldn't help but smile. 'Who's Meredith?' she repeated, approaching the table and taking a seat.

'She's our head of security. Rose called her to investigate the attack,' said Caspar.

'And Jon goes red and says stupid things whenever she's around,' said Elliot.

'Even more stupid than normal,' added Caspar.

Elliot laughed. Then he jumped up and said to Amari, 'You must be starving. I was just about to make us some lunch. Quiche and salad. Hope that's okay?'

'Sounds wonderful,' said Amari. She petted the large, shaggy mongrel who'd forced his head into her hand. 'What are the dogs' names?'

'Charlie and Delta,' said Caspar. 'The one you're petting is Charlie.'

'Like from the phonetic alphabet?'

Caspar chuckled. 'Yep. We've always had dogs, but the arguments about names got out of control.'

'It would take weeks, and was all anyone would talk about,' said Rose, entering the kitchen.

'So Rose put her foot down in the late eighteen hundreds. She makes us cycle through the phonetic alphabet so there's no arguing,' said Caspar.

'It's mostly fine,' said Elliot. 'We're only on our second time around, so it hasn't got old yet, although people in the park give you weird looks when you call for a dog named Hotel!'

Amari laughed, although it sounded tense, even to her own ears. 'How many of you live here?'

'We move around a lot,' said Caspar, 'but anywhere from half a dozen to twenty, depending on what's going on.'

'It's unpleasant when we get that full,' said Elliot.

'How many de … people like you are there?'

'We don't know for sure,' said Rose, 'and the number fluctuates. Brand new demons occasionally awake, and older demons are either killed or die. And, of course, there are demons like you, who are incarnated but asleep.'

'You can die, then? In a … final way?'

'Everybody dies eventually,' said Rose, as though this were obvious. 'It just takes us longer than everyone else. But to answer your question, there are a few hundred in the Pagan Nation, and we think most other major nations are about the same size. The Buddhists probably have more, the Aztecs maybe a few less; they have a tendency to kill each other.'

'And the Egyptians,' said Caspar. 'Some nations have fire in their blood.'

'Are nations like countries?' Amari asked.

Charlie put a paw up onto the edge of her seat, edging as close to her as he could.

'Not really,' said Rose. 'They operate more like religions, and are often affiliated with religions. Although each nation does have their own distinct territory.'

'Most nations have their headquarters in their area of origin,' said Caspar. 'Pagans here in London, Buddhists in Asia, Aztecs in South America, Egyptians in Egypt …'

'How many nations are there?' asked Amari.

'We don't know for sure,' said Rose. 'Sometimes people defect and form new nations. Sometimes nations are wiped out through wars or too many defections. But there are probably ten or eleven big ones.'

'There are loads of smaller ones too,' said Elliot, placing two oversized quiches on the table. 'Discount them at your peril.'

Caspar smiled a knowing smile.

'I used to be an Aborigine,' Elliot explained, seeing Amari's confusion.

'And Meredith was a Wakan when she first awoke,' said Caspar, 'an American Indian.'

'The smaller nations can provide an edge in times of war,' said Rose.

'What do you fight about?' asked Amari. 'What does each group want?'

'What don't we fight about?' laughed Elliot.

'Natural resources, philosophy, theology, powerful people,' said Caspar.

'What are you fighting about now?' asked Amari.

'The Templars are aggressive. They always want more: more power, more control, more resources, and damn the consequences,' said Caspar. 'We see things differently. We want to use the world's resources in a responsible way. For everyone to have enough.'

'We're idealists,' Elliot said, grinning.

'But when the Templars start stomping all over our territory, we can't let them get away with it,' said Meredith, striding in from the back of the room. 'We lead the Pagan Nation, and we need to keep our people safe.'

'I thought there was some rule about politics at lunch,' said Jon, one step behind Meredith. He sat next to her at the table.

Caspar and Elliot shared a meaningful look.

Jon glared at them.

Elliot put a green salad, a Greek salad, and a tray of baked eggplant with yoghurt and pomegranate seeds on the table.

'Wow, this looks delicious,' said Amari.

'Elliot likes to feed us,' said Caspar, as Elliot pulled a batch of freshly baked rolls from the oven.

'I could live for a million years and that smell would never get old,' said Meredith, inhaling deeply.

Elliot slid the rolls into a basket and placed them on the table, along with a jar of homemade chutney. A rush of sensation filled Amari. She tipped her head forward and closed her eyes, another memory flashing before her. She saw a table much like this one, the same food laid out, the same smell wafting up from the table. She snapped her eyes open.

Caspar put his hand on her arm. 'You okay?' he asked. There was no worry in his eyes, only mild concern.

'Fine,' she said. 'Another flashback.'

'This was always your favorite kind of meal,' said Elliot.

'And ... chilis,' said Amari softly, mostly to herself. 'I put them on everything.'

Elliot smiled a broad smile, picking up a red chili from the counter and putting it in front of her. 'Bravo.'

Amari frowned. Those words had been out of her mouth before she'd even thought about them … Was she being pranked by one of those magicians who planted ideas in your head? Was the room full of con artists and cameras? Because the alternative—that this was all true—was starting to sound plausible, and that was too ludicrous a prospect to entertain.

After lunch, Rose called Meredith to her office. Elliot and Jon returned to their jobs, and Amari asked Caspar to show her the courtyard she'd seen from the bedroom window.

He led her out the back of the kitchen, through a beautiful room made mostly of glass and packed full of plants, then into a set of cloisters. Amari hadn't realized there was a covered walkway around the garden when she'd been looking from above.

The walkway ran the full perimeter of the square courtyard, with only one entrance point into the garden on each side. The courtyard itself had carefully constructed cobbled paths, cut through geometrically spaced flower beds that were bursting with plants. The circular fountain was at the center of it all, providing sound, movement, and calm.

The strange familiarity returned with full force as Amari took it all in. Her head spun, and then everything went black …

'Amari!' said Caspar, somewhere through the haze in her mind.

Amari opened her eyes to find Caspar crouching over her, his hands on her face. Had her legs given way?

'What happened?'

'You collapsed.'

'I think I need to sit for a minute.'

'Can you walk? There are benches.'

Amari nodded, letting him help her to her feet and lead her to the solid granite benches around the fountain. The smell of lavender invaded her lungs, forcing her to put her head between her legs and take deep breaths.

'What's happening to me?' she gasped.

'Your brain's fighting itself. You spent a lot of time here—in the cloisters and courtyard—in previous lives. You've always loved to be outside.' He chuckled. 'You went through a poetry phase in the seventeen hundreds. You'd come out here every day, rain or shine, and wouldn't let anyone else be here while you worked. You said our closed minds would *chase away your inspiration*.'

Amari sat up and Caspar was close. Too close. He placed his hand atop hers. 'Don't fight the memories,' he said quietly, 'it'll make it harder. And don't fight me.'

He ran his thumb across her skin.

Amari snatched her hand away and moved a few inches along the bench. 'I'm married,' she said, looking away.

'But not for the first time.'

'You're delusional. All of you; it's the only logical explanation.'

'If you say so.' Caspar got up. 'I'll give you some space … you don't like it when people crowd you.'

Amari huffed out a breath as he walked away. 'Wait. I have more questions … just, sit over there,' she said, pointing at the next bench over. *Because I can't think when you're near*, she didn't add.

Caspar sat. She watched his face for any victorious twitch, but his features gave nothing away.

'I don't even know where to start …'

Caspar just sat there, watching the water.

'I'm going to entertain the notion that everything you've told me is true,' she said eventually, turning the gold band around her finger.

'How gracious.'

She threw him a warning look. 'Don't push your luck.'

His lips quirked.

'What?'

'You've always been feisty; it's one of the many things I love.'

Amari's pulse raced. 'I have a husband,' she said. 'Please don't say things like that. It's inappropriate.'

Caspar raised an eyebrow. 'If you say so,' he said again.

'Urgh. Fine. If you can't do that, let's address it: you and me. We were married?'

A shadow passed behind Caspar's eyes. 'We were, more than once. And as far as I'm concerned, we still are.'

'Well, I disagree.'

'You won't when you wake.'

'Assuming that ever happens.'

'I assure you, it will.'

'Jesus, this is …' She paused, gripping the edge of the bench in frustration. 'I mean, assuming all this is true, what am I supposed to do about Dean? He loves me, and I love him.'

'Do you?'

She screamed inwardly, working hard to keep her face neutral. He was infuriating. 'Yes! Of course I do.'

'Did.'

'Do.'

'Really? Because I heard you wouldn't let him anywhere near you last night. Which, by the way, means you didn't consummate your marriage, so an annulment is definitely on the table.'

'An annulment?'

'Yes. Especially as he got on a plane and flew away from said unconsummated marriage mere hours after it occurred.'

'His work is important, and he cares about the people he helps.'

'And you got married in a *hotel.* Does that even count as a real wedding?'

'Stop baiting me.'

'My dear, I assure you, I'm doing nothing of the sort.'

'Don't call me that.'

'My favorite wedding of ours was under the stars, on the French Riviera.'

The French Riviera … something about the French Riviera … 'Oh God … the perfume?'

'See, your sleeping brain remembers.'

'Wait … the perfume … the hair and makeup artists? You sent them?'

'No, I didn't. I told them not to get involved, but they're impossible.'

'You're lying.'

'I most certainly am not. I'll call them here right now. You can ask them yourself.'

Amari took a deep breath, trying to slow everything down. 'I guess it's not important.'

They sat in silence, the only sound the trickle of water from the ancient stone fountain. Amari watched it, emptying her mind of anything but the ripples. She stood, and Caspar's eyes darted to her. She sat on the foot-high pool edge, dipping her fingers into the cool water.

A flashback caressed at the edge of her consciousness, this one different from the brutal attack of the others. She closed her eyes and let it in, curious to see what the fountain would bring back.

She was walking with a man around the cloisters. It was cold, and they were bundled up in cloaks, frost on the ground. She felt an overwhelming love for him, a love she could choke on, a visceral thing. But she was nervous: she wasn't sure he returned her feelings, and she felt ... guilt.

They meandered into the garden, stopping to look at a winter rose, then a set of carvings. Gut-wrenching tension grew between them. She was shaking by the time they stopped at the fountain, like she might burst into tears at any moment. She dipped her fingers into the water, relishing the cool, crisp bite; anything to ground her.

'Raina,' said the man, pulling her up to face him, holding one of her shaking hands between his. His eyes ... they were Caspar's rich brown eyes.

'Caspar,' she said, her voice pleading.

He put a finger on her lips, then lowered himself to one knee.

A sob escaped her, relief breaking the dam holding her emotions.

'Raina, we've been to hell, and we both know it was you who took us there. I was angry, I won't deny it. I hated you. You tore my heart from my chest, threw it to the ground, and pressed your heel upon it. It shattered into countless pieces, never to be whole again.'

Raina sobbed once more, dropping to her knees, her hand caressing his face. He looked down, pressing into her touch. His eyes were cloudy when he looked at her again.

'Those fragments that you left behind, they ached. Every minute of every hour of every day, they ached for you. I'd shut my eyes and see the curves of your countless bodies, recall words you'd uttered just for me, study the memory of your stormy green eyes. I was sick with grief.'

He closed his eyes, pulled himself together, and when he opened them again, there was a newfound resolve.

'Raina Halabi, I will love you until the end of time, across countless lifetimes and countries and conflicts. I want nothing in this world aside from you.'

He pulled a battered band of gold from his cloak and slid it onto her finger.

'Marry me, and let us put this mess in the past.'

Raina's euphoria crashed into Amari, pummeling her chest. 'Yes,' she whispered, through another sob, pulling Caspar's lips to hers. 'I'm sorry,' she breathed. 'I love you.'

Caspar's hands went to her neck, caressing her skin as she relaxed into his deep, languid kisses. She sighed, opening her mouth to him, letting him claim her, pushing for more.

'Amari?'

Amari opened her eyes to find Caspar crouching before her. She was flushed, the sensation of the kiss still pressing on her lips. She flicked her eyes to his mouth, violent lust from the memory coursing through her.

Caspar ran his hand across her hair, his face only inches from hers, and she wanted him to kiss her. More than anything. She wanted to reach up and pull him to her, like Raina had; to hell with the consequences.

She wanted his hands in her hair, his tongue in her mouth, his teeth on her neck. She wanted him to take her upstairs, to feel his weight on her. She wanted him. Her eyes flicked again to his lips, so close.

His hand slid to her neck, hopeful eyes boring deep into her soul. He gasped.

'What?'

'Your eyes,' he said, gently tipping her head back to expose them to more light.

'What about them?'

'They're changing.'

I'm changing, she thought. *Can I stop it? Do I have any choice?* 'What … what did she do?'

Caspar's brow furrowed. 'Raina?'

Amari nodded. 'That flashback; you proposed to her, right here. You said she'd done something terrible.'

He looked away. 'It's complicated. For you to fully understand … there's so much I'd need to tell you …'

'How did I die?' she demanded.

Caspar looked confused at her change of tack.

'My most recent death. How did it happen?'

Caspar bowed his head. 'I wasn't there,' he said.

He pushed himself back and sat next to her on the edge of the pool.

'You don't know?'

'I heard rumors.'

'Which were?'

'You were being chased, we think by Templars. They'd been hunting you for some time. I don't know why, not for sure. They had you cornered, and you killed yourself rather than be taken.'

'I … killed myself?' A shudder ran through her.

'It wasn't the first time.'

'This is … Jesus, this is …'

She stood, a flash of anger catching hold of her. She bunched her fists against the rage. She didn't have the words for what this was. It was frustrating, and … abnormal. She hated that everyone here had this expectation of her—that she would wake up. To them, every moment she was herself, she was nothing but a disappointment. It wasn't a feeling she was used to.

'I told you it would seem fantastical.'

'That doesn't even begin to describe what this is,' she snapped.

Her phone buzzed in her pocket. She pulled it out, growling when she saw who it was. 'It's Dean.'

'I'll give you a minute,' he said, walking away.

Amari resisted the temptation to hurl the phone at his head.

Amari took a breath, pulling her furious emotions back under control, then answered the call. 'Dean, hi!' she said, too brightly. 'How was the flight?'

'Hey baby. It was fine; on time at least. How are you feeling? Are you still at the hotel? Leila said she was going to try and get the room for another night.'

'I'm ... still feeling kinda strange, I guess.'

'Has the doctor given you anything today?'

'No. I haven't seen the doctor again. I didn't really like him.' It wasn't a lie.

'But you're getting some rest?'

'I'm working through it.'

'I wish I was there.'

Amari's insides churned at the thought. The truth was, she was glad he'd flown away. The idea of him touching her was too much to bear.

Tears filled her eyes. This was so unfair; she'd been happy. She'd loved Dean more than anything, had been so excited for her life with him. She'd wondered whether their children would inherit his height, easy demeanor, delectable smile ... but now, the memory of his smile made her shudder. It was a cheap, disposable thing next to the memory of Caspar's lips on hers.

'Amari?' Dean asked, concern lacing his tone. 'You still there?'

'I'm still here,' she said, although she wasn't sure that was true.

'You ran like a baby,' said Jon, laughing as Caspar recounted his conversation with Amari.

Jon wouldn't have been Caspar's first choice as a confidant, but he couldn't find anyone else.

'I gave her privacy so she could speak to her ...'

'... husband,' finished Jon, taunting him.

'Fake husband, from a soon-to-be-annulled marriage.'

'Sure about that?'

'Yes. As soon as she wakes up, she won't want to be married to that loser. She's Raina Halabi: queenmaker, power broker, business mastermind, grand strategist. Wars have been won and lost because of her. She won't want some run-of-the-mill human rights lawyer.'

'But will she want you?' said Jon, his tone more serious.

'She will eventually, but I don't know if it'll be in this lifetime.'

He wasn't sure he could stand another lifetime in the doghouse.

'Rose wants to see us in her study,' said Jon, looking at his phone.

They walked down the stone corridor that led to a string of offices on the ground floor. Rose's office was unassuming, although it contained more than one priceless artifact: artwork that experts assumed lost, figurines carved for fun by famous sculptors, a necklace she'd acquired from ancient Egypt.

Dark wooden bookshelves covered most of the walls. The flagstone floor was covered with plush Persian rugs. The dogs lay in front of a big stone fireplace.

Jon and Caspar slumped into beaten up old tartan chairs, sitting opposite where Meredith, Talli, and Rose already sat in similarly worn seating.

'What's up?' asked Caspar, taking in their somber expressions.

'We've received two CCTV clips from the Metropolitan Police,' said Rose. 'There's more to come, but our contact wanted to share what they had as soon as possible.'

'Does it show who attacked us?' asked Caspar.

'Yes and no,' said Meredith. 'We've got a blurry face that our contact's running through facial recognition software. But obviously, that will only tell us so much, if anything at all.'

'Did they look young?' asked Caspar. The older they were the better, assuming they were a demon. If the attacker was young, recently reincarnated, then their face would be new, and less likely to be in the Pagans' own database.

'Quite young. Looks around thirty,' said Meredith, 'although the quality of the footage isn't great, so it's hard to say for sure.'

'Did it show anything else?' asked Caspar.

'They had what looks like a cuff on their right wrist. Again, it's hard to tell for sure, but …'

'… Templar,' said Jon, enthusiastically.

'Or a copycat,' said Meredith, 'or a human. Could be Slayers trying to stir up bad feeling between the nations, hoping we'll declare war and start killing each other.'

'So the footage tells us nothing helpful,' said Jon.

'Oh, to be young and melodramatic,' said Caspar.

Jon threw a cushion at Caspar's head. Caspar caught it, dropped it behind him, and leaned back.

'We can search for the attacker's face now we know it, and cross-reference it against our database of demons,' said Caspar.

'And our contact in the Met can do the same,' said Meredith.

'And we can ask the Registerium to cross-reference the face against their database,' said Rose. 'Although, they're unlikely to be registered, unless whoever's responsible is trying to send a message.'

'And we can be prepared when they attack again,' said Meredith, 'which reminds me ... do you all remember the protocols? What to do if you're attacked? Who to call?'

'Of course,' said Jon, as though this were a stupid question.

'I could probably do with some combat training,' said Caspar, shooting Jon a *stop trying so hard* look. 'I've never trained in this body.'

'Some of us keep ourselves well oiled,' said Jon.

Caspar shook his head, embarrassed for Jon.

'You could give us a demonstration with Meredith later,' said Caspar, a smirk pulling at the edge of his lips.

'Great idea,' said Rose, not giving Jon or Meredith time to protest.

Caspar's face split into a full, beaming grin. 'Wonderful,' he said.

'And afterwards, I can fight you,' Jon said to Caspar.

'Afterwards, everyone can train,' said Meredith. 'Amari should train too.'

Caspar nodded. 'I'll let her know.'

Amari entered the hall to find a crowd already gathered: Rose, Caspar, Jon, Elliot, Meredith, and Gemma. They greeted her when she arrived, and she smiled back, walking over to where Caspar sat with Rose on a low bench.

'Hey,' Caspar said. 'Good nap?'

Amari had told him she was tired after her call with Dean, but really, she'd just wanted to be alone. She'd sat in her bedroom, crying her eyes out, trying not to make too much noise. The last thing she needed was for everyone here to think she was tragic.

'Yes, thanks. So,' she said, looking around, 'what's all this about?'

'Combat training,' said Caspar, 'although I guess that sounds, I don't know, military or something. Doesn't suit these times. Anyway, Meredith likes to ensure we've all got some hand-to-hand combat skills, should we be attacked. In light of recent events, she's running a refresher course.'

'And she's got some new moves she wants to teach us,' said Jon, plonking himself down next to Amari. 'Her method's one of a kind; it's a mixture of everything she's ever learned, from all the martial arts across the world.' His eyes tracked Meredith as he talked.

Caspar rolled his eyes and Amari suppressed a smile. 'I've never done any martial arts,' she said.

Caspar snorted. 'Your subconscious has.'

'What's that supposed to mean?'

'That once you wake up, no one's going to want to face you in a fight,' said Jon. 'You're almost as good as Meredith.'

Caspar leaned in and murmured, 'You're better; you just got bored of showing off in recent lifetimes.'

A shiver shot up Amari's spine, adrenaline flowing through her blood. She'd always been competitive. An irrational part of her wanted to put Meredith flat on her back to prove how good she was. This was obviously ridiculous, given she'd be worse than useless in a fight … she'd have to subdue her competitive side until her old memories came back.

Oh God, her *old memories*? Was she beginning to believe this craziness?

'Pre-Midsummer celebration. Here. Tomorrow night,' came Talli's singsong voice as she entered at the back of the room.

'Bring your wild side,' said Christa, embracing Meredith and Gemma.

'Do I need to be worried?' Amari asked Caspar.

'With those two? Always,' said Rose, before Caspar could respond.

'Amari!' said Talli. 'We're so glad you're here! You're not cross, are you?'

Amari looked between Talli's mischievous features and Christa's guilty expression. 'It's nice to see you too,' she said.

Talli clapped her hands in glee, pulling Amari into an awkward hug. Then she sat on the ground right in front of Amari, her long skirt billowing out around her. She pulled Christa down too, linking their arms.

'This should be fun,' said Talli, as Meredith summoned Jon to the middle of the room.

'He's going to get his ass kicked,' said Christa, loud enough for Jon to hear.

'Hey, a little faith, please,' said Jon, limbering up.

Meredith turned to where everyone now sat in a crowd at the side. 'The session will proceed as follows,' she said, in a tone that nobody was going to argue with. 'Jon and I will fight, which will take all of two minutes.'

'Hey!' said Jon.

Meredith ignored him. 'Then, I'll use Jon to demonstrate some new moves. After that, everyone will pair up and fight, and I'll train Amari. Any questions?'

Silence.

'Great. Ready, Jon?'

But Jon was already launching an attack from behind. Meredith sidestepped him, and he lurched a few paces past where she stood.

Talli clapped loudly. 'Spirited start, Jon, bravo!'

Jon didn't respond; he was already launching his next attack. Meredith spun him over her arm. Jon landed hard on the floor.

The crowd groaned. 'That's got to hurt,' said Elliot.

'At least she puts mats down these days,' said Christa. 'Remember that Christmas? I guess it must have been in the fifteen hundreds.'

'No,' said Elliot. 'I wasn't alive in the fifteen hundreds.'

'Oh, well, anyway, she kept throwing us onto the stone floor of this church—can't remember where it was. Said it would toughen us up.'

'Until she broke my back,' said Rose.

'She let us have padding after that,' said Christa.

'Well done, Jon. Up you get,' sang Talli. 'Take a step back. Make her come to you.'

Jon didn't respond, but he waited for Meredith to attack.

Meredith sauntered towards him, one eyebrow raised. 'Ready for me to finish it?' she asked, getting close, her tone seductive.

Jon looked at her, their eyes level, and everything went still. His arm shot out, trying to punch her stomach, but she blocked him, flicked his legs out from under him, and left him in a heap on the floor.

'So, now we've got that out of the way,' said Meredith, 'Jon, if you'd be so kind as to get up and stand in front of me.'

Jon did as he was told, Meredith wrapping her arms around him from behind.

Jon raised a cocky eyebrow at the crowd.

'You know you're about to end up on the floor again, right?' said Elliot.

'Don't even care,' said Jon, just as Meredith demonstrated how to drop an opponent to the ground. He groaned. 'Okay, I care a little.'

Meredith demonstrated two further moves before telling Jon he could sit down.

'Talli, Gemma, you're up,' said Meredith. 'Try to incorporate the new moves as you fight.'

'Go Tals! You've got this!' said Christa, as Talli jumped up and danced to the middle of the matted area. Gemma followed her.

Amari leaned into Caspar. 'Isn't that a bit unfair? Talli versus Miss Warrior Princess?'

Caspar chuckled. 'Just watch.'

Talli and Gemma spun around the floor. Amari was amazed to see that Gemma was hanging back, wary even.

Talli would circle in, land a blow, and circle away again, before Gemma could respond. Talli's movements were fluid, flowing, like a dancer's. She unleashed uncompromising kicks and punches, all while looking like it was a choreographed routine.

Gemma held her own, landing her share of punches, but Talli had the edge. She finished it with a karate kick to Gemma's chest, throwing her backwards onto the mat.

Christa clapped and whistled loudly. 'That's my girl!'

Talli hopped her feet together, held the sides of her skirt up, and curtsied to the crowd.

'That felt wonderful,' she gushed, gliding back to her seat.

'Now you've seen the moves in action, it's your turn,' Meredith said to the rest of them. 'Rose with Talli, Caspar with Christa, and the two young'uns.'

'We're not that young anymore,' Jon grumbled, walking to the other side of the room with Elliot.

'Younger than the rest of us,' laughed Talli.

Meredith took Amari to the back, showing her the basics of self-defense while the others sparred. Amari picked it up quickly, her muscles seeming to instinctively know what Meredith wanted her to do.

'Not as bad as I'd feared,' said Meredith, after an hour. 'We can add in a few attacking moves next time too.'

'Thanks,' said Amari, feeling good after the exercise. Her muscles would ache in the morning, but it was nice to get her blood pumping.

'Did someone say it was dinner time?' asked Talli, picking herself up from where Rose had deposited her on the floor. Amari couldn't quite believe it.

'Never underestimate the power of experience,' Caspar whispered, his body so close she could feel his breath on her ear.

Amari closed her eyes for a split second, the memory of a queen dressed in all her finery flashing before her eyes. The monarch was striding towards a dais, where her throne awaited. Amari quickly opened her eyes; she'd had enough memories for one day.

Dinner was beef Wellington, mashed potato, and green beans. Amari had no idea how Elliot had managed to cook it to perfection in between training.

'I'm confused about the boundaries,' said Amari, as they tucked into a dessert of summer pudding and clotted cream. Her stomach was already bursting at the seams, but it didn't seem right to pass up something so delicious. 'How do they work?'

'The boundaries?' asked Jon.

'Between nations. Where does Pagan territory stop and Templar territory start, for example?'

'In that particular case,' said Rose, 'the boundary is through the middle of the Atlantic, up almost to Iceland and Greenland, where the Viking's territory begins. Everything below Denmark and above the Mediterranean is ours, right the way along to the far side of Poland, down through Ukraine, Romania, Bulgaria, and Turkey.'

'So, in some countries, more than one nation owns territory?' asked Amari.

'Of course,' Rose replied. 'Modern borders were drawn long after our territories were agreed. And, of course, if a nation is wiped out, or goes to war and is defeated, our territories have to be redrawn, so they move around over time.'

'An organization called the Registerium keeps the official record, in case of dispute,' said Caspar.

'Although, a lot of the new or tiny nations don't register until there's some benefit to them,' said Elliot. 'So even the Registerium isn't a complete picture.'

'Are people from other nations allowed to travel in Pagan territory without asking first?' asked Amari. 'Is there some kind of demon passport?!'

'That's a grey area,' said Talli, giving Amari a meaningful look. 'They're supposed to ask for official permission, but people rarely bother these days.'

'The problem is, it's impossible to track unregistered demons,' said Meredith. 'As long as everyone respects the Registerium's rules, we generally overlook trespassing.'

'What are the rules?' said Amari, scraping up the last morsels in her bowl.

'No war unless there's good reason,' said Christa.

'The Registerium gets to decide what constitutes a *good* reason,' added Talli.

'No exposing us to humans. And no fighting with anything other than knives—guns draw too much attention,' said Christa.

'Christa used to work for the Registerium,' said Talli.

'Yep,' Christa confirmed. 'And each nation has a representative on the Registerium's council. Generally, demons sit for one lifetime; it's an interesting job.'

'Too political for me,' said Talli, screwing up her face. 'People lying to you all the time, trying to register false identities, fabricating rule contraventions, trying to get their territory increased when they're not entitled to …'

'… but I got to see who was trying to get the Registerium to back what cause,' said Christa. 'When a nation's gearing up for war, it's helpful to have the Registerium on side. A lot of the smaller nations will follow whatever the Registerium decides. Even if the Registerium decides not to fight, they might impose fines and sanctions, which can really help turn the tide of a war.'

'And you said the Templars are causing trouble?' asked Amari, putting down her spoon and leaning back in her chair, trying to relieve the pressure on her stomach.

'Unfortunately, yes,' said Rose. 'They've been antagonizing us for the past hundred years or so, testing

79

us, seeing how much we'll let them get away with. We think they're going to try and take this island, but everything's gone quiet. Random attacks are their only communication.'

'What?! As in England, Scotland, and Wales?' said Amari, in disbelief.

These people went around *taking* countries?

'Why?'

'There's a lot of magic here,' said Rose. 'Islands are prone to magic.'

Amari's expression was skeptical, like Rose had crossed a line.

Rose laughed. 'My dear, what, if not magic, do you think supports our reincarnation?'

'Like wands and potions and flying on broomsticks?'

'No broomsticks,' said Talli, 'and no wands, but small magics. Herbs, energy, healing crystals, music and vibrations, projections, that kind of thing.'

'Have you ever had a thought about someone pop into your head, entirely at random, and then find out something significant happened to them at that moment?' asked Caspar.

'Or just known something was wrong, but didn't know what?' said Christa. 'And then gone home to find your house flooded?'

'It's magic,' said Talli, her eyes flashing playfully.

'Mind blown?' laughed Jon, taking in Amari's expression. 'Wait and see what weird shit this one's going to pull tomorrow night.' He nodded at Talli. 'She's kind of like our spiritual leader.'

'Just call me Priestess,' said Talli, with a smile.

Amari thanked Elliot for dinner, then told everyone she was going to bed.

'I need to grab a couple of things from your room,' said Caspar, following her out, ignoring the watchful eyes of the rest of the table.

'Where will you sleep?' asked Amari, as they climbed the first set of stairs.

'There are plenty of spare rooms,' he said. 'I'll be in the one just across the landing.'

'I could sleep in another room if you'd prefer,' said Amari. 'It seems unfair to kick you out of your bedroom.'

'It was your room first, actually,' said Caspar. Not to mention the hundreds of little things in there that might cause a flashback, or—please Gods—her full awakening.

'If you're sure …'

'I am.'

He followed her up the second set of stairs, giving in to the temptation of watching her as she climbed in front of him.

They entered the bedroom and Caspar moved around, opening drawers, pulling out clothes and a couple of books.

Amari sat on the bed, watching him. She shuffled back so her head rested against the headboard.

'I think that's all I need for tonight,' he said, heading for the door.

'Sit with me for a while,' said Amari, the words rushed. She added, almost shyly, 'I still have a lot of questions … if you don't mind.'

'Of course.'

He placed his belongings on one of the button-backs and sat on the bed, as close as he dared.

Her body, with its fiery, Mediterranean features, suited Raina to a T. Caspar smirked as he remembered a short, White, toneless body Raina had once found herself in. She'd been aghast, but try as she might, she'd never managed to get it into shape. Raina had always said that body was spiteful, that it had wanted her to look bad. Caspar had liked it; he'd quite enjoyed the curves.

'What?' said Amari. 'What's funny?'

'I was just thinking how well that body matches your personality, and remembering one that didn't suit you quite so well.'

'Didn't suit *Raina*, you mean,' she said, looking at her hands.

'It's the same thing,' he said, shifting forward, but catching himself before he touched her.

'Will I even remember who I am when Raina comes back? Assuming this isn't some weird reality TV show.'

Caspar laughed.

'I'm only half joking.'

'I know,' he said. 'You'll be exactly the same person when you wake. You're Raina, even now. Your personality is her personality, you just don't have all the memories and experiences that nuance her. You're more heavily influenced by this life, rather than a collection of all of your lives.'

'So I won't be wiped out?'

'You'll be the same, just with vastly improved combat skills, and some different opinions. Your subconscious is Raina; you and she are one and the same.'

'Different opinions about what?' she said, searching his eyes.

'About me,' he joked.

She tilted her head. 'What will I think about you when she wakes?'

'You've been pretty angry at me for the last couple of lifetimes,' he said, raising his eyebrows.

She appraised him, looking from one of his eyes to the other.

'What did you do?' she said.

Caspar went rigid, clasped his hands, then turned his body away. He couldn't talk about this with her; she didn't remember her side. When Raina came back, she'd accuse him of trying to manipulate her.

'Hey,' she said, crossing her legs and leaning forward, briefly touching his arm. 'I'm sorry, I didn't mean to make you uncomfortable.'

'It …' he started, then paused. 'I don't know how you'll react when you wake up. It terrifies me.'

Silence stretched between them.

'How did you know it was me?' said Amari. 'I get that hunters have special abilities, but did you know it was me, right from when we first met?'

'Yes,' he said, without hesitation. 'Awake demons feel magic more keenly, and your magic's almost as familiar to me as my own. When we shook hands, I could feel it, and I recognized your eyes. And as soon as you started talking, I was absolutely certain.'

Amari sat back and looked up at the ceiling. 'What's the point of all this?' she asked, rubbing her face with her hands. 'I mean, it's hard enough to contemplate the meaning of a single life. But endless lives? Did I irritate a divine being somewhere? Is this my punishment?'

Caspar shifted to face her. 'It's no different for us than anyone else. We all have to work out what's important to us, what we want to do with our lives.' He paused until she looked at him. 'And it's not a punishment. Never think that.'

'Why?'

'We get second chances,' he said, 'and a chance to make a difference.'

He looked away, fisting a hand in the bed covers, seeking an outlet for his frustration.

'Like what? What difference can any of us really make?'

'We can try; we can fight for equality, to stop people like the Templars from taking over. And we get to learn, to love, to take care of the people who matter to us, to laugh, dance, sing, and … we get to be together.'

Silence settled over them once more.

'All I ever wanted was a family,' said Amari.

'Yeah?'

'I wanted kids, with Dean, more than anything. Did we ever …?' She avoided his eyes as she said the words.

Caspar's heart pounded. 'It's rare for demons to have children. Even if they do conceive, there's no guarantee the child will be demon too.'

'Oh.' She bowed her head. 'It's weird … I've never been into other peoples' kids. Honestly, I find most of them repulsive; I'm the worst kind of person, I know.'

Caspar shrugged, like it was probably true. Amari shoved him.

'The idea of my own kid though … it's … something I want.'

Caspar's hand went to the front of his shirt, clutching at the fabric; children were what every demon wanted but knew they would never get. It burned a hole inside them all.

He searched for words. 'It … might happen. But what's more likely is that a hunter will find a child who everyone thinks is mentally ill, because they keep talking about a past life, or because they're having strange dreams, or they know too much for someone their age; a new demon, who needs a mother.'

Amari shook her head. 'No. That's not what I mean.'

Chapter 8

The following morning, Amari jogged down the stairs, breezed into the kitchen, and announced to Meredith and Gemma that she would be returning to her hotel room to pick up her stuff.

Meredith and Gemma tried to talk her out of it, told her they would go instead, but Amari was adamant. Eventually, Amari just walked out, seeing as she wasn't a hostage.

Caspar entered the kitchen just as she did so, left with little choice but to follow in her wake.

They took a taxi to the hotel, Gemma and Caspar waiting outside while Meredith went in with Amari. Caspar had wanted to go in too, but Amari had put her foot down. She didn't need him looking at all her personal stuff, and Dean's parents could still be kicking around. She didn't need them seeing her with another man.

Meredith swept the bridal suite while Amari waited in the doorway. Amari resisted the urge to roll her eyes. She had to remind herself that yesterday they'd been attacked. *Was it really only yesterday?*

Once Meredith gave the all clear, it took Amari only a couple of minutes to pack her things. She followed Meredith back into the elevator only ten minutes after they'd entered the lobby.

The elevator doors opened, and Meredith stepped out, striding towards the exit. Amari was right behind her, until a hand clamped down on her arm. Amari whirled around, and her blood ran cold. She found, to her dismay, Dean's sister Jade, glaring at her in the way only teenaged girls could.

'Jade, hi!' said Amari, too enthusiastically.

'Where have you been?' Jade demanded. 'Leila told us you went off with some *man*. We've been waiting for you to get in touch and explain yourself.'

Explain myself? Amari almost laughed in her face. 'Given your brother's working, I decided to do the same. That man was a colleague.'

'But you were ill,' she said, 'and Leila didn't say he was a colleague.'

'Because Leila didn't know,' said Amari, forcefully. 'And, by the way, I don't have to explain myself to either of you.'

'Leila's really hurt, you know. She thought you would've confided in her.'

Was she for real? 'About what, exactly?'

'If you're having an affair and didn't want to marry my brother.'

Amari barked out a laugh. 'I am not, nor have I been having, an affair. So take your teenaged melodrama and leave me alone.'

Amari left the hotel, her back riddled with the daggers Jade thew from her eyes.

'What was that about?' asked Meredith.

'Dean's little sister,' said Amari. 'She's always hated me, and now she's decided I'm having an affair.'

'If anything, Dean was the affair,' said Caspar. Meredith punched him on the arm. 'Ow, what?'

'You're an idiot,' said Meredith.

87

Amari had already hailed a taxi and was getting in, Gemma hot on her heels.

'Where are you going now?' asked Gemma.

'To my ... Dean's house, to get some clothes.'

'That's absurd,' said Caspar.

'That's the first place someone would go if they were trying to find you,' said Gemma.

'That's why you guys are here, isn't it?' said Amari, getting in the car and telling the driver the address. 'Come or stay, it's up to you, but I'm going.'

She held her breath; she really didn't want to go alone.

'Get in the front,' Meredith told Gemma, pushing Amari into the middle so she could climb in beside her.

Caspar went to the far side door, huffing loudly and muttering under his breath.

'Wait here,' said Meredith, as they pulled up at the top of the street. 'Keys and security code please.'

Meredith and Gemma got out. They each took a side of the road, stalking towards the townhouse where Amari's rehearsal dinner had been held only two days before.

Finally satisfied the area was clear of threats, Meredith entered through the front door and Gemma ducked round the back.

Caspar and Amari sat in the cab, the driver looking bored.

'How long are we going to sit here?' the driver asked. 'Not that I mind ... just want to know what kind of wait I'm in for, that's all.'

'Only a few minutes,' said Caspar, his tone clipped.

Amari threw him a stern look; there was no need to take his irritation out on the driver.

'We shouldn't be here,' Caspar hissed, low enough that the driver couldn't hear. 'It's reckless.'

Amari shrugged. 'I need to get some of my things.' *Before Dean gets back and burns everything I own*, she didn't add.

Dean. What was she going to do about Dean? She still wasn't certain the Pagans weren't some cult. Maybe this was how they got people to join … maybe she should go to the police.

Meredith appeared at the door, signaling that it was safe for them to go in. Amari didn't hesitate, throwing the door open and striding down the road. Caspar scrambled to catch up.

Amari walked in through the front door, feeling like an intruder in her own home. Because, it wasn't her home any longer.

She looked at the artwork on the walls, most of which she and Dean had bought together. She ran a hand over the fabric of the sofa they'd had for years. She looked at the photos of her and Dean on numerous holidays, and with friends and family, that she'd lovingly placed in frames and dotted around the place to make it feel like home.

She walked up the stairs, into the master bedroom, feeling guilty as she looked at Dean's side of the immaculately made bed. Cufflinks sat in a little bowl on his nightstand, most of which she'd given him.

His slippers were next to the bed, a half-read book on international relations sat on the chest of drawers. Looking around, she could pretend that nothing of the last two days had happened. She could lie down and imagine that she and Dean were blissfully happy; about to embark on a wonderful life together.

But she'd never been one for burying her head in the sand. She pulled out a Mulberry travel bag and started stuffing clothes inside. She didn't take much, just everyday clothes, pajamas, comfortable shoes, a favorite pair of earrings.

She already had most of her toiletries from the hotel, but she packed a few extra things from the bathroom, inhaling the familiar smell of Dean's aftershave. That smell had been part of her life for so long ... the thought was like a knife in her gut.

She left the house, tears pooling in her eyes, grieving the life she'd lost. Whatever happened now— even if it did all turn out to be a cult—her life could never go back to the way it had been.

She walked down the steps outside, deep in thought, when Callie came rushing out of the house next door.

'Mari! Mari!' Callie called gleefully. 'Are you okay? Nana said you were sick.'

Amari crouched and pulled Callie in for a hug, her tears threatening to overflow. She hadn't considered that she might never see Callie again. 'I'm fine, munchkin. Did you like the wedding?'

'Yes! I'm going to wear my dress every day. Well, not today, because Nana's washing it, but every day I can. And I danced with Dean, and Leila, and loads of people. And I ate two pieces of cake! I tried to get another one, but Nana wouldn't let me. And you looked like a princess!'

'Thanks, sweetie. You looked like a princess too.'

'Nana said you couldn't go on your special holiday. Is that true?'

'Dean had to fly to America to help someone, but he'll be back soon.'

'And then you'll go on holiday?'

Amari pulled her in for another hug, then pushed her to arm's length. 'Did you grow?'

Callie giggled gleefully. 'I'm nearly as big as you!'

'Maybe it was all that cake.'

Caspar walked up behind Amari, surprising her when he crouched down next to them.

'Hey!' he said. 'What's your name?'

'Callie,' she said proudly. 'I was one of Mari's bridesmaids.'

'You were?' he asked.

Callie nodded enthusiastically.

'I bet you were the best bridesmaid of them all.'

Callie giggled again. 'Who are you?' she asked.

'I'm Caspar, Amari's friend.'

'Were you at the wedding?'

'I couldn't be there, but Amari and I are doing some work together. In fact, we need to get going … but, will you do something for me?'

Callie laughed. 'What?'

'Will you put this in some water?' He held out a daisy he'd picked from the verge.

Callie made a grab for his hand and pulled it free. 'I'm going to put it in my flower press so I can keep it forever.'

Caspar laughed. 'That sounds like a great idea. It was lovely to meet you, Callie.'

Callie hummed with delight, giving him a hug before Amari pulled her in again.

'I can't wait to see that once you've pressed it,' said Amari.

'I'll come over and show it to you,' she said.

The tears threatened again. 'Sounds wonderful.'

They got up to leave. Amari chatted briefly with Callie's grandmother, who was standing at the door, patiently waiting for Callie to return.

Callie ran up the steps, through the door, then appeared seconds later at the window, waving wildly.

Caspar and Amari waved back.

'She's got spirit,' said Caspar, as they walked towards where Meredith waited a little further up the street. Gemma followed behind.

'She's one of a kind,' said Amari. 'I'm going to miss her.'

Amari held it together until they got back to Cloister Cottage, but only made it as far as the kitchen, where the smell of rosemary made her strangely nostalgic. She burst into tears.

Caspar was there in an instant, indicating to the others that they should leave.

'I know this is confusing,' he said, rubbing her arms, 'but it'll be easier when you wake.'

'Because I'll forget everyone I care about?'

'No, of course not. I don't think you'll ever forget Callie, or the bond you have, but when you wake up … I don't know … I just think all the other memories will make it easier.'

At that, the tears started coming thick and fast. Caspar pulled Amari to his chest, wrapping his arms around her. She pressed into him, sobbing into his t-shirt.

They stayed there a while, Caspar stroking her back, making soothing circles, holding her tight.

'I'm sorry,' said Amari, pulling back, wiping the tears on her sleeve.

'Don't apologize; crying's healthy. Shall I make tea?'

Amari nodded.

'And I'm sure Elliot's got something delicious in one of these tins,' he said, rummaging around. 'Bingo!' He pulled out a pink floral biscuit tin and set it on the table. 'Chocolate shortbread.' He picked up a piece and took a large bite as he walked back to the Aga.

'Honestly, any time you need to cry, you should embrace it. Everyone here's lived enough lives to know crying's medicine.'

Amari smiled. 'Thanks,' she said, sitting in front of the tin and taking a piece of shortbread.

Her phone buzzed. A deep sense of foreboding filled her when she saw the name. 'It's Dean; I'll go outside.'

'Stay,' said Caspar, setting a steaming mug of tea in front of her. 'I'll give you some privacy.'

He left through the door that led to the stairs.

Amari took a deep breath and picked up the call.

'Hey, Dean.'

'Hey, baby,' said Dean.

Amari winced.

'What's been going on?'

'What do you mean?' Amari said, suddenly jumpy. Did he know something?

'Just wondering what you've been up to. You sound kinda off … is everything okay?'

'Yeah, fine, just tired after the wedding,' she said, fiddling with the shortbread crumbs on the table.

'I wish I could be there with you. Actually, no, I wish we were lying by a pool right now, sipping cocktails.'

'Me too,' said Amari, and she meant it. A luxury hotel, the sound of lapping water, sun on her skin, an elaborate cocktail … that all sounded pretty great right about now. 'Do you know when you're coming back?'

'It's impossible to say, but it's going to be at least another week. I would tell you to get on a plane and come see me, but we're working stupid hours ...'

'I know,' she said. She got up and walked to the window. 'I'm working here too, keeping busy.'

'You sure you're okay? You haven't been messaging much, and you sound ... flat.'

'It's been a busy couple of days,' she said absently.

She watched a bird scratching in a flower bed in the courtyard; if only her life were so simple.

'Babe, I've got to go to a meeting. Speak later?'

'Sure.'

'I love you.'

'I love you too.'

Amari felt sick. How was it possible that so soon after meaning them, those words were a lie?

Chapter 9

Amari entered the hall, feeling more than a little ridiculous. Talli had sent her a simple, white, floor-length dress to wear, along with a crown made of eucalyptus, laurel, and dainty white flowers.

The dress tied at the waist with a gold cord and was unnervingly similar to the dresses she'd had her bridesmaids wear at her wedding. She went barefoot, as instructed, and had sprayed herself liberally with a perfume Talli had left for her. It smelled like orange and geranium, and Amari couldn't get enough of it.

The moment she set foot inside the hall, her trepidation fell away. It had been transformed into a medieval banqueting hall, a long table stretched down the middle, flowers hanging above, suspended from the ceiling. Candles were dotted among the flowers and along the table's length.

The table was set with the most beautiful, rustic, handmade pottery, copper-colored cutlery, and old, heavy glassware. A pink rose and sprig of rosemary perched on top of each linen napkin.

The table was laden with endless platters of food: fruit, cheese, pies, bread, cured meats, chutneys. Decanters of ruby red wine sat among the food, alongside yet more flowers.

The rest of the hall had been decorated in an equally breathtaking manner, the smell of summer wafting amid the flowers and lit candles.

A large copper bowl sat at each of the four compass points, flames roaring in the northernmost bowl. Musicians warmed up their lutes and panpipes at the opposite end, a patch of floor in front of them left clear for dancing.

Caspar handed Amari a heavy glass of red wine. 'Talli and Christa never fail to amaze,' he said.

'It's breathtaking. Were they wedding planners in a former life?'

Caspar laughed. 'In a manner of speaking, they were. But they rarely wait for someone to employ them; usually they just take over. Or, Talli does, and Christa goes where Talli leads, swept along like the rest of us.'

'How many lifetimes have they been together?' asked Amari.

'Only three or four, actually; their love is still young.'

Amari laughed. 'If you say so.'

'Compared to ours, it's minutes old.'

Amari didn't know what to say to that … 'What have they got planned for the evening?'

'Who knows,' said Caspar. 'They like to keep us guessing. But some combination of eating, rituals, and dancing is how these things go.'

'Rituals?'

'Pagan rituals.'

'Oh yeah, right.' The thought made her uncomfortable; she'd always thought Paganism was a joke. 'Who are they?' she asked, pointing to a cluster of five or six new people. Aside from the musicians, she knew everyone else in the hall.

'Bodyguards,' said Caspar. 'Meredith's best team.'

'Sit, everyone, sit!' said Talli, dressed exactly like Amari, like all the women were. 'First we feast.'

Amari waited expectantly to hear what came second, but Talli didn't continue.

They took seats at random, Talli not seeming to care who sat where. She flitted around, into and out of the kitchen, adjusting flowers, relighting a candle that had fluttered out, checking in with the musicians—who began to play—before finally landing at the head of the table.

Talli picked up a sprig of rosemary and an ornate knife, and a sudden silence cut through the din. Even the musicians killed their instruments, perfectly on cue.

A shudder ran down Amari's spine, a tingle of anticipation kindling in her stomach. She looked to Caspar, who she found was watching her, handsome in the candlelight.

Her insides contracted as she took in his predatory features. She held his gaze, momentarily lost in the depth of his eyes, made mysterious by the flickering light. He was perfectly still, yet poised, drinking her in, ready to pounce.

Talli moved and Amari turned back to watch. She was holding the knife over her head, walking slowly towards the flaming bowl.

The silence was absolute as Talli used the knife to cut a circle in the air in front of the fire. She did it quickly, using her whole body, as though it were part of a dance. It looked as though there was resistance, something pushing back against the knife, and something sparked in Amari's memory. She shook it away.

Talli finished the cutting, then dropped to one knee, saying words that Amari didn't understand. Talli stood, thrusting her arm through the circle, dropping the sprig of rosemary into the flames, chanting the whole time. She pulled her hand back, then fanned her arms out to either side, tipping her head back as her chants crescendoed.

The air in the room went tight, energy potent, the hairs on Amari's arms rising. Everyone leaned in as Talli started swaying, faster and faster to match her words.

Christa rose from her seat, carrying a copper bell suspended on a short piece of rope. She moved towards Talli, her white dress hiding her feet, giving her an ethereal air in the flickering candlelight.

Christa stood behind Talli, lifted the bell, and struck it once. Talli dropped to the floor, no longer chanting. Christa let the bell ring, the deep, crisp *dong* resonating around the hall.

Amari was held in a trancelike state, unable to tear her eyes away. It felt so natural, and yet so strange. Only days before, she would've laughed at the thought of attending a ceremony such as this ...

The ringing finally ceased and Talli rose to her feet. She swiveled to face Christa, and they kissed. Amari felt uncomfortable, like an intruder on an intimate moment, but no one else batted an eye. In fact, much to her surprise, Elliot kissed Gemma, Jon kissed Meredith, who, weirdly, didn't protest, and everyone else was at it too. Even Rose was kissing one of the bodyguards.

Caspar was suddenly close, leaning towards her. 'It's just part of the ceremony,' he whispered, the spicy scent of his cologne intoxicating. 'Meredith would punch Jon in the face if he tried to kiss her under normal circumstances.'

His eyes flicked to her lips and she tingled with anticipation. Her whole body tensed. He leaned forwards, then paused.

Her breathing hitched, heart racing. Her eyelids fluttered closed, wine fogging her thoughts, chasing her inhibitions away.

He pressed his lips to her cheek, a small huff escaping her at the shock of the contact, and then he pulled away, tracing a finger down her arm, gently squeezing her hand before breaking all contact.

Amari fought the urge to pull him back, lace her fingers with his, rest her head against him.

Every part of her deflated. Her lips prickled, angry at being denied the contact they sought. Her head swam, the music and wine and candlelight almost hypnotic. But a thought of acute clarity forced its way in, the searing light of it stark against the candlelit gloom, carving an image across her mind. The image of a man, wearing a suit, waiting for her to walk down the aisle towards him: her husband, Dean. What was wrong with her?

Talli and Christa returned to the table and the kissing ceased. Jon and Meredith were the last to relinquish each other. To Amari's surprise, Meredith didn't look at all put out.

As soon as Talli and Christa sat, they all dug into the feast with gusto, grabbing handfuls from the platters, knocking back wine, chatter and laughter filling the air.

Amari picked at the food, feeling nervous, like an outsider among them. They were so comfortable with each other, never running out of things to say, understanding one other in a way Amari couldn't begin to.

'Everything okay?' asked Caspar, leaning in again, his voice low.

'Yes,' said Amari, avoiding his eyes. 'It's just … I'm a few lifetimes short of fitting in.'

Caspar stifled a laugh. 'Sorry,' he said, resting a hand on her forearm at her hurt expression.

Amari's focus narrowed to the spot where their skin met. He absently rubbed his thumb back and forth.

99

She took a deep breath, ignoring the sensation pooling inside.

'I'm sorry you feel that way. It's only funny because normally the boot's on the other foot.'

'Well, I'm not that person now,' she said, pulling her arm away.

'You are,' he said, grabbing her hand, holding it in both of his. 'You'll wake up soon. Your eyes are gaining flecks all the time; you'll be back to ruling this place any day now.'

That doesn't help me now. But she gave a small nod and turned back to the table, putting an end to the topic.

When Talli deemed the feast to have gone on for long enough, she stood, motioning to the musicians to up the tempo. They sprang to life, the music shifting from mellow sounds that faded into the background, to loud, vivid strokes of the violin and fast drumbeats.

Talli took to the open area in front of the musicians and danced; leaping, circling, clapping, swaying, her dress flowing around her legs, hair bouncing wildly with her movements. The others watched, clapping, laughing, and cheering her on.

Jon was next to take to the floor. He swung Talli around, lifting her, spinning her, then they circled apart, each dancing their own dance. It didn't take long for the rest of the table to join in.

Caspar offered Amari his hand. She didn't even hesitate, her hand going to his without conscious thought. *Maybe that was Raina*, thought Amari, as Caspar pulled her in, wrapping his arms tightly around her shoulders, swaying them in time to the music.

Amari hesitated, conflicted about the proximity. Her body was so firmly pressed up against his, feeling every hard muscle and line of him through their clothes.

'It's only dancing,' he said in her ear, running a hand down her tense back.

It was too much … his smell, his body, the deep seductive tone of his voice rumbling through her. Desire flooded her, but guilt chased it, the sensation making her nauseous. She was about to pull away, to say she needed a drink, when the music changed. It wasn't so different from the song before, with the same upbeat, Celtic feel, but Amari's mind and body reacted instantly, as one.

An electric thrill of excitement ran up her spine. Her eyes seemed to open wider. Her mind seemed to process more. And out of nowhere, her hands tightened around Caspar. She pressed herself against him, let his hands guide her, swayed her hips like a temptress.

Amari was there, but also not. It was like being in a flashback, but in real time, her conscious brain yielding entirely to the dominance of what lay beneath.

Caspar felt the change and didn't hesitate, whirling them around, moving them as one, ignoring everyone else. The others were too caught up in their own dancing to pay Caspar and Amari any attention anyway.

The hall came alive with reeling, pulsing energy, the music, and alcohol, and maybe even a little magic, making them high. The energy bounced from person to person, everyone contributing to the rising tide.

Amari felt it all vibrate through her, her blood beginning to sing, reveling in the feel of Caspar's solid body against hers. She shifted, sliding her leg in between his, delighting in the hardness she felt there as he rocked them from side to side.

Caspar growled into her neck, one hand sliding lower, covering her backside, pulling her writhing hips against him. She gasped in his ear, burying her face in his neck, moving with the beat.

The music slowed and she pulled back, placed a hand on Caspar's face, and looked seductively up into his smoky brown eyes. She would have pulled his lips to hers, would have kissed him, was inching towards him, not caring who was watching, or that she was married, or that she'd only just met him. But the song came to an abrupt end.

Whatever had held Amari's mind released, and her inhibitions snapped back into place. She dropped her hand and stepped back, Caspar's features turning ashen as she slipped away.

Amari held his gaze, trying to apologize with her eyes, hoping he would understand. And then she fled.

The following morning, Amari—her head pounding—sought out Meredith. She found her in the kitchen, drinking a suspicious-looking concoction of raw egg and something green.

Meredith was more than happy to oblige Amari's request to train, muttering something about Jon having got the wrong impression and needing a distraction anyway. Amari smiled, but didn't probe for details.

'We'll start with a jog,' said Meredith. 'We won't be able to do anything constructive until our heads are clearer.'

'I thought it wasn't safe to go out?' said Amari, her hopes picking up at the thought of leaving the confines of Cloister Cottage.

'We'll be quick, and I'll be with you,' Meredith replied. 'We'll take Gemma too, and the dogs.'

'No, you won't,' laughed Talli, entering the kitchen, dropping to the floor to pet the dogs.

Meredith gave Talli a look, demanding more information.

'Gemma's in Elliot's room. I doubt she wants to be disturbed.'

Meredith rolled her eyes. 'Looks like it's just you and me then,' she said, 'unless you want to come for a jog, Talli?'

'I'll come,' she said, jumping up. 'Just give me a minute to change.'

A few minutes later, they were heading for the river. It was still early enough that the city commuters were few and far between. In an hour, the place would teem with life, people streaming purposefully off tubes and into office buildings.

The dogs were the most well-behaved animals Amari had ever seen, trotting obediently along, without the need for leashes.

'Rose trains them,' said Meredith, following Amari's gaze. 'No one else can inspire the same levels of obedience, despite endless attempts.'

Amari laughed. 'It's amazing.'

They jogged along in silence for a bit before Amari's curiosity got the better of her. 'Are Elliot and Gemma together?' she asked.

Talli laughed. 'They've been trying to figure that out for three lifetimes.'

'Gemma's shy,' said Meredith.

'And Elliot's too much of a gentleman,' added Talli.

'But it was always going to happen eventually.'

'They make such a delicious couple,' said Talli. 'I hope they give it a go this time around.'

'I'll have to bench her for at least five years,' said Meredith, sourly, 'which is inconvenient, given we're all but at war.'

'Oh, give it a rest,' said Talli, 'you're as delighted for them as I am. Don't you dare pretend otherwise, especially not to Gemma's face. She looks up to you, and if you ruin this for them, you'll have me to answer to.'

Meredith laughed. 'You're such a little Cupid.'

'Don't try and turn this round on me, or I'll get Rose to marry you off to a Templar. Although, I guess that might *cause* a war, rather than make one less likely …'

'Is that a thing?' asked Amari, shocked. 'People being married off to form alliances?'

'Yes, for pretty much the whole of time,' said Talli, with a sarcastic edge.

'And before you ask,' said Meredith, 'yes, it still happens today; even among non-demons.'

'Does it?' asked Amari, skeptically.

'Yes,' said Talli.

'It can get pretty nasty with demons, though,' said Meredith. 'There's so much history between everyone; you never know if someone's let go of an old grudge or not.'

'Have I ever been part of a marriage alliance?' asked Amari.

'I don't think so,' said Talli, 'although, there was some stuff with the Templars, one or two lifetimes ago. Rose wouldn't tell us the details, but Caspar was *mad*. I think it had something to do with an old lover of yours …'

'… I thought it had something to do with an old lover of Caspar's,' said Meredith, 'which was why he was so wound up …'

'You'll have to ask Caspar, or Rose,' said Talli. 'Rose has the best memory of all of us. It's hard to remember things when you've lived for so many lifetimes—not everything sticks.'

'And things can get confused,' added Meredith.

'You never know if someone else remembers the same details as you,' said Talli. 'And even if they do, they might have interpreted them in an entirely different way. Or they might have forgotten altogether.'

'We keep records of everything,' said Meredith. 'Although some people are better at updating their journals than others.' She looked pointedly at Talli as they ran onto London Bridge, heading for the South Bank.

'Most people get better at it after they've been burnt a couple of times,' said Talli, sticking her tongue out at Meredith's back.

'So, everything that's happened in my past lives is recorded somewhere?' asked Amari, her pulse leaping.

'Oh, well, yeah, I guess,' said Talli, 'but I wouldn't go reading about the past; it's not healthy. We write things in a heavily biased way.'

'We're only supposed to access them in the event of a dispute, or a war, or something similarly momentous,' said Meredith.

'How I'd love to get my hands on those,' said Amari. 'I have so many questions. Do you … interfere with elections? Break laws?'

'Some nations do. The Templars, for example. Their main goal is to expand their power and influence, and grow their empire,' said Meredith. 'Even if they justify it differently.'

'We don't generally do things like that,' said Talli. Meredith laughed and gave her a look. 'Okay, well, we do, but only for the greater good.'

'As determined by us,' countered Meredith.

'Yes, but our goals are equality, respecting the earth, living good lives; we're not out to rule the world. Although,' said Talli, 'Raina got very into queen-making for a while. Said it was only fair that women got to have a shot too. Caspar was against it ... he thought you took it too far.'

'I'm not Raina,' said Amari, almost without thinking.

'You are and you aren't,' said Talli.

Amari let it go. She didn't want to argue the finer points of reincarnation, not when she was at such a disadvantage. 'What does Caspar want?'

'Aside from you?' laughed Talli.

Amari gave her an exasperated look, her eyes returning to the pavement just in time to dodge a stack of cardboard boxes. Talli laughed harder.

'How are things going with you two?' asked Meredith.

Talli looked keen to know the answer too.

Amari didn't mind; she was enjoying having people to talk to. 'Honestly, it's all so strange, because I don't know him. He feels familiar, I feel drawn to him, and my God he's nice to look at—do not tell him I said that.'

'He got a good body this time, it's true,' said Talli.

Amari laughed, feeling lighter than she had in days. 'But he's a stranger. I don't know anything about him, and he's trying so hard to be nice to me, which ... I don't know, I just want him to be real, to be himself, so I can get to know him. And he keeps deflecting my questions. I think Raina's mad at him?'

Meredith and Talli kept quiet, waiting for her to continue.

'I guess that means it's bad,' said Amari, her good mood faltering.

'We didn't say that,' said Talli. 'It's just ... most demons have learned the hard way to stay out of other demons' business.'

Silence settled over them. Amari watched two motor boats pass on the river. Life on the water always seemed so simple. Maybe she should get on a boat and head out to sea ... discover where the wind and tides would take her. Probably onto a load of jagged rocks, knowing her luck.

'What are you going to do about Dean?' Talli asked, pulling Amari back from her thoughts.

Amari paused before responding, casting around for the right words. 'I know you don't know Dean,' she said, her voice hesitant, 'but we got *married,* not even forty-eight hours ago. I loved him, had an awesome life with him, was excited for our future. I can't stand that I'm lying to him, but I can't talk to him about any of this. And I can't break up with him out of the blue, and definitely not over the phone; we just vowed to spend the rest of our lives together.'

'Do you still love him?' asked Talli, as they turned onto Waterloo Bridge, crossing back onto the north side of the river. It was beginning to get busy, so they increased the pace.

Amari paused. It felt like a betrayal of Dean, of their relationship, to be speaking like this with two relative strangers. But even the thought of Dean's arm around her sent a shudder of repulsion down her spine.

'I feel differently now than I did on Friday night. Then, I was blissfully happy. In love. My feelings were like a magnificent, ancient tree, and my tree was a lovely thing to look at, and sit under, and climb. But with Caspar ... it's like a forest, so big I'm lost.

'And not only that, but I'm blindfolded, and running. I'm going too fast, certain to trip, or run into something. I don't know if Caspar will be the one to catch me when I fall, or the one to trip me up.

'Caspar and Raina are fighting. Once I wake, maybe I'll have no choice but to hate him.'

'Caspar's a good man,' said Meredith. 'I won't get involved in things that are none of my business, but I'll go as far as to say that everything he did was because he was convinced it was the right thing to do. For you. For everyone. He's the one that keeps us together when things are falling apart, and he loves you, unconditionally. Never forget that.'

The mood was suddenly heavy. Amari had a million questions, but before she could work out where to start, Talli cut across them.

'Ooh, I love this bakery,' she squealed. 'Let's get breakfast for everyone, especially as Elliot's not going to surface much before lunch.'

They bought croissants and freshly made bread, then power walked back to Cloister Cottage. The food smelled too good to continue training, so they headed straight for the kitchen. The dogs made a beeline for a promising spot under the table, lying in wait.

Caspar and Rose were the only ones in the kitchen, the air between them tense.

'Everything alright?' asked Talli, plonking their purchases down on the table. 'Meredith, be a love and put the kettle on.'

Meredith rolled her eyes, but did it, then grabbed plates, jam, and butter, and put them on the table.

Caspar was holding Rose's gaze; they seemed to be having a silent conversation. 'What's for breakfast?' Rose eventually said, giving Caspar a small nod.

The tension evaporated.

Amari caught Caspar's eye, dying to know what was going on … if it had anything to do with her. His eyes flamed, but told her nothing other than that he was furious. His pupils dilated as he held her gaze, his anger shifting to something else entirely. Amari's cheeks heated. She looked away, grabbing a croissant.

Meredith made the tea, then came to join them at the table. She poured, dishing out steaming mugs. Amari appreciatively wrapped her fingers around hers.

'How can this place still exist here, in the City of London?' Amari asked, taking another bite of croissant, savoring the flakey, buttery deliciousness.

'Oh, it's not easy,' said Rose, buttering a slice of sourdough. It looked mouthwateringly good; Amari would have one of those next. 'We have a number of measures in place: small magics and wards, bribery, old and very thorough contracts, deflection, demons in high places. We could move to a new home—one that would be far easier to hide—but demons are sentimental creatures. I can't imagine giving the place up.'

Before Amari could ask a follow-up question, her phone rang. Dean. Fuck. It was still the middle of the night in New York ... She went into the cloisters and answered the call. 'Hey,' she said, shuddering inside.

'Where are you, Amari?'

'Huh?'

'I just got off the phone with Leila. She told me you left the hotel with some guy yesterday morning. And Jade said the same thing. Jade said you shouted at her, that you told her to leave you alone.'

Amari's mind reeled, refusing to provide words.

'Well?' he demanded. 'What's going on?'

His tone riled her, snapping her mental faculties back into place. How dare he speak to her like this, especially without getting her side of the story first.

'Dean,' she started, her voice low, quiet, dangerous, 'I did leave the hotel with a guy, the one who showed up at our rehearsal dinner. He's from the government. I'm doing work for them ...'

'... what does the government want with a food critic?'

She gritted her teeth. 'I can't talk about it.'

'Well, what about Jade? And Leila?' His tone was still accusing, but more hesitant.

'Jade confronted me at the hotel. She accused me of having an affair, so I told her to get lost. And Leila thinks I should be wrapped up in cotton wool; she's just annoyed I won't let her take care of me. But the only thing wrong with me is that my husband took off to the other side of the Atlantic the morning after our wedding. What do you want me to do? Sit around and pine for your return?'

Dean paused. 'You've just been so ... distant. You haven't been messaging. So when both Leila and Jade called, and told me there was another man, I guess I ... thought the worst.'

Amari let the silence stretch. It went on for so long, she wondered if the call had dropped.

'I'm sorry,' Dean eventually said. 'I guess I'm under a lot of pressure with this case, and jumped to conclusions. But why didn't you tell me?'

'We've both been busy. We've only had a few snatched minutes since you left, and I didn't want to add to your stress.'

'Mari, I'm ... I'm really sorry.'

'I'm busy too, and under pressure.'

'I wish you could tell me about it. You always feel better when you get things off your chest.'

Amari's chest tightened, tears pooling. 'I really do ... I wish I could tell you, but I don't want to get thrown in jail ... that would only add to your workload.'

Dean exhaled, his relief palpable, even down the phone line. 'Okay, well, I've got to go, but try to keep yourself out of prison ... at least until I've wrapped up this case.'

'I'll try.'

'I love you, Mari.'

'Love you too.'

Amari hung up and began to shake, leaning against the cloisters for support. She hated lying. She hated that her textbook existence had been turned upside down, that everything was so out of her control. She hated feeling so isolated, so alone, so exposed. She badly needed someone to talk to, but no one she knew could possibly understand.

Her eyes welled with tears, then overflowed. She let them run free. She sank to the floor, leaning against the cloisters, head in her hands.

She was the worst kind of human. Not only was she a liar, but the way her heart raced every time she set eyes on Caspar, she was probably a cheat too.

Caspar was in the kitchen when Amari returned inside, petting one of the dogs and reading a morning newspaper.

'Everything okay?' he asked, taking in her blotchy face and steely features.

'Of course not,' she said. 'I need to go to my office. If I'm going to be here for days on end, I need something to do with my time. I've got reviews to write, and the notes I need are in my office.'

'Meredith will be happy to go …'

'… you misunderstand me,' she said, striding towards the door. 'I'm going to my office, right now. Come if you must, but I've had enough of hiding away.'

'Amari, please don't do this.'

'There's no evidence to suggest the man who attacked us was after me,' she said. 'I might be in no danger at all.'

Caspar's blood ran cold. She was right. If he was the target, his presence could put her in greater danger. But if the attacker *was* after her, and there was no one there to protect her ...

'I'm coming,' he said, jumping to his feet. He phoned Meredith as he trailed after Amari. It went to voicemail.

'Shit,' he said into the phone. 'Meredith, Amari's going to her office. She's not listening to reason. We need backup. Call me as soon as you get this.'

He called Gemma. No answer.

'Shit,' he said again, under his breath, stepping through the front door, onto the cobbles.

He called Talli.

'I'm on a train to Surrey with Christa,' said Talli. 'We'll never get there in time. I'll call round the bodyguards. You call Rose.'

Caspar did as she suggested, a pace behind Amari as she hurried towards the main road.

'I'm in the West End with Meredith and Gemma,' said Rose, picking up on the first ring. 'We're on our way, but we won't be there in time. You need to stall her.'

'I'll do my best to slow her down,' said Caspar. But by the time he reached the main road, Amari had already flagged down a black cab. He only just managed to catch her before she drove away without him.

He grabbed her arm, stopping her from ducking inside. 'Amari, what's going on? Why the rush?' he asked.

'I need to do something on my own schedule. I need to be in control of some part of my life,' she said, pulling away from him. She got in and gave the driver the address. Caspar had no choice but to follow.

Amari's office was at Chancery Lane, only a mile away. Luckily, they got stuck in commuter traffic; it would take forever to get there at this rate. Caspar relaxed a little as another traffic light went red. Amari drummed her fingers on her leg.

'Amari, you know this is dangerous, right? It's a needless risk.'

'Were we even attacked before?' she said, looking out of the window, like she wasn't really talking to him. 'The whole thing could have been a fabrication, just to get me to go with you.'

Caspar looked at her but didn't say anything, because, what was there to say?

'Well? Was it all a work of fiction?'

'We both know that's not what this is about. You're angry, so you're being reckless; it's in character, in case you were wondering.'

'Fuck off.'

'What did Dean say?'

'Can you pull over, please?' Amari called through the glass to the driver.

The driver stopped next to St. Paul's Cathedral, and Amari used her phone to pay for the cab. She jumped out and launched into a run along Cheapside, not far from her office now. She didn't even look back at Caspar.

'Amari, wait!' shouted Caspar, taking off after her, hampered by his loafers. Amari still wore her trainers from the morning run, but he slowly gained ground, both of them having to weave in and out of the sea of commuters. They attracted a number of strange looks.

Amari slowed as they approached Chancery Lane tube station, turning suddenly down a side street.

Caspar caught her arm, pulling her to a halt, both of them out of breath.

'Amari, what are you doing?' he panted.

'I'm trying to get away from you, in case you hadn't noticed.'

'Why? What have I done?'

A shadow crossed behind her eyes. She shook her head, yanking her arm away. 'Nothing,' she said, storming off up the street.

Caspar followed. 'Talk to me. Tell me what happened.'

'It's none of your God-damned business.'

'It might be good for you to get it off your chest; you always find that helpful.'

She whirled around. 'Don't pretend you know me; you know nothing about my life. And I didn't want you around in my last two lives, so maybe you should take the hint and leave me alone.'

Her words stunned him, ripping a hole in his chest. He didn't even bother to look around, to see if anyone else had heard her speak of multiple lives. *She doesn't know*, he reminded himself. She didn't know all that had gone before. But that didn't make the words hurt any less.

Amari turned, walking up a set of worn stone steps into her office building.

'I'll leave you alone,' said Caspar, 'I promise, but not until the others get here. I can't leave you unprotected. If anything happened …'

Amari paused at the top and turned to face him, but something over her shoulder caught Caspar's attention.

'Down!' he shouted, pulling a knife from his sleeve and throwing it, just as a blade hit the wood of the door frame next to Amari's head.

Caspar's knife struck their attacker in the shoulder, forcing him to drop his second blade. But another figure appeared out of the shadows, dagger in hand.

Caspar grabbed Amari's arm. She was frozen to the spot, and for a short, terrifying moment, he thought she would fight him. He hauled her down the steps, and, to his relief, she sprang into action as soon as her feet hit the bottom.

They ran, Caspar glad of the people everywhere. They'd travelled almost a hundred meters before he had space to glance back over his shoulder. Both attackers followed.

'Shit,' he said, 'they're still coming. We need to get to the tunnels.'

'Where?' asked Amari.

'The post office in Clerkenwell. There's a tunnel that'll take us to Liverpool Street.'

They made a series of quick turns, weaved in and out of the suit-clad army, and dashed across a busy road just as the lights changed, much to the outrage of the morning traffic.

They had to wait to cross the next road, the traffic in full flow. Amari looked behind them, frantically scanning for any sign of pursuit.

'Caspar, I can't see them.'

The lights changed and he grabbed her hand, pulling her across the road, down an alley next to a busy café, pushing her back out of sight. He peered around the edge of the building, scanning the crowd.

'I can't see them either,' he said, pulling out his phone. 'Rose is close. She knows where we are. We'll wait here. If they're still around, hopefully they won't risk a fight in the open.'

Caspar tore his eyes from the road and glanced back at Amari. She was backed against the wall, her head pressed firmly against it, fists clenched at her side.

It was so easy to forget she was new to all of this. So easy for her to think that normal rules applied, that people wouldn't throw knives at her for no obvious reason. Raina would have fought back, would have easily taken them down.

In truth, the assassins had been sloppy. If they'd been better at their jobs, both Amari and Caspar would be dead, but Amari didn't remember that yet. And Caspar had been distracted. If anything had happened ...

He turned his head back to scan the crowd. 'Still nothing,' he said, trying to adopt a soothing tone. 'They most likely decided a chase was too conspicuous; too likely that someone would pull out a phone and film us. We're safe here, and Rose is two minutes away.'

Amari didn't respond. Caspar wasn't even sure she'd heard him, but he kept talking to her, reassuring her, until the welcome trio of Rose, Gemma, and Meredith appeared from the back of a dark blue Jaguar with diplomatic plates. The car swiftly departed.

'What happened?' asked Rose.

Meredith and Gemma surveyed the area, refusing to turn their backs to the street.

'Two assassins were waiting at Amari's office building,' said Caspar. 'They threw a knife at Amari. I hit one of them in the shoulder, then we ran. They chased us, but not for long; I guess there were too many witnesses, and one of them was bleeding.

'They both had leather cuffs around their wrists, although I didn't see the markings. I didn't recognize either of them, and they didn't speak. They were amateurs; we caught them off guard.'

The sound of hyperventilating interrupted them, and Caspar turned to find Amari crouched in the gutter.

'It would be very convenient for us all if she would wake up,' said Rose.

Caspar threw her a dirty look, then went to Amari's side. He helped her stand. She was pale and shaking.

'We need to get back to the cottage,' said Caspar.

'Car's here,' said Meredith, from the mouth of the ally.

Gemma scanned for threats from the other side of the street.

'Okay,' said Amari, letting Caspar lead her.

They piled into the back of a spacious seven-seater minivan. One of Meredith's team of bodyguards was driving, another jumping out to slide open the side door.

Rose, Meredith, and Gemma sat on the back row, Caspar and Amari taking the seats in front. Amari was still shaking.

'Do we have a blanket?' asked Caspar. 'Or a coat?'

One of the bodyguards passed back a lightweight coat, and Caspar put it over Amari's lap. She didn't even look at him.

The driver maneuvered the van out into the traffic, the silence loud in Caspar's ears. Amari leaned her head against the window, staring blankly out.

Caspar was paralyzed, conflicted. Should he take her hand? Wrap his arm around her? Would she push him away? Would he make it worse?

She was in shock, that much was clear. But she was teetering on a knife edge … he didn't want to be the one to push her over.

Eventually, he reached out and placed his hand on hers. She stiffened, then flipped her hand over, lacing their fingers. Caspar's heart thumped.

Rose deployed Meredith and one of the bodyguards when they neared Amari's office building.

'Search it and see what you can get in terms of CCTV,' she said, 'and see if you can find a trail of blood from the shoulder wound.' She turned her attention to her phone, typing furiously, presumably contacting her demon in the police.

'Didn't think we'd be seeing you so early,' said Jon, nudging Elliot on the shoulder.

Elliot remained silent.

'Did she kick you out? Come to her senses?'

'Rose needed me,' said Gemma with surprising force, as she, Amari, and Caspar entered the kitchen.

'Shit, sorry,' said Jon, his face going red. 'Um … I've got to go to work. You know I'm just messing around though, right? I'm really happy for you guys.'

Gemma gave Jon a dirty look as he left.

He sent one last apology over his shoulder.

'Rose wants to speak to you,' Gemma said to Elliot.

They left the room together, Elliot's hand placed lovingly on Gemma's lower back.

Amari and Caspar stood still for a moment, the enormity of what had almost happened weighing heavy. Amari walked to where the dogs lay by the unlit fire. She sank to the floor, pulling her knees up to her chest. Delta rolled over, begging her to scratch his tummy.

Caspar put the kettle on, giving both of them a few solitary moments. He made tea, adding a large teaspoon of sugar to Amari's, then placed it next to her on the floor.

Caspar sat too, careful not to crowd her, leaning back against the fire surround. Charlie got up and moved to where Caspar sat, flopping down heavily, partially on Caspar's legs. They sat in silence, letting the minutes tick by, drinking their tea, stroking the dogs.

Caspar waited for Amari to talk first. He would have sat there all day, waiting, not wanting to press her.

Eventually she looked up at him, a new understanding in her eyes.

'I never thought ...' She faltered and looked away. 'I didn't think we were in real danger. I didn't see the first attack. I convinced myself you were exaggerating.'

Caspar scratched behind Charlie's ear. 'What happened?' he said softly. 'This morning, when you were in the cloisters?'

Amari looked straight into Caspar's eyes. 'Dean accused me of having an affair.'

Caspar's heartrate shot up. 'Ah ...' He tried to find the right words, but she continued before he could, dropping her gaze to Delta.

'I was angry, and I wanted ... no ... needed to ... to do something, to break out of here, to vent.' She took a breath. 'I'm sorry. That man ... he was aiming at *me*; it was me they wanted.'

Tears rolled down her cheeks. She lowered her head, wiping them quickly away.

'Why do they want me?'

Caspar scooched up next to her, still careful not to get too close. He rubbed her back in soothing circles. 'Hey, it's okay, we got away.'

She sobbed, turning herself into him, shifting closer.

Caspar's chest ached as he wrapped one arm around her, his other hand stroking her hair.

'Honestly, I don't know why they want you, but at least now we know it's you they want. That narrows our search significantly.'

Another sob wracked Amari's body. 'I'm sorry; I don't usually cry all the time.'

He kissed the top of her head and squeezed her arm. 'Crying's good, remember? You're in shock, and your brain's waging an internal war; it would be weird if you weren't crying.'

'And I'm in limbo,' she said. She sat up and wiped her eyes. 'I'm going to go mad, cooped up in here with nothing to do. How long do we wait, sitting around, hoping I'm going to wake up?'

'Considerably longer than we have so far, given you've only been here for a couple of days.'

'And what if I don't wake up before Dean gets back? Do I end things with him based on something that might never happen? What if I never wake up?'

'You will,' said Caspar, with more force than necessary. *Everyone woke up eventually ... didn't they?*

'You don't know that.'

'There are still things we can try. The other night, when we were dancing ...' Caspar broke off; this wasn't the time.

'That wasn't me,' she said, hotly.

'I know,' he rushed to say. 'That's what I was going to say. It was Raina; I felt the shift in you. And then the song ended, and she went back to sleep. Every day, more flecks appear in your eyes. Every day we get a little closer. It won't be long now.'

'And I'm supposed to sit around doing nothing, trapped in here, just ... hoping?'

'There are things we can do.'

'Like what?'

'Well, for starters, there are plenty of artifacts around the place for you to study. Some should bring back memories. And, if nothing else, most of them are pretty to look at.'

Amari sniffed. 'Fine,' she said, giving her face one last wipe. 'Show me the way.'

Caspar led Amari to a study further along the corridor from Rose's. It was bigger than Rose's and had two desks, one at each end, with a seating area of low couches in the middle.

One end was neat, everything put away, books lined up, clear space on the desk. The other was a state, with books, papers, coffee cups, and ancient treasures strewn everywhere.

'I take it that's your desk?' Amari teased, feeling more like herself at the prospect of doing some work.

'It is,' he laughed. 'And the one over there is yours.'

'As in, it was Raina's?' she asked, both keen and apprehensive to explore.

'Yep. For the last few lifetimes, anyway.'

Amari walked to the desk and put her hand on it. She braced for a flashback, but none came, at least not until she sat in the chair and put both hands on the leather-topped wood.

The memory was only a flash across her mind, but it was intimate, Caspar's eyes in an unfamiliar body, his hands pushing her back onto the desk, skirts up around her hips.

Amari's face flushed crimson. Caspar looked away and pulled out a set of keys.

Drawers and glass display cases covered the far wall from floor to ceiling. The wood was dark, reminding her of the drawers in Caspar's other office, the one where the first attack had taken place. The drawers each had a little brass plate with a keyhole in the center, and a rush of excitement filled her as her brain conjured images of what might be inside.

Caspar went to one of the drawers, unlocked it, and pulled out a piece of pottery. It was a small, thick-sided bowl, almost perfect, aside from a couple of chips around the rim. It was pinkish orange and glazed, with light ridges pressed around the outside.

'Oh my God,' said Amari, as Caspar put the bowl on the desk in front of her. 'How old is that?'

Caspar laughed. 'Only about a thousand years.'

'Jesus ... you're not even wearing gloves!'

'Why would I? I made it.'

'You made it?' Amari's brain struggled to keep up.

'It's a wedding cup. The bride and groom both drink from it.'

'This is so exciting!'

Amari could barely contain herself. Having access to artifacts like this, along with the person who made it ... it was ... well, there were no words to describe what it was.

'That ring on your finger,' said Caspar, pointing to the gold band Amari still couldn't bring herself to take off, 'is considerably older than this.'

Amari ran her thumb over the band, trying to take it all in. 'And there are other things here, like this? So old?'

'My dear, this is the boring tip of the iceberg in comparison to the veritable treasures stored in this building. The only reason this is of note is because it might spark a memory.'

'The tip of the iceberg?' Her pulse raced, her mouth dry, head spinning.

'Recognize that painting behind you?' he asked, with a mischievous smile.

Amari stood and whirled around, her eyes locking onto the hazy image of a bridge. 'Oh my God. Is that ... is that a Monet?'

'It is,' he said, walking around to her side and perching on the edge of the desk. 'And not just any Monet. This is one of the series Monet painted of Charing Cross Bridge. I bought it and left it to a museum when I died. It was stolen from that museum, and to this day the police have no idea who did it.'

Amari scowled. 'You stole it from a museum?'

'Heavens, no! I tracked it down and stole it back, for a bit of fun. I even faked its destruction. Many believe it was burned in a fire. Little do they know it's hanging, safe and sound, behind your desk. I thought you might like it.'

'I love it,' said Amari, without thinking. 'It's beautiful.'

'It won't help bring you back. You hated me when I bought it, so this is the first time you've seen it. But it might bring you some joy.'

Amari smiled. 'It already has.'

'Good. Now touch the cup.'

'Without gloves?' It seemed wrong.

Caspar thrust it into her hands. 'Yes, without gloves.'

Amari reverently took hold of the priceless artifact. After a moment, an image popped into her mind. She was momentarily disoriented, but not sure if it was her, or Raina, who felt that way.

She looked down and saw a hand—Raina's hand—placed on top of a man's. They stood before a priestess, next to a river, a small crowd standing around them.

The priestess—who might have been Talli—was tying their hands together with a length of embroidered cloth, saying words that Amari couldn't make out. She could have understood them, if only Raina had been paying attention. But Raina's whole being was focused on the sensation of Caspar's skin against hers. Their hands bound together caused an inferno in her blood, consuming her. She itched to be alone with him, to douse the flames.

The memory ended abruptly, and Amari placed the bowl on the desk, disappointed not to have seen more.

'It was so short,' she said to Caspar. 'I think Talli was tying my hand to yours?'

'Pagan hand-tying ceremony,' said Caspar. 'It was probably one of our marriage ceremonies. We've had a number of them. Now, let's see, what next ...'

'Next? I want to talk more about the wedding.'

'Later. We might have to work through every drawer on that wall, so we need to keep moving.'

Amari took in the vast number of drawers. There must have been hundreds, all different shapes and sizes; they were going to be here for days.

'And once we're done in here, if you're still not awake, we can ask the others what they've got that could help. Some of us like to hoard more than others. Believe it or not, you and I take a streamlined approach, relatively speaking.'

'If you say so,' said Amari, glancing again at the drawers. 'Okay, what's next?'

Amari sat in bed that evening, staring at her phone, which told her she'd missed three calls from Dean. She knew she should call him, but she'd had such an emotional day, she wasn't sure she could take any more.

A knock sounded from the door. Relieved, she threw down the phone. 'Come in!'

'Hey,' said Caspar. 'Just delivering the books you wanted. Meredith got them from your office.'

'Thanks. On the table's great.'

'Have a good night,' he said, turning to leave.

'Caspar,' she blurted, 'do you mind ... staying for a bit?'

Caspar faltered, surprised. 'Of course,' he said, sitting on the end of the bed.

Amari clenched her fingers. 'I really am sorry about earlier.'

'Don't be,' said Caspar, waving her apology away. 'It was barely even a scrape versus some of the things we've been through.'

Amari shuddered. 'That doesn't make me feel any better.'

'Sorry. I could lie to you, but I'm not sure that would help.'

She smiled. 'I wish you would do that more.'

'Lie to you?!' He laughed.

'No!' She threw him a chastising look. 'Say what you're really thinking. I feel like you walk on eggshells around me, scared you might offend me. I know I've been crying a lot, but I'm not fragile.'

Caspar took a deep breath. 'I know you're not, and I'm not walking on eggshells.'

Amari arched an eyebrow.

'Honestly. It's … I don't know how to act around you. I can't act the way I want to … the way I used to …

'If you were awake, I would've given you hell for the shit you pulled earlier. But now, it wouldn't be fair; you didn't know any better.'

'You would've given me hell?' teased Amari.

'And then some.'

Amari cocked an eyebrow. 'I would've liked to see that.'

'That's nothing compared to the things I'd like to see.'

Amari's stomach contracted. She looked into Caspar's tortured eyes.

'You really want me to tell you what I'm thinking?' he said.

'Yes,' she breathed.

Silence descended as each studied the other, eyes locked, air tense, loaded with adulterous potential.

Amari looked away, inhaled, broke the spell. 'Thank you, for showing me the artifacts.'

She'd had four flashbacks in total, including the ones from the desk and the wedding cup. The third had been because of a fur muff, and had shown her a midwinter festival, where she'd danced with Caspar under the stars, fires blazing all around.

The fourth had been in response to an elaborate Asian dagger with a swirling flower pattern across the handle and sheath. In the memory, Raina had thrown the dagger, and it had lodged in a woman's back. Amari had never felt rage like it, and had come back to the present consumed by bloodlust. She'd been unable to concentrate after that, so had gone to find Meredith for a training session, needing an outlet.

'They're as much your things as they are mine,' said Caspar, 'and anyway, I want you to wake up as much as you do. Maybe even more.'

'I wish more of them had brought back memories.'

'We don't remember everything,' said Caspar. 'A demon's brain isn't any bigger than a normal person's, and I'm sure there are things you can't remember, even from this single lifetime, let alone things that happened hundreds of years ago.

'The things we remember the best are steeped in emotion: rage, despair, love, lust, guilt, happiness. The emotions around the memory need to be strong enough to break through. Raina may have forgotten many of those artifacts entirely.'

'The gold bangle you showed me … what did you want me to remember?' Caspar had looked particularly hopeful when he'd slipped it onto her wrist, desperate almost.

His eyes lit up with impish delight. 'You'll remember when you wake.'

'Spoil sport.'

Amari leaned back and looked up at the stars above the bed, the flashback they'd caused coming back to her.

'Who was Jamie?'

'Jamie?'

'When you first left me alone in here, those stars brought back a memory. I was lying on the beach, staring at the stars, waiting for someone called Jamie. I was in a pink evening dress and he wore a tuxedo. We both had American accents.'

Caspar was up and moving before Amari had time to blink.

'Caspar? What is it?' She hadn't even told him about the kiss …

He turned to face her as he swung the door open. 'You want me to tell you what I'm thinking?'

'Um … yes?'

'I'm thinking I'm going to kill Rose.'

Caspar stormed into Rose's office, not caring that she was in the middle of a meeting with Meredith, Gemma, and the rest of the bodyguards.

'You lied to me,' he roared.

Rose calmly took in Caspar's words, then flicked her eyes to Amari, who stood by the door, looking confused and guilty.

Rose's mouth quirked into a hard smile. 'You're going to have to be a little more explicit, I'm afraid.'

'You told me Raina wasn't in any danger.'

'Could you narrow it down to a lifetime, at least?'

'The last one, or the one before. Hopefully it'll be fresh in your memory.'

'And what particular danger would you like to discuss?'

'You sent her to America, to the Templars.'

'Ah,' said Rose. 'Raina accompanied me to America for talks with the Templars. As I recall, it wasn't especially dangerous.'

'Then why was she waiting for Jamie alone on the beach?'

Rose furrowed her brow, eyes flicking once again to Amari. 'Now that, I couldn't say,' she said.

'You expect me to believe that?'

'I don't give a damn what you believe. We went to America, the talks were disappointing, we came home. It was two lifetimes ago. Raina was there to gain intelligence. Given her relationship with Jamie, she was the ideal person to take along.

'I didn't know she met him on the beach at night. That seems to me a needless risk, although I'm sure she had her reasons. We can only speculate about what those were until Raina comes back to us ... unless Amari has anything further she can add?'

'Um ... no,' Amari said awkwardly. 'I'm sorry, I didn't mean to cause any upset.'

'I could never work out why the Templars killed Raina in her last life,' said Caspar. 'Why would they go to the trouble? They could have killed her—eternally— and you knew something but chose to keep it from me.'

Rose took a deep breath. 'You're understandably upset. But, as you know, I have little tolerance for theatrics. We don't know for sure that it was the Templars who killed her. My advice would be to stay focused on bringing Raina back. And before you do anything rash, I suggest you consider what Raina's reaction to that rash behavior will be, once she wakes.

You've been in the doghouse for some time and say you'd like to be let out. I'd think about that, if I were you.'

'I need answers.'

'Then wake Raina up and get them.'

Caspar thundered out of the room, leaving Amari standing in the doorway, shell shocked. One minute everything had been fine, more than fine—he'd started opening up to her—the next, it had all blown up in her face.

'He has a tendency to let his emotions get the better of him, at least where you're concerned,' said Rose, whose tone indicated that Amari was dismissed.

Amari gave an uncertain half nod, then followed Caspar back upstairs. She hesitated when she reached the landing outside their bedrooms. He'd been so angry. But more than that, he'd been hurt, and she'd caused it; she hadn't stopped to think. Of course he would be upset by Raina meeting another man on the beach at night. Wouldn't she fly off the handle if her husband had been doing the same?

She steeled herself, then knocked on his door. Several moments passed. Amari began to wonder if he'd gone out. Maybe to get some air. Maybe to find someone to spar with.

She was about to turn away, to go back to her room, when a floorboard groaned. Caspar swung the door open, fixing her with a cold, impassive stare. He didn't invite her in.

'I'm … uh.' She was taken aback by this new side to him, with his closed expression and hostile body language. Tension filled the air, and not the romantic kind. He'd been nothing but considerate, accommodating, and lenient with her ... until now.

Her stomach sank, dread gnawing at her insides. If he turned away from her, refused to help her, what would she do? What would happen to her? Who would care? The thought scared, no ... it terrified her.

'I'm sorry,' she said. 'I shouldn't have told you. I should've thought about what I was saying.'

'I'm glad I know.'

'Right,' said Amari, his short answer compounding her fears. 'Is there ... ah ... anything else I can do? To wake Raina, I mean.'

Caspar looked squarely into her eyes, his expression unreadable.

'You can kiss me.'

Amari drew back, shocked by his tone: it was pure challenge. He wanted to get under her skin, to fight, to vent his anger, and it made Amari forget her fears, made her see red.

'Goodnight, Caspar. I hope, for all our sakes, that your mood has improved by the morning.'

Amari had to resist very hard the temptation to slam her bedroom door. She threw herself furiously onto the bed, looking up at the troublesome stars, made ever angrier by the knowledge that sleep was a distant dream.

Amari woke up late the following morning. By the time she made it downstairs, the others were finishing breakfast, discussing something intently.

'As soon as Midsummer's over,' said Rose, 'I'm sending envoys to all nations. We need to gather allies ... the Templars want war.'

'There's nothing else we can do?' said Elliot. 'There's no way to make a deal?'

'They'll only deal with Raina,' said Rose. 'It's been that way since Jamie took over. So, unless they change their stance, no, I don't think so.'

Amari felt the guilt again. It irritated her; she was doing everything she could.

You can kiss me.

Well, almost everything.

'There's no way Raina can go to the Templars. They killed her in her last life,' said Caspar.

'He's right,' said Rose. 'There's a high chance they'd kill her on sight.'

'Why?' asked Jon. 'What happened? I thought they liked Raina?'

Amari walked to the Aga and put the kettle on to boil. Every head swiveled towards her.

'Morning,' she said.

'Morning,' the others chorused.

Amari grabbed the teapot from the table. 'I'd like to know that too,' she said. 'What happened with the Templars?'

'I'm afraid I don't know,' said Rose. 'One minute you were a key part of our team to build relations, the next, you were dead.'

Silence descended as Amari filled the teapot. It was so uncomfortable she felt the room might combust.

'Where are you sending us?' asked Elliot.

'I'm working through the details,' said Rose, 'but I need to go to the Registerium before deciding anything. Hopefully we won't have to act without their backing.'

'Did you find anything from the attack?' asked Amari.

The whole table turned their attention back to her.

'No,' said Meredith. 'The CCTV footage wasn't great. Neither of the attackers matched the one from the attack in Caspar's office. And although they had wrist cuffs, we couldn't make out what was written on them.'

'We checked the admissions records from every hospital within a hundred miles,' said Gemma. 'Several patients were admitted with knife wounds, but none of them matched the description of your attacker.'

'Any facial recognition matches?' asked Amari.

'No,' said Rose, taking a heavy breath. 'Not for any of them.'

Chapter 10

The next week passed in a blur of training, eating, and memory hunting. The others had taken to telling Amari their favorite Raina memories, most of which felt familiar, but none of which resulted in a flashback.

Caspar had apologized for his behavior, and they'd fallen into a steady daily rhythm. They got up early, trained, ate breakfast, worked through artifacts, had lunch, trained again, worked through more artifacts, ate dinner, then sat around reading or chatting with the others.

They kept busy, but by the end of the week, Amari was frustrated and full of angst. She felt trapped in Cloister Cottage … and inside her own head.

Amari had had more flashbacks, and Caspar said there were more flecks of gold in her eyes. But she didn't *feel* any different.

Caspar filled her in on Rose's plans, answered her endless questions, and talked with her for hours, but something had shifted, those words always between them: *You can kiss me.*

Amari had had extensive internal conversations on the topic. She could quite easily kiss him, like an actor would kiss an onscreen lover. But that's not how it would be. Even if it was for her, it wouldn't be for him.

And she had too many conflicting emotions about him, not least because she was still married.

Still married. That's how she'd come to think about her relationship with Dean, like it was something that would come to an end. She couldn't bring herself to say the words out loud, nor think about the details, not yet, but her marriage was going to end.

She'd only spoken to Dean twice, and had ignored the rest of his calls. Each time, the distance between them increased.

Leila had called her five times, leaving a message each time. She wanted to know where Amari was, if she was okay, and what was going on with Dean. Dean had called Leila, asking where Amari was. She'd told him the truth: that she didn't know, and that she was worried.

Amari couldn't bring herself to speak to her cousin. What would she say? That she was working for the government? Leila would pick that story apart in seconds. And Amari had to distance herself from everyone she loved; she didn't want to put them in danger.

But there was a part of her that still wouldn't let her believe in the Pagans, in reincarnation, in her lives with Caspar. Despite all the things she'd seen, and felt, a part of her wondered if she was just some pawn in a bigger game: it could be a cult ... they could be drugging her ... she could be mentally ill.

'Amari?' asked Caspar. He leaned against the headboard. He'd come into her room after dinner, needing to collect a book.

'Sorry. Lost in thought.'

'Anything I can help with?'

'No.'

'Are you ready for tomorrow? Do you need Meredith to get anything else from your house?'

'She went earlier,' said Amari. 'I'm all set. I can't wait to get out of here, and I'm excited to see Maltings.'

'Me too,' said Caspar. 'We've been cooped up here for way too long, and it's so beautiful there.'

'Tell me about it,' said Amari, leaning back and closing her eyes.

A comfortable silence settled over them. Caspar's suggestion that she kiss him, for once, wasn't making her uneasy. Maybe she was too tired for such inhibitions—the last few days had been relentless, draining. She was exhausted, could feel sleep tugging at her, awareness of her surroundings diminishing.

'Amari?' Caspar said, his voice low.

Seconds passed before Amari realized he'd said anything. Her conscious brain had to swim against the tide, back to the surface.

She tried in vain to put together a response, but soon forgot what she was struggling to do, her thoughts slipping back to the depths.

Darkness circled. She gave in.

Amari's head slid to one side, coming to rest on Caspar's shoulder. Caspar shifted, about to move away, but she frowned in protest, wriggling her head against him to get more comfortable.

He could stay for a few minutes—until she was properly asleep—and then slip away.

'Okay,' he breathed, wrapping an arm around her, more to himself than to her, resisting the temptation to bury his nose in her hair.

Caspar woke the following morning to find himself lying on Amari's bed. His arm was around her, her head on his shoulder, her leg slung over his. His heart pounded, every nerve in his body savoring the contact. He'd been craving the feel of her against him for longer than he could bear to remember. He hadn't been like this, with her, for two agonizing lifetimes. He didn't dare move a muscle lest it end.

He breathed her in, fighting the urge to wrap his other arm around her, to press her more fully against him, or tip back her head and lift her lips to his.

He closed his eyes, cherishing these snatched moments, which would surely come to an end as soon as Amari opened her eyes. He fought the despair of that thought, focusing instead on where their skin touched, on the sparks careening through his blood, setting him on fire.

Amari stirred, then stiffened.

Caspar held his breath, praying she wouldn't immediately push herself away.

She shifted her weight.

He fought the urge to hold onto her, disappointment coursing through him as he felt her pulling back. But then she relaxed, her hand settling on his chest, the weight of her head returning. Caspar breathed a deep sigh of relief.

'Good morning,' said Amari, playing with a button on his shirt.

His mind went blank, unable to focus on anything but her fingers, willing her to continue.

'I had the most invigorating dream,' she said, her tone flirty, fingers walking to the next button.

Caspar caught her hand, halting her movements. He rolled her onto her back, rolling half of the way with her, looking down into her eyes.

'Don't tease me, Amari. Not if that's all you're going to do.'

She looked seductively up at him, dropping her gaze from his eyes to his lips, then back again.

'Kiss me,' she breathed.

Caspar's heart nearly stopped. 'Do you mean that?'

'Yes,' she said, moving her hand to his neck, drawing him down to her.

Caspar's breath hitched. He couldn't comply fast enough, and their lips crashed together. He came alive at the contact, every sense heightened, every nerve alert, unleashed desire chasing through him.

There was nothing gentle about it, his lips demanding everything of hers, their mouths opening together, fitting perfectly, somehow knowing what the other wanted. Amari moaned and the sound resonated to his core.

He rolled on top of her, his weight pushing her into the mattress, and she moaned again, her hips lifting to meet him. Every part of him sang. He wanted her more than life itself.

'Wait,' Amari breathed, between kisses. Her hands were on his chest, pushing him back.

'What?' he rasped, moving his mouth to her neck.

She gasped. 'Caspar, we should stop.'

It took every ounce of self-control he had to pull back from her, craving her touch as soon as he broke contact. He put his head in his hands, trying to regain some semblance of composure.

'Hey,' she said, pulling his hands from his face, holding onto them. 'What is it?'

'I ...' he looked away. Did she regret the kiss?

'Caspar,' she said, leaning in, kissing him again, a deep, slow, reassuring kiss.

It turned heated, and this time Caspar pulled away, because otherwise he'd pull her onto his lap. And if that happened, he wasn't sure he'd be able to stop.

Amari pressed her forehead against his, her hand on his neck. 'I'm so confused. I've only known you for a week, but it feels ...'

'You've known me a lot longer than a week,' he said, running a hand down her cheek.

'So my subconscious keeps telling me. Nearly all the memories involve us kissing,' she said, kissing him again, 'or ... doing other things ...'

Caspar growled, squeezing her neck. 'Don't say things like that.'

Amari laughed. 'What? Kissing? Or is it the *other things* you'd rather I didn't reference?'

'I told you not to tease me,' he said, nipping her lip.

She gasped, then ran a nail down his neck.

'Amari,' he breathed, 'we should stop.'

'I know,' she whispered, kissing him one final time.

And then, too soon, she was gone.

'So, let me get this straight,' said Amari, through a mouthful of toast and orange marmalade. 'You comb the world for genius kids, because they're more likely to be demons than genuine prodigies?'

'Yep,' said Jon.

'That's kind of sad,' said Amari.

'I know,' said Talli. 'It's so much nicer to think they're remarkable.'

'But when you do find a genuine one, it's even more awesome,' said Christa.

'So, wait, what about the famous ones? Mozart? Pascal? Picasso?'

'All demons,' said Jon, with a shrug.

'Are they still around? Can I meet them?' asked Amari, realizing the possibilities.

'Mozart and Pascal are both dead. They were already old when they did their cool stuff, hence why they could do their cool stuff. They died of natural old age,' said Jon.

'That's really a thing?' asked Amari.

'Of course,' said Christa, 'everyone dies eventually.'

'How old are we talking?'

'Oh, a few thousand years at the upper end,' said Talli.

'A lot don't make it much past a thousand though,' said Christa.

'How old's Raina?' asked Amari, an edge of panic creeping through her.

'Over a thousand,' laughed Talli. 'But she's got a good millennium in her yet, don't you worry.'

'How can you be so sure?'

'People usually die early because they want to,' said Talli. 'Raina's not the type to give up on life.'

'Okay, good. And what about Picasso? Is he still alive?'

'Thought to be,' said Elliot, 'but he's gone to ground.'

'That's artists for you,' said Jon.

'Hey,' said Talli, 'you're young. You'll probably have an artist phase too, you know.'

'Doubtful,' said Jon. 'I'm more of a businessman than an artist.'

'Do you have any idea how pompous you sound?' asked Talli.

'You're a textbook young demon,' said Meredith. 'Money, success, showy cars, yachts in the Med, big houses, lavish parties …'

'There's nothing wrong with any of that,' said Jon, defensively, 'and it keeps everyone here fed.'

They all laughed at that.

'You'll become an artist soon enough,' said Christa.

'An artist?' asked Amari.

'Second phase of a demon's progression through life,' said Christa. 'People lose interest in money and look for ways to express themselves.'

'I think you'll make a good artist,' Meredith said to Jon, cocking a provocative eyebrow.

Jon flushed. 'Well, I guess, maybe, under the right circumstances,' he spluttered.

They erupted into laughter.

'I'm looking forward to my artist phase,' said Elliot.

Gemma smiled encouragingly at him. Knowing looks were shared up and down the table.

'In fact, I might start today; I'm bored of money.'

'Good for you,' said Talli.

'Did I have a long money-obsessed phase?' asked Amari.

They laughed again.

'You?' said Talli, banging the table. 'You were the worst of us all. And you didn't stop at money. You liked power: king—and queen—making, running business empires, investing, dabbling in politics.

'You're the reason we don't have to worry about putting food on the table, and never will have to. You would've been a natural Templar ...'

Amari wasn't sure if that was meant as a compliment or an insult, but it stung.

'What about my artist phase?'

'Short and sweet,' said Caspar as he entered the room. Their eyes met for a split second before he looked away, the thrill of this morning hanging between them. 'You produced some beautiful works, but you destroyed most of them shortly afterwards.'

'Why?!' Amari had been about to ask if she could see them.

'Because you're a perfectionist, and you didn't think any of them were good enough. But I managed to smuggle a couple of them out,' said Caspar, looking pleased with himself.

'Can I see them?' asked Amari.

'There's one at Maltings,' said Caspar. 'You can see it later.'

'What happens after the artist phase?' said Amari.

'Everyone gets deep and meaningful and wants to find the purpose of life,' said Jon. 'They disappear for lifetimes on end, meditating in the Himalayas, desperately trying to come up with an answer.'

'I did that,' said Meredith. 'It's where I learned some of my best fighting moves.'

'Oh, well, I didn't mean you. You came back with something to show for it.'

The laughter tipped Jon over the edge.

'I'm going to work. Where, I'll have you know, I'm one of the top-earning traders in the city.'

'He's a way off his artist phase yet,' said Elliot.

'Has Raina worked out the meaning of life yet?' asked Amari, jovially.

The energy plummeted. Amari looked around, worried she'd said something terrible.

'I'm not sure anyone's really worked that out,' Talli said kindly. 'But you focused more on the people you care about. That's what mattered to you—protecting them.'

Caspar and Amari travelled to Somerset in a Range Rover with Talli, Christa, and Meredith. Meredith drove, Amari in the front with her, the other three piled into the back.

Amari was preoccupied by Caspar's searing presence behind her, wondering if he'd reach out and touch her, both wishing he would and praying he didn't.

They hadn't been alone since that morning, and Amari couldn't stop thinking about it. She could still feel the kisses on her bruised lips; she hadn't been kissed like that since ... had she ever been kissed like that?

Amari looked down at her hands, eyes wandering to the rings on her fingers. The ones on her left hand tied her to Dean, the one on her right to Caspar. Only one of them she couldn't live without ... not that it helped with the guilt.

She had to tell Dean, and it had to be done face to face. Until then, she couldn't let anything else happen with Caspar. She'd kissed him, in part to see if it would finally wake her. Seeing as it hadn't, there was no justification for doing it again.

They were mostly quiet during the journey, Talli the only one to attempt conversation. 'What's got into you lot?' she asked. 'There's some weird energy going on in here.'

'If you say so,' said Meredith.

The rest of them remained quiet.

'Even you?' said Talli, turning on Christa.

'I just want to stare out the window, Tals,' said Christa, kissing the back of Talli's hand.

Talli huffed, leant her head against Christa's shoulder, and went to sleep.

Eventually, they reached the tiny Somerset village of Buttercross, which was no more than a handful of well-kept cottages, a church, a village hall, and an old malt house. It was a beautiful, immaculate place. Flowers draped from window boxes, the road signs were made of wood, the hedges were perfectly clipped, and the roads were swept.

Meredith maneuvered the Range Rover down a small, rugged track next to the malt house. The track was packed earth and gravel with a runner of grass growing down the middle, fields on either side. They followed it to its termination at an old, rambling, crumbling farmhouse.

Amari felt prickles of familiarity and anticipation as they approached. It had cut-stone mullion windows and a square, wooden front door. The drive afforded them a good view of the front of the house and lawns, then took them round the back, where they parked in a graveled courtyard. A series of stone outbuildings dotted the perimeter, and a five-bar gate led to paddocks beyond.

Amari couldn't take it all in fast enough. Caspar had said they owned the house together, and, strangely, it felt like it was hers—like it was home. She drank in every detail of their surroundings. A low wall grabbed her attention, then a pile of terracotta pots, then a delicate yellow rose climbing the side of the house.

'Want to see inside?' asked Caspar, watching her every move.

Amari flicked her gaze to him. She was sure she looked like an excited child, but didn't care. Caspar laughed as she practically skipped to the back door.

'Finally,' called Talli, 'some energy! This is more like it!'

Caspar held the door open for Amari, stepping back so she could enter the boot room first.

'Not the most glamorous entrance, but it's easier than walking round to the front,' said Caspar.

Amari looked around the square little room, with its walls lined with empty pegs. She took in the low wooden benches, a wooden bucket in the corner, and, set off to one side, an ajar door to the downstairs loo. It had the sad, empty feel that a house got when you moved out of it; a space devoid of anything that made it a home.

Amari followed the flagstones through a white wooden door with six glass panels at the top, down a short, wide corridor, and into the kitchen.

Her heart sank; the kitchen had seen better days. It was falling apart. If it had been well maintained, it would've been stunning, worthy of a lifestyle magazine. It had all the right features: a central island with herbs hanging from a rack above, an Aga, a rustic kitchen table and full-height dressers, a free-standing butcher's block, and windows above the sink that overlooked a walled kitchen garden beyond.

But two of the windows had cracked panes, the herb drying rack looked like it could fall at any minute, one of the table legs was propped up by pieces of wood, the dressers had doors hanging off at odd angles, the garden was a jumble of weeds, and a thick coating of cobwebs and dirt covered the whole place.

'How did it get like this?' demanded Amari, whirling to face Caspar, anger running hot in her veins. *Jesus ... why do I even care?*

Caspar took a step back in surprise. 'Well, I mean, I suppose it's seen better days, but everything still works.'

'The place is falling apart.'

'It's not that bad,' he protested, but Amari had already stormed past him, down the corridor and into the front entrance hall.

She took a left and found herself in a long sitting room, with window seats, beams, and an inglenook fireplace. The room was in a similar state of disrepair, although at least all the window panes were intact.

She crossed to the other side of the room, through a door that led to a study. It too was a state. Her eyes took in the moth-eaten curtains, ruined desk, and sun-damaged books, but when her gaze flicked to the far wall, she was brought up short. Hanging there was a painting: an abstract countryside scene in a plain gold frame. It had rolling hills, the possibility of water, and a stormy summer sky. It called to her like a homing beacon.

'I'm sorry,' said Caspar, entering the room. 'I should've got someone to fix the place up before bringing you here. I didn't even think. I've made a couple of calls, and there'll be a team here to sort the place out ASAP. They're going to start later today. I didn't come here in my last life … it was too … Amari? Are you okay?'

Amari hadn't even turned around. The painting was captivating. It held her, reminding her of the brush strokes she'd made, of where she'd been, how she'd felt when she'd painted it.

'Amari?' said Caspar. He placed a hand on her shoulder.

His touch snapped her out of her trance. 'That's the painting you were talking about, isn't it? The one I painted? The one you saved?'

Caspar's eyes flicked to the painting. He gave a small nod.

'It's beautiful. I'm glad you rescued it.'

'Did it bring back a memory?'

Amari turned back to look at it. 'Not really … not like the others, but I can remember painting it. It's almost like my hands would know what to do if I picked up a brush.'

'Want to try it?' he asked, eagerly.

'Maybe later. I want to see the rest of the house.'

Caspar showed her around, apologizing again and again for the state of the place.

Once she'd finished looking at the dining and drawing rooms on the ground floor, he showed her the four large bedrooms, three bathrooms, and dressing room upstairs.

Strangely, Amari's favorite place was the upstairs landing. It was wide and cozy, a plush Persian rug covering the floor, a chaise longue along the wall. She lay back on the chaise and looked out through the window, taking in first the gardens, and then the rolling fields beyond.

'You loved to watch the sunset from there,' said Caspar, from where he waited halfway down the stairs.

'This spot ... it makes me feel content,' she said. 'It's the weirdest thing.'

The rest of the day was spent cleaning, tidying, directing the clean-up team that had magically appeared, and deciding what modernizations needed to be made.

Amari was a house renovation pro; she and Dean had flipped several properties during the London property boom. So she didn't waste any time before making a list of things to change.

Top priority were carpets, improved plumbing, additional radiators, a new boiler—thank God it was summer—an upgrade to the wiring, new mattresses—there were mice in more than one of the existing ones—new curtains, and new linens and towels.

She and Caspar drove to the nearest supermarket to make a dent in the list, as well as to pick up a bucketload of cleaning essentials and some basic food items.

Amari was invigorated. It felt so good to have purpose, to be in charge of something, and Caspar seemed delighted that she was taking the lead.

'Where will the others stay during Midsummer?' asked Amari, as they drove back to the house. 'They won't all fit in our house …'

Her face turned red. *Our house.* How had she come to think of this place as hers so soon? How was it that she felt so comfortable playing house with Caspar?

Caspar smiled, then reached out to take her hand. He was hesitant, and that more than anything pushed Amari to let him entwine their fingers. A hum of belonging buzzed through her as he did.

'Every house in the village is owned by demons,' said Caspar. 'Rose owns one, and so do Talli and Christa. Meredith, Jon, and Elliot will stay with us, and I guess maybe Gemma too. But they won't be here until closer to the celebration, so it'll just be Meredith for now.'

'And what about everyone else?' asked Amari. 'From the way Talli talks, it sounds like there'll be hundreds of people.'

Caspar barked out a laugh then rubbed his thumb across Amari's skin. She had to try very hard to focus on his words, ignoring first the excitement, and then the pang of guilt that accompanied his movements.

'It won't be quite that big. There'll be about a hundred of us. Anyone who doesn't fit in one of the cottages will either rough it in the malt house, bring tents, or stay in one of the local pubs or bed and breakfasts.'

'And Talli runs the show?'

'Heaven help anyone who tries to get in her way!' said Caspar. 'The main celebration will take place in the field behind the malt house. It has a brilliant view, and the energy's perfect; it's on a ley line that leads directly to Stonehenge.'

'I'm sorry, what?' She was expected to believe in ley lines now?

'Ley lines? Lines of power that traverse the globe?'

'Yes,' snapped Amari, 'I know what they are. You're saying they're real?'

'Of course. Power pools around the lines; it's how magic travels around the world.'

'Right.'

Caspar laughed. 'You don't believe me?'

'I'm not sure what to believe any longer.'

Chapter 11

By the time Amari and Caspar got back to the house, the team had worked miracles. The pegs in the boot room were loaded with Barbour coats and down-filled jackets. Piles of flat caps and wax and woolen hats sat on a shelf above, rows of wellie boots underneath. The wooden bucket in the corner had even been filled with walking sticks with elaborately carved tops.

It turned out most of their cleaning supplies were obsolete; a local cleaning firm had come in with their own products. They'd cleaned the place from top to bottom, and the surfaces practically sparkled.

The rest of the team had fixed anything they could find that was broken, taken out things that were beyond repair, cut the grass in the garden, and someone had even purchased new mattresses for all four bedrooms.

'This is wild,' said Amari, taking in the transformation. 'How did you get these guys here on such short notice?'

'We employ them to look after all the properties in the village. Seeing as it's Midsummer, they'd already lined up reinforcements. They're human, but we pay them well enough that they don't ask questions. Before today, I told them not to bother with this place, given that I wasn't using it, and didn't want anyone else to use it either. I couldn't come here and not think constantly of you ...'

When they'd finished looking around downstairs, Amari went back to the kitchen, looking for the bed linens they'd bought. Her shopping wasn't where she'd left it.

'Did you move the sheets?' asked Amari.

'No,' said Caspar, 'but I know some people who probably did.'

'You're kidding. Already?'

'They're efficient.'

One of the team, a middle-aged woman called Helen, entered the kitchen. She was short, plump, and stern-looking, her lined face forming a formidable expression.

'We're going to borrow a spare duvet and pillows from one of the other houses,' said Helen. 'The ones here need to be replaced. We'll buy new ones for you tomorrow.'

'We'll need two beds,' said Amari quickly, before events could run even further away from her.

'Three,' said Caspar. 'Meredith's staying too.'

'Three duvets it is, then,' said Helen. 'What would you like to do about curtains and paint colors? Shall I pick out the fabric and colors, or would you like to?' She looked expectantly at Amari, as did Caspar.

'I'd love to pick them out,' said Amari. 'And we probably need to get some of the furniture re-upholstered, and some throw cushions to make it feel more homely.'

'Right you are. I'll bring samples with me tomorrow,' said Helen, heading for the back door.

Caspar and Amari watched her go.

'Wouldn't want to get on the wrong side of her,' whispered Amari.

'Me neither,' Caspar agreed, smiling conspiratorially. 'Right. Seeing as everyone else has done the hard work, let's cook dinner. We're sure to have company in a bit.'

As it turned out, Caspar was brilliant in the kitchen. He chopped, stirred, flavored, and even made mayonnaise, without breaking a sweat.

'Elliot loves it, so we let him do all the cooking,' said Caspar, when Amari remarked on his abilities, 'but most demons have had to learn at some point in their history. Almost all of us were born in a time before microwaves and convection ovens and convenience foods. We had to cook in brick ovens, or over open fires.'

'Well, I still think your knife skills are exemplary,' she said.

She rummaged in cupboards and drawers to find the newly cleaned cutlery and crockery, and set them on the newly repaired table.

Caspar made a big vat of chicken, mushroom, and pea risotto. Amari made a green salad to go on the side, along with some delicious-looking bread they'd bought.

'Ooh, something smells good,' said Talli as she marched into the kitchen, not bothering to knock. But then, seeing as the demons' finances were a community affair, Amari supposed the house must belong to her too, technically. She'd have to ask Caspar how it all worked.

'Risotto,' said Caspar, taking the huge pan to the table as Meredith and Christa entered the room. 'You're just in time.'

'Were you expecting an army?' asked Christa, looking at the mountain of food.

'I forgot it was just us,' said Caspar.

'Leftovers for lunch tomorrow,' said Talli. 'We can have deep-fried risotto balls. Oh yes, let's do that!'

Amari caught Christa's eye and smiled at Talli's perpetual enthusiasm: she was one of a kind.

Not long later, they sat back in their chairs, stuffed with the risotto they'd washed down with two bottles of wine.

'So, how does reincarnation work?' asked Amari, filling the comfortable silence. 'I mean, you two,' she indicated towards Talli and Christa, 'are roughly the same age in this life, as are Caspar and I. Does that always happen? What if one of you dies much earlier than the other? Are there usually gaps in time between reincarnations?'

'That got heavy quickly,' laughed Christa.

'Nobody knows how it works, exactly,' said Caspar.

'It is magic after all,' said Talli.

'Sometimes there are big gaps between incarnations, sometimes it's immediate,' said Caspar. 'It varies each time. So yes, sometimes there are big age gaps between demons who used to be the same age. I think our biggest was twenty years. You were older.'

'Surely that could get weird,' said Amari, 'when a ten-year-old is in love with a thirty-year-old.'

'Yes,' said Caspar, 'but that rarely happens.'

'Most demons, once they've reincarnated, take a decade or two to wake up in their new bodies. Those who wake up sooner—as children—usually stay with their biological families. It's just easier that way,' said Christa.

'I mean, would you have wanted to abandon your birth parents when you were ten, or twelve?' said Meredith.

The thought made Amari shudder. 'Absolutely not. Do I have to abandon them now?'

'Of course not,' said Talli, 'but you can't discuss your demon life with them.'

'And for those who wake up earlier,' said Christa, 'it depends on their nation. Pagans are strict about respecting the rules of society, including the age of consent, regardless of how many lives a demon has lived.'

'After that, it's up to the demons involved to do what they want,' said Meredith.

'We've had some interesting age gaps,' laughed Talli. 'Our biggest was thirty years!'

'We got some strange looks,' said Christa.

'That was a breeze in comparison to when you came back as a woman in the eighteenth century,' said Talli. 'Hiding same-sex relationships back then was so difficult—everyone in everyone else's business … no privacy.'

'Do all demons change sex sometimes?' asked Amari.

'Not everyone,' said Christa. 'But quite a few.'

'You never did,' said Caspar, preempting her next question.

'Shame,' said Amari. She'd love to know what it was like to be a man.

Talli and Christa eventually left for the night, and Meredith took the bedroom furthest from Amari and Caspar. Amari went into her room—the room that had been hers and Caspar's in previous lives. Caspar followed her in.

153

'Have you got everything you need?' he asked, casting around for a reason to linger.

'Yes, thanks,' she said, raising an eyebrow. 'Would you like to stay for a while?'

'You're not too tired?'

Amari climbed onto the bed, propped up the pillows, and leaned back against the wooden headboard, patting the space next to her.

The bed was less elaborate than the four-poster at Cloister Cottage, and Caspar liked it better. He sat next to her, leaning back, her summer scent washing over him, making his breath catch in his throat.

'What do you think of the house?' he asked.

'Aside from the fact you've let it crumble,' said Amari, sternly, 'it's awesome. The rooms are so welcoming, and there's so much personality and history.'

'You always loved it here.'

'Do you realize how many priceless artifacts there are, strewn all over the place? You know I had to stop Helen from throwing away a three-hundred-year-old vase earlier?'

'It was probably a piece of junk.'

'It's three hundred years old! It deserves more respect than to be thrown in the trash.'

'How sentimental you've become.'

'I dread to think the things you lot have destroyed, with no regard for those who might like to appreciate them.'

'What do you suggest? We could leave things outside museums, like you would with clothes at a charity shop?'

'Not overly subtle,' said Amari, 'and I'm guessing that would lead to some awkward questions.'

'Okay, well, work out the logistics, and let me know what you think is best.'

'Maybe I will.'

A comfortable silence settled over them, and Caspar slipped his hand into hers. She let him, but hesitated first. Caspar tensed.

The silence stretched, an edge of discomfort pervading the cozy space, a prickle of anxiety shooting up his spine. Whatever was going to happen next wouldn't be good; he could feel it in the air. It wound tauter with each passing second.

Amari retrieved her hand, wringing it with the other in her lap. 'What were we arguing about?' she asked. 'In our last lives? Why wouldn't I talk to you for an entire lifetime?'

Caspar's anxiety turned to nausea. He'd thought they were making progress … they *were* making progress, but this …

He took a deep breath. 'Amari, no good can come from talking about it.'

'Are you ever going to tell me what you did?'

Caspar went up on his knees, facing her. He almost reached for her, but knew she'd kick him out in a heartbeat if he did.

'Can't we leave that fight until you wake up?'

'How am I supposed to trust you when you're keeping things from me?'

'It would be impossible to tell you everything … for you to understand the context. And if I tell you my side, when you wake, you'll accuse me of trying to brainwash your subconscious. I can't win either way.'

'Is it bad? Did you kill somebody?'

Caspar laughed. He knew it was a bad idea, but he couldn't help it. 'Raina's killed enough people in her lives … that would barely make her blink. I made a choice she disagreed with. I was trying to protect her. It didn't play out as I'd hoped, and she blames me for the consequences.'

'Would you do it differently? If you could do it again?'

Caspar had asked himself that so many times.

'I'd like to say yes, but honestly, I don't know. I would do anything to protect her … to protect you. Maybe if we'd worked it out together … we both acted from emotion …'

There was a long silence, the past haunting him.

'I'm tired,' said Amari, shutting him out.

They'd been getting somewhere. But now she was sending them right back to the start.

'Okay,' he said, lingering for a few moments—hoping she'd change her mind—before heading for the door. 'See you in the morning.'

'Caspar,' she said, stopping him. 'Thank you for today. I feel at home here, despite the chaos.'

'I'm glad to hear it,' he said, then forced himself to leave. Maybe all was not lost after all.

By the time Amari made it to breakfast the following morning, the kitchen was awash with people.

'Finally,' said Helen, who had the air of a ticking time bomb. She threw a dirty look at Caspar. 'May we go upstairs now?'

'Please, carry on,' said Caspar, his eyes glinting with amusement.

'Um … were they waiting for me to come down?' asked Amari.

'Prince Flipping Charming over here wouldn't even let us get started in the other rooms until you woke up. He didn't want you to be disturbed,' said Helen, storming past, her team in tow.

Amari's cheeks flushed. 'Oh, sorry.'

She rounded on Caspar once they were alone.

'Don't do that again. I don't want Helen to hate me.'

'Oh, don't worry about her. She loves to have something to complain about. Sleep well?'

'Yes actually, I did.'

'Raina always slept well in that room. She said it was something to do with the ley lines.'

'If you say so,' said Amari, putting the kettle on.

Caspar moved next to her, standing close, their arms almost touching. He leaned across her to put bread in the toaster, and Amari's senses heightened.

He placed a hand on her shoulder, twisting her to face him, looking into her eyes, only inches away.

'Are you cross with me?' His tone was flirtatious.

'Maybe,' she said, matching it.

'Are you going to make it hard for me to get back in your good graces?'

'Maybe,' she said, quieter this time, her body reacting to the heat radiating from him, the closeness.

She turned her head away, but his hand came up to her face, pulling it back to look at him. Her eyes flicked to his lips—she couldn't help it—and his eyes dilated.

He slowly leaned his head towards her, stopping only when their lips were so close she could feel his breath on her skin.

Her eyes fluttered closed, but still he waited. She stayed still, her mind racing, telling her to pull away. Her body refused to listen. It wanted to close the gap and never look back.

The back door slammed, and Amari jumped. She dropped her head, placed her hands on Caspar's chest, balled her fists in the fabric, then pushed herself away, turning just in time to see Elliot, Meredith, Jon, and Gemma enter the room.

'Hey,' said Elliot, hesitating for a split second as he took in the scene. 'We brought supplies!'

He held up two shopping bags crammed full of bread, croissants, eggs, bacon, and sausages.

'We're going to need sustenance before Talli gets her hands on us.'

'Sounds good to me,' said Amari.

She knew her enthusiasm sounded forced, but she was busy fighting her body's vigorous urging to pull Caspar into the nearest secluded space.

She found, when she turned back to the kettle, that Caspar hadn't moved a muscle. His eyes bored into hers, releasing an injection of happy chemicals into her blood.

'You make the tea, and I'll help Elliot,' she said.

Her fingers brushed against his as she moved away. He caught them, held them briefly, then released her.

After breakfast, they walked down the drive to the malt house, meeting Talli, Christa, and a team of other demons, most of whom Amari didn't recognize.

Talli didn't hesitate for a moment before putting them to work, building tents and gazebos, stringing up lights, building bars and stages, creating fire pits, placing hay bales around the place, making flower decorations and crowns, cleaning out the malt house, and erecting an enormous may pole. Everything was carefully positioned by Talli, and no one dared deviate from her carefully constructed plan.

Talli focused her attention on the stone circle where the rituals would take place, ensuring the flowers and ceremonial bowls were positioned correctly. She liberally smudged the area with herbs, using a knife to cut the air, and ringing bells to purify.

Nobody walked through the circle, knowing from years of experience that to do so would bring Talli's wrath down in full force. Amari almost committed the crime, but Christa caught her arm just in time.

By the end of the day, they'd made good progress, but there was still much to do. Talli gave out orders for the following morning as they sat around the kitchen table.

'Anyone heard from Rose?' asked Jon, sipping his after-dinner coffee.

The others shook their heads.

'Nothing,' said Christa.

'Is that unusual?' asked Amari.

'Not really,' said Caspar. 'She's at the Registerium. You're not allowed to take in communications devices.'

'She's probably locked in endless boring talks,' said Talli.

'They're probably burying their heads in the sand, hoping the problem will disappear,' added Meredith.

'Has she gone because of the attacks on me?' asked Amari.

'That, and the rising tensions with the Templars,' said Christa. 'They're reneging on deals, trespassing extensively, and threatening to cause upset in the non-demon world through trade tariffs, stock market manipulation ... that kind of thing.'

'What do you think will happen?' asked Amari. 'I'm assuming there's still no evidence about who was trying to kill me?'

'No,' said Caspar. 'And the Registerium will stall.'

'But Rose has to raise the issue now, so if things go south, she's already warned them,' said Christa.

'The Registerium's the body that oversees all demon nations, right?' asked Amari.

'Yep,' said Christa, 'but the Registerium only has a limited number of its own followers. Most demons would rather be affiliated with one of the nations. It's exciting to be part of a nation, and there's more freedom.'

'But you said each nation always has a representative there?' asked Amari.

'Yes,' said Christa. 'Currently it's a guy called Malcolm for us. He's only been there for five years though, so I'm not sure how much help he'll be to Rose.'

'And the representatives make decisions collectively? Who's in charge?' asked Amari.

'The Registerium has an elected council, led by the Registrar,' said Caspar. 'They're elected by the Registerium's followers, from within their own ranks, and deal with all the administration that goes along with running the place.

'They keep our records, organize and chair meetings, and ultimately have the power to make decisions, if the representatives from other nations disagree.'

'Can anyone join the Registerium and become one of their followers?' asked Amari.

'Yes, in theory,' said Caspar, 'although they'd have to give up their allegiance to any other nation, and devote at least ten lifetimes to the Registerium.'

'Ten lifetimes?!' exclaimed Amari.

'Most of them are a bit weird,' said Jon.

'Often they're disillusioned with their nation and want a break,' said Christa.

'And the guy in charge is a total crackpot,' added Jon.

'He's not that bad,' said Caspar.

'Yes, he is,' said Jon. 'Remember the time one of our demons was murdered, with half a dozen demon witnesses to say it was the Aztecs, but he refused to do anything?'

'Because he didn't want to start a war,' said Meredith.

'What's the point in having rules if the Registerium doesn't enforce them?' said Jon.

'There's no rule that says we can't kill each other,' said Meredith, 'only that we can't draw attention from non-demons when we do.'

'Fat lot of good that does anyone,' said Jon.

'We're free to go to war if we want to,' said Meredith.

'But it's suicide if the Registerium doesn't give the go ahead.'

The rest of them watched Meredith and Jon with interest.

'And if the Registerium doesn't give the go ahead,' said Jon, 'everyone might side with the murdering bastards who started the dispute to begin with.'

'Life comes with risks,' Meredith said with a shrug.

'Maybe we need a new Registerium that has some balls,' said Jon.

The other demons laughed.

'Good luck with that,' said Talli. 'Have you got any idea how long it took, or how many people had to die, or how suspicious the non-demons had to get before we agreed to form the Registerium in the first place? All the big nations need to be on board for any change to happen.'

'And the Registerium would try to kill you,' said Christa.

'Not to mention, it would probably unite all the other demon nations against you,' said Meredith.

'But it's so broken,' said Jon.

The old demons laughed again.

'Every political system that's ever existed is broken,' said Meredith. 'You think you've got a better way?'

That night, Caspar didn't follow Amari into her room. She waited for him, wondering if there would be a knock on her door, hoping there would be, but it never came. Eventually, Amari decided she would go to him.

'Come in,' said Caspar's surprised voice.

Amari pushed the door open to find Caspar topless and in bed. She closed the door softly behind her, the house now fully occupied with the other four sharing the two spare rooms.

'I can't sleep,' she lied.

He shifted to make room for her. He didn't reach for a shirt.

'What's on your mind?'

You. 'Nothing in particular.'

'There's somewhere I want to take you tomorrow,' he said, pulling back the covers for her. She climbed in, laying the duvet, warm from Caspar's body, across her legs.

'You think Talli's going to let you get away with that?'

'We'll have to sneak away. We can pretend we're going to get supplies.'

'Where are we going?'

'It's a surprise.'

'Hmm,' said Amari, narrowing her eyes. 'Will I like it?'

'You'll love it.'

His eyes lingered on hers. They watched each other, seconds ticking by.

'What were we arguing about, before you proposed by the fountain? What did I do?'

Caspar took a long breath. 'Amari, do you really want to talk about this stuff? You'll remember soon enough.'

'I want to know. Raina's pissed at you for something you've done ... but I guess she's done bad things too.'

'We've both made our share of questionable decisions. And I want to forget them.'

'Caspar, just tell me. What did I do?'

Caspar bared his teeth. 'You ran away with an old lover; I don't really know why.'

Amari felt an intense pang of guilt.

'I guess I was focusing on work. Raina was fed up with international politics, and wanted me to give it up too. I thought I was close to a breakthrough with the Russian Spirituals and felt compelled to keep going.'

'So she had an affair.'

'It was someone from her distant past, although she wouldn't tell me his name. They had a fling before I even met her ... she said that's how she'd always thought of it, anyway. Turns out he'd always wanted more. He showed up at a time when our relationship was turbulent.'

'Have you ever had an affair?'

'Only once, after I found out Raina had left. It made me sick, and I've never done it again.'

'Have you been tempted?'

'No.' He met her eyes. 'You're the only one I want.'

'Raina's pretty great, huh?'

She dropped her eyes to his toned, naked chest. It was begging for her to reach out and touch it. Her cheeks flushed.

'You are Raina,' he said, taking her hand, playing with her fingers.

He leaned in, invading her space, the heat of his skin radiating towards her, lips so tantalizingly close, but she dipped her head. She wanted nothing more than to kiss him, but she couldn't.

'I need to tell Dean it's over,' she said, meeting his gaze. She raised a hand to his cheek, stroking his skin, finally vocalizing the words she'd been hiding from. 'I feel horrible enough as it is.'

He rested his forehead against hers. 'Will it make any difference?' he asked, closing his eyes, raising his hand to her face, mirroring her touch.

'I don't know.'

He had a point. She was going to break Dean's heart either way.

Chapter 12

Amari came down early the following day, not wanting to incur the wrath of Helen, who'd laid out fabric, carpet, and paint samples in the sitting room. After making a cup of tea and grabbing an apple from the kitchen, they sat together to make some decisions.

An hour and a half later, they'd been all over the house, holding up samples to get a sense of how each would look, and how different colors and textures would work together.

Amari was nothing if not decisive, and by the time they'd finished, she'd made most of the important decisions. She'd chosen textured carpets, muted wall colors—most of which were similar to the rooms' existing colors—and patterned and floral fabrics for the curtains. She'd kept it mostly traditional, but with a twist here or there.

'I need more tea after all that,' said Amari, turning to see if Helen would like one too, but she'd already disappeared. 'That woman has boundless energy,' Amari said to Caspar, who was loading food into a picnic basket.

'Be right back,' he said.

He sneaked the fully laden basket out of the back door and into the car while there was no one around to see.

'Subtle,' laughed Amari as he returned, giving her a high five.

'Hey! I'm a criminal mastermind.'

'I'm sure.'

'We'd should leave now, or we'll be discovered.'

'Good plan.'

'Here,' he said, holding out an insulated metal cup so she could take her tea.

'Did you pack some of Elliot's flapjack? I'm hungry.'

'Yes, of course,' he said, ushering her out of the kitchen. 'Come on, let's move.'

Amari giggled. 'I feel like we're teenagers, sneaking out behind our parents' backs.'

'Because that's pretty much what we're doing!' laughed Caspar, starting the Range Rover. 'The most difficult bit will be getting past the malt house, but I'm thinking we speed through and stop for nothing.'

'Don't speed. It'll draw attention. Just drive through at a natural pace, like we're going on an errand for Talli.'

'That could backfire. If Talli sees us, she'll jump onto the bonnet; I've seen her do it before … but she won't if we're travelling at speed.'

'You people are crazy.'

'Yes. I don't think any of us would argue otherwise.'

'Whatever. But if you kill someone, it's nothing to do with me.'

Caspar floored it past the malt house, and it turned out he was right to; Talli hurled a projectile at the window as they passed.

'Jesus Christ!' screamed Amari, thanking all her lucky stars that the window held.

Caspar laughed loudly. 'I knew she'd be lying in wait.'

'She threw a brick at the window!'

'It bounced off. Bullet-proof glass. She just wanted us to know she's pissed.'

'Message received.'

'We'll be back after lunch, and she's got an army of people arriving today; they'll be done in no time.'

They drove down the pretty Somerset lanes, the Range Rover high enough that Amari could see over the hedgerows.

'It's beautiful around here,' said Amari.

'Have you spent much time in the countryside?'

'Not really. I grew up in London, worked in London, and went on holidays abroad mainly. What about you?'

'Raina and I lived all over the place. You were born in the Middle East. I was born in France, or at least, what's now called France, but since then, we've lived all across the world. We both did a stint in Nepal, finding ourselves.'

Amari laughed. 'Of course we did.'

'We lived in a castle in Scotland for a bit. We've had houses in Devon, Cornwall, Pembrokeshire, Hertfordshire, East Anglia. We've travelled to pretty much everywhere in the UK, and we've lived abroad too.'

'Do people usually reincarnate in the same place they died?'

'Generally, it's wherever they considered to be home when they died, but it's not straightforward. You could have several homes, or might not feel like you have a home at all.'

'I guess that's why there are hunters.'

'Yep.'

'They have a terrible name, by the way.'

'Better than the Slayers.'

'True.'

Caspar turned the Range Rover onto a side road, ignoring the big sign saying, *Private. Keep out.* He drove to the end of the tree-lined track, stopping in a wide area next to a big metal gate.

'Where are we?' asked Amari.

'At the most perfect picnic spot you'll ever find.'

Caspar retrieved the basket and a blanket, then led her through the gap at the side of the gate, into the woodland beyond.

They walked for maybe two minutes—Amari glad she'd worn sensible shoes—then came out into a beautiful clearing next to a lively stream.

Caspar turned downstream, halting alongside a natural pool. There was a little waterfall where water flowed in, the sound soothing, and a lip at the other side, over which the water flowed out. The pool in the middle looked deep and wide and perfect for a dip.

'I didn't bring any swimming stuff,' said Amari, disappointed.

Caspar laughed, laying out the picnic blanket. 'You're not normally concerned with such things.'

Amari scowled. 'Well, I am now.'

'I'll turn my back and avert my gaze, I promise. And I've got towels.' He unhooked them from the bottom of the wicker basket, and held them up for her to see.

Amari sighed. 'Oh, fine. Seeing as you promised.'

'Quick dip before we eat?' Caspar suggested, kicking off his shoes and unbuttoning his shirt without waiting for a reply.

Amari watched with interest, but turned quickly away when his hands went to his belt buckle. Caspar laughed.

'Flipping Pagans.'

'Wait until tomorrow; you haven't seen anything yet …'

'I dread to think,' she said, beginning to strip off her clothes.

Caspar jumped into the water with a splash.

'Bloody hell!' he gasped. 'It's freezing.'

Amari giggled. 'Turn around.'

Caspar reluctantly turned his back, panting and splashing as his body got used to the temperature. Amari pulled off her underwear and walked to the water's edge. She dipped in a toe, then pulled it quickly back.

'You're right; it's too cold for a swim.'

Caspar began to turn around.

'Don't you dare!' she shrieked.

'You've just got to go for it. Jump in; it's the only way.'

'It's cold. Unpleasantly cold.'

'I'm turning around.'

'No!'

'Three, two, one.'

Amari jumped. The cold hit her like a wall. She surfaced, struggling for breath, her feet not quite reaching the bottom.

'Fuck, fuck, fuck,' she whimpered, trying to breathe.

'It'll be okay in a minute,' he chuckled, taking her in. 'My body's adjusted already.'

Their eyes met across the pool, and Amari's mind was hijacked by a memory. She and an Italian man with Caspar's eyes were swimming in a natural pool. It was night, and it was colder than she'd expected. She was complaining about the temperature.

The man laughed loudly, prowling towards her, lit only by the moon. Waterfalls created mist that cooled her further. She moved away from the spray, ducking into the water, keeping a careful eye on Caspar's progress.

Caspar altered his course, ceaselessly and wordlessly stalking her. Her heart raced as he got within range. She splashed him and dove away, squealing as he caught her foot, preventing her escape.

Her feet went to the bottom, forcing him to relinquish her, but his hand ran up her leg, across her backside, to her waist. She shivered, wrapping her arms around his neck, letting him pull her naked body flush against him.

Caspar lifted her, enfolding her in his arms, and she wrapped her legs around him. They kissed, and it was deep and leisurely and healing. She was his and he was hers, and they needed nothing more than that, but they needed it, each other.

They needed to touch, to feel the fierce heat of their bodies pressed together, to entangle themselves and lie together, holding each other. It energized and restored them, just being near the other. It brought safety, belonging.

Feeling throbbed in Raina's chest, filling it with pressure, pushing against her ribs, threatening to crack her open. *Love ... such an inadequate word for an extension of your soul*, thought Raina, pulling back far enough to look at him. *For someone who'd be yours until you turned to dust.*

Amari snapped out of the memory to find herself in Caspar's arms. She didn't think, wrapping herself around him, holding him to her.

'Hey ... it's okay,' said Caspar, running a hand across her back. 'Another memory?'

'I told you I didn't want you to see me naked,' sobbed Amari, overtaken by a swell of emotion. 'I never cry. How have you turned me into such a mess?'

'I thought, on balance, that you'd prefer for me to see your naked body than to drown; you dropped like a stone. Anyway, I can't see much; you're too close for a good view.'

'I guess,' she said, desperately holding onto him, holding onto the feeling from the memory, trying not to think about their nakedness.

Silence settled over them.

'Want to tell me about it?' Caspar asked gently.

'We were at some outdoor pools,' she said into his neck. 'There were waterfalls. It was night and it was cold. You looked Italian.'

'Oh. Terme di Saturnia,' said Caspar, quietly, 'hundreds of years ago.'

She pressed her lips against Caspar's beating pulse, breathing in the smell from the memory.

He shivered.

'You've felt that way for hundreds of years?'

Caspar's lips brushed her ear. '*We* have; you and I.'

Amari could still feel how they'd felt for each other in every inch of her body; a craving like nothing she'd ever known. She wanted to entwine their bodies, to crawl inside him, to join themselves in every possible way.

Her body burned hot everywhere they touched, desire fierce and demanding, rampaging through her veins. Her brain shut down; she couldn't think, could only act.

She kissed his pulse again, then lifted her head, pulling back so she could look into his eyes, not caring that her breasts were in full view.

His breath hitched, eyes going black as she put a hand on his cheek, ran a thumb across his lips. He closed his eyes, took a breath, opened them, ran his gaze over her naked flesh.

She took his head in both her hands and pulled his lips to hers. They kissed like they had in the memory, like there was nothing else in the world, like all that mattered was this.

Eventually, the cold forced them from the pool. Caspar jumped out first, grabbing one of the big, fluffy towels, wrapping it around his shoulders.

He practically tackled Amari as she climbed out, forcing a delighted shriek to escape her lips. He pulled her into his chest, closing his arms around her, the heat shocking after the cold bite of the air.

Caspar trailed his fingers up and down her skin, sending a searing bolt of desire to her core.

She kissed him, pressed her body against his, spurred on by his reaction to her touch.

He groaned into her mouth, pushing her backwards. Amari's hands circled his back, clinging to him, driven by instinct alone.

They reached the blanket and Caspar hooked his leg around Amari's ankles, tripping her, catching her weight as she crumpled backwards, lowering her to the ground.

He kissed her neck, cupped her breast. Amari gasped as he pinched her nipple, bucking her hips against him.

His mouth replaced his hand, teasing her nipple as his fingers traced the contours of her body, exploring her skin with small, tantalizing movements. He slid across her hip bone, into the hollow beside it, along the crease at the base of her belly. She raised her hips, urging his fingers lower. Instead, he walked them up, across her stomach, stepping from one rib to the next.

His lips kissed upwards, to her collarbone, then sucked and kissed and licked the skin just below it.

Amari gasped in surprise as her muscles clenched. He chuckled and she grabbed his hair. He growled into her neck, taking a breast in his hand, massaging, flicking, rolling.

He nipped at her neck, and she tipped her head back, giving him more room.

He slid his hand down across her skin, laying his palm flat on her stomach, the weight of it sparking a delicious sensation between her thighs.

His hand slid lower, ever closer. Her hips bucked when he reached her core, and she moaned, arching into him, writhing against him. His lips met hers, tongue probing into her mouth, and sensation filled every inch of her, driving her crazy.

Her hands went to his back, pulling at him until he finally rolled on top of her, the weight of him pressing her down. She hummed with pleasure, feeling him hard between her thighs. She raised her hips, tried to make him give her what she wanted.

He breathed a laugh into her ear. 'What's the rush?' he murmured, making small, infuriating movements.

She grasped a handful of his hair, forcing him to meet her eyes. 'I want you.'

He held her gaze for a beat then lowered his lips to her mouth, their kisses long and deep as he nudged at her core.

He pushed inside, and they both gasped. Amari wrapped her legs around him, wanting more. His movements were slow, deliberate, reverent.

His lips went to her ear, huffs of breath caressing her skin. He slipped his hands under her backside, lifting her, pushing deeper, increasing the pace.

He groaned into her neck and the sound ripped through her, setting her alight. He sensed it, his movements becoming faster, fiercer, winding her tighter, ever closer to the brink, until a hard, deep thrust finally gave her release. He followed her over, and together, they rode wave after wave of pleasure.

Amari and Caspar travelled back to Maltings in silence, each lost in thought, their hands linked together.

They'd finally pulled apart, wrapped themselves in the towels, and dug into the picnic. They'd touched at all times, Amari leaning against Caspar as he lounged on the blanket.

Caspar had packed every delicious thing he could find: Scotch eggs, Comté and Manchego cheeses with crackers and homemade chutney, raspberries from the canes that had been uncovered in the overgrown garden, quiche, flapjack, and a bottle of crisp white wine.

After they'd eaten, they'd laid together, cuddling, taking turns to instigate long, luxurious kisses, trickling water and chirping birds the soundtrack to their bliss.

Amari couldn't find words to match her feelings. She could barely remember what Dean looked like, and the thought sickened her. How could that be possible, in such a short amount of time? But what she'd felt in the flashback ... there was nothing that could compare, not if she lived ten thousand lifetimes.

She loved Caspar. My God, she did. She loved him. How could that be? It wasn't like the feeling from the dream ... not yet. But she wanted it, that feeling, needed it, like an addict, craving more after her first taste of a potent drug.

They got back to Maltings, driving straight past the crowd of demons now sitting round a central bonfire, talking, singing, dancing, and eating. Talli was dancing around the maypole, seeming not to notice the Range Rover as it sailed by.

Caspar parked by the back door and helped Amari out, not bothering to retrieve the picnic basket. He threaded his fingers through hers and headed straight for the stairs.

Amari followed in a trance, not caring if the whole world saw them, caring only that she was with him. He led them to Amari's bedroom, closed the door, and pulled her around to face him.

'Are you sure?' he asked. 'Now we're back here … you still want this? Still want me?'

She reached up and pressed her lips against his, a feeling of rightness settling over her, of relief.

They moved to the bed, Caspar gently lowering her down, turning her over, stripping off their clothes.

He straddled her, his weight resting on the top of her legs, caressing her, massaging her pressure points, kissing every sensitive spot, hands roaming across every inch of flesh.

Amari basked in the contact, glorying in the feel of his strong, deft hands, little moans of pleasure escaping her lips. She wanted them to lock themselves away, here, together, for days, weeks on end.

His fingers turned teasing as they explored her, ghosting her sensitive spots, coming tantalizingly close to her breasts, before skirting away, his lips kissing their way down her spine.

She felt him stiffen against her and he shifted his weight, lying on top on her, his hard, naked torso flush against her back. His weight pressed her down, and she mewed in gratification, doing it again when she felt him brush her core. She pressed back into him, lifting her hips as much as she was able, rocking against him.

She exhaled, fisting her hands in the sheets. 'Caspar,' she breathed.

He entered her, whispered her name, bit her neck. Neither of them lasted long.

Caspar rolled them to the side, tucking her in front of him. She sighed contentedly. He kissed her hair, stroked her skin. She couldn't remember a time when she'd felt so perfectly peaceful, equalized, happy.

A welcome breeze from the window cooled them, then made them shiver. Caspar covered them with a sheet.

Life felt suddenly simple—this was all they would ever need. They fell asleep, tangled, and sated, and serene.

Chapter 13

Caspar woke early, before dawn, to a knock at the door. Whoever it was moved on, and Caspar looked down at Amari, her head on his arm.

Her hair was strewn out around her, covering her cheek, shading her face from view. He pulled it back, tracing his fingers along her cheekbone, pushing the hair behind her ear.

She shifted in her sleep, pouting her lips, frowning. A smile tugged at his mouth and his heart nearly burst. He'd seen her face do this exact transition in countless bodies.

He ran his thumb across her lips and they parted. He kissed her without thinking, his body reacting to hers. He sucked on her bottom lip, feeling her lips respond as her conscious mind awoke. He started to pull away, but she stopped him, her hand running lazily up his neck, into his hair.

'We've got to get up,' he murmured.

'We're never leaving this bed.'

'It's the Summer Solstice.'

'I don't care.'

She wrapped a leg across his, pinning him in place.

'We can't miss it,' he said, his lips working their way from her neck to her collarbone.

'I beg to differ.'

She arched into him.

'They'll come in here and drag us out naked.'

His hand skirted her breast, down across her waist.

'No, they won't.'

'They've done it before.'

His lips reached her breast. She moaned as he sucked a nipple into his mouth. Her head tipped back, pressing into the pillow.

'You people are batshit crazy.'

'Be that as it may,' he said, sitting up and pulling her with him, her hair falling in an arc around her face, 'you really don't want to miss this.' He held her head in his hands and kissed her lips, which were pouting again. 'Trust me.'

'Oh, fine. I'm going to have a shower.'

'Be quick. I would come with you, but we haven't got long until sunrise. I'll shower next door.'

'What happens at sunrise?'

'You'll see.'

Amari showered, not bothering to wash her hair, then dressed in the flowing white dress and flower crown that someone had left outside her bedroom door. The dress cinched in at the waist and had beautiful tulip sleeves that brushed her fingertips.

Caspar appeared at her door as she slipped on a pair of sandals, wearing a simple linen shirt and cutoff trousers. He moved into her space, hands going to her waist. Amari breathed in his freshly washed smell.

'You look beautiful,' he said, kissing her briefly. Then he took her hand and led her down the stairs.

'About flipping time,' said Meredith, turning as she heard them enter the room. Her eyes flicked to their joined hands, then to their faces. She raised an eyebrow, but said only, 'We have to go.'

Meredith wore a dress similar to Amari's, although Meredith's had additional paneling across the front, and slits up the sides so her legs could move freely. Her flower crown was smaller than Amari's, but it suited her.

They left through the back door to find Elliot and Gemma canoodling, whispering quietly to each other, while Jon paced feverishly.

'Thank all the Gods,' Jon said when they appeared. 'These two are driving me crazy.' He spotted Amari and Caspar's joined hands. 'For the love of all that is holy … you too?'

Caspar smiled, Amari wrapping her arms around his waist.

'You've got Meredith,' said Caspar, his tone even.

Jon narrowed his eyes, then turned and stalked off in the direction of the malt house. 'We've got to get going, or we're going to be late,' he called back to them.

Meredith took one look at the two couples and rolled her eyes, following in Jon's wake.

By the time they reached the field next to the malt house, the sun's rays were smudging the horizon. A crowd had gathered around the main bonfire, and Talli and Christa were dancing around it in dresses similar to Amari's.

Talli thrust an elaborate knife into the fire, then pulled it back, along with a stick that was already burning. She walked to the stone circle, both knife and stick held high.

Copper element bowls awaited at the four compass points outside the stone circle. Talli lit the fire bowl using the stick, waiting for it to roar to life before standing, now holding only the knife.

She walked slowly around the circle, holding the knife up above the stones, cutting the air, completing a full turn, coming to a stop when she once again reached the fire bowl.

Talli pulled the knife toward her chest, blade pointing upwards, both hands on the handle. She walked, bare foot, slowly, in her fluid way, to the flat altar stone in the middle of the circle, then spun dramatically to face east, towards the sunrise.

Someone in the crowd started drumming, the beat slow and methodical. Another drum joined the first, then another, and another.

The drummers, a mix of men and women, walked forward until there were ten of them surrounding the stone circle. Amari shivered and Caspar pulled her back against his chest, wrapping his arms around her.

Talli remained in front of the altar, still as the stones, head bowed, waiting. As the light of dawn peeked over the horizon, the tempo of the drumming increased, slowly at first, the crowd swaying in time with the beat.

As the rays intensified, so did the drumming, faster and faster, some demons starting to dance, either alone or in pairs, energy cracking palpably all around.

Amari rested her head back on Caspar's chest. She let him sway her, drumbeats reverberating through them, willingly following his lead.

Talli raised her arms above her head, blade held between her hands. She dropped to her knees, arms still overhead. The drumming ceased in perfect unison. The demons stilled, watching, waiting.

The sun came over the horizon, beams of light glinting off the blade in Talli's hand, making it seem like the source of light itself. Talli began chanting in words that Amari neither knew nor understood. The crowd joined in until the whole place resonated with the deep, rumbling, hair-raising sound.

Anticipation, hot and tingling, filled Amari, gooseflesh spreading like wildfire across her skin. She felt uneasy, like maybe she wasn't supposed to witness this.

And then Talli stopped, and the place went dead.

Talli plunged the knife into the earth, and a wave of power surged across the gathering, followed by complete stillness for four long beats. Then the place erupted; the drummers resumed, others joining in with pipes and strings and voices.

Demons took to the makeshift stages, dancing, jumping, swooping, and swaying. Euphoria swept through them, the world outside irrelevant, foreign, forgotten in the face of such emotion. Amari danced ceaselessly with Caspar, inhibitions spirited away by that fearsome surge of power.

At last the cavorting died down, coinciding, not surprisingly, with the appearance of a breakfast feast.

Three long banquet tables had been artfully laid with rustic candle centerpieces, divine floral creations, linen napkins, heavy silver cutlery, and hearty pottery.

Waiters brought platter after platter of delicious food. Along with fruit and yoghurt were cold meats, cheeses, pies, whole sides of smoked salmon, and an array of breads and pastries. And then came the cooked food: sausages, bacon, eggs, fried bread, grilled tomatoes, mushrooms sautéed with butter and cream.

Amari's stomach rumbled in delight. She grabbed an oven-fresh roll, slathered it with creamy butter, pressed two slices of smoked bacon inside, then bit down. She closed her eyes as the flavors and textures and juices hit her tongue.

Caspar placed a mug of steaming tea in front of her, then dropped down next to her, kissing the palm of her free hand.

Amari smiled lovingly at him. She reached for him, kissed him. Maybe she'd died and gone to Pagan heaven.

Amari and Caspar sat at the table already occupied by their friends. Caspar had grabbed them hooded, floor-length blue cloaks from the malt house, because, despite the fact it was Midsummer, it was early morning, it was England, and it was cold. The others had also wrapped themselves up so they could enjoy their breakfast in comfort.

Amari and Caspar huddled together, as close as they could get on separate chairs.

Rose arrived with little fanfare, taking her rightful place at the head of the table, next to Talli, apologizing for missing the morning ceremony.

'I only just arrived back from the Registerium,' said Rose. Her features were haggard, despite her immaculate appearance. 'I haven't even had time to change.'

'What happened?' asked Jon.

Rose waved a hand. 'I'll debrief you tomorrow. Today, let's just enjoy Midsummer.'

'I'll get you a cloak,' said Caspar, jumping up.

'I'll get you some tea,' said Talli, 'and a flower crown.'

Talli caught up to Caspar as he entered the malt house. A flock of younger demons had been assigned to catering duty. They were busy ferrying food out, and empty platters back in.

'What the hell are you playing at?' said Talli, grabbing Caspar's arm.

'It's none of your business,' Caspar hissed.

'It'll blow up in your face. You're both going to get hurt.'

'You think I don't know that?'

'She'll use it against you.'

Caspar rounded on her, glaring into Talli's eyes. 'What if Raina never forgives me? What if this is all I'll ever have of her? I've been alone for two lifetimes. If she rejects me again ... I ... at least I'll have had this.'

'She'll say you took advantage of her.'

Caspar hung his head. 'Honestly, I don't know what she's going to say. I haven't seen her in a hundred years. What if she's changed? What if she's moved on?'

'She'd never do that,' said Talli, her tone softening. 'She just needs time.'

Caspar took a deep breath, looking at Amari, who was laughing at something Christa had said.

'What about what I need? I don't know how much more I can give.'

After breakfast, most people dispersed, presumably to get some rest before the evening's festivities. Caspar and Amari chatted with the others until the sun was high in the sky and the crowd began to return.

People lounged about, playing games, singing and dancing, knitting, basket-making, and setting out stalls full of traditional pottery, clothing, and jewelry. There was food for sale too: honey and marmalade, herb and tea blends, hedgerow jellies, chutney, fudge, bread.

Groups sat making flower wreaths, singing, reading, carving wooden objects, drinking homebrewed beer, elderflower cordial, or potent, home-distilled-gin cocktails. The place had the atmosphere of a relaxed festival.

Amari and Caspar took a blanket, spread it under one of the few trees, and made themselves comfortable. Caspar had informed Amari that this was where they'd spend the rest of the day. She hadn't complained, snuggling up against him, squashing any residual resistance that her conscious mind tried to mount. *Dean, Dean, Dean*, it said to her, on a loop, until she silenced it. Every other part of her sang the name *Caspar*.

By mid-afternoon, the field was abuzz. 'The artists are arriving,' said Caspar, as a crowd of ten or twelve made their way into the field. 'They're the middle-agers.'

'I see,' said Amari.

She watched as the group set up camp on the far side of the field. They didn't have any particularly distinguishing features, nor did they crack out easels and paintbrushes as she'd half-expected them to.

'Elliot should go and make friends, now he's decided to start his artist phase.'

'I think Gemma might have something to say about that,' laughed Caspar. He looked to the yurt on the tree line behind them, into which Gemma and Elliot had disappeared.

The field was sectioned loosely into areas. The malt barn stood at one end, the banquet tables in front of it, then the stone circle, with the main bonfire directly behind that. Off to one side stood the maypole, around which was an open space for dancing, with two makeshift stages bounding that area, one at each end.

To the other side of the bonfire, stretching all the way into the wood that ran along the field's edge, was an area scattered with yurts, tents, and picnic blankets, all well-spaced to afford privacy. The far end of the field contained a makeshift market and game space.

Bonfires were dotted across the field, and a line of fire torches circled the perimeter.

A thrill ran through Amari as she thought about what the place would look like later that night, flames dancing, casting ancient shadows.

She lay back, looking up through the leaves, watching the slow progress of the occasional clouds across the clear blue sky. Caspar lay next to her, holding her hand, seemingly unable to let her go.

'It's so strange,' said Amari, as Caspar stroked her fingers.

'What is?'

'I feel like I know you deeply, and yet I know nothing about you.'

'You know everything there is to know about me, and probably more, knowing you. It's all in there somewhere,' he said, stroking her temple.

'What didn't Raina like about you?'

'Absolutely nothing,' said Caspar, in mock outrage. 'She thinks I'm practically perfect in every way. At least, when she isn't mad at me.'

'Only practically?'

'Modesty is an amiable quality, or so I've been told.'

'Come on, seriously. There are niggles in every relationship. My mother would hit the roof every time she found my dad's wet towel strewn across the bed. No matter how many times she told him, he'd forget at least a third of the time.'

Caspar laughed, then turned thoughtful, shadows clouding his eyes. 'She thought I was married to my work. She said I prioritized that over you, over us.'

'Did you?'

'Probably.'

'Would she think that now, if she were here?'

'You are here,' he said, rolling over to kiss her.

Amari hummed. 'You know what I mean,' she said, between kisses.

'You tell me. Have I been working too much since we met?'

'No,' she said, running her hand through his hair. 'You've spent almost all your time with me. But I guess I am your work right now: Rose gave you orders to wake Raina. Maybe when that happens—if that happens—you'll forget all about me.' She gave him a playful pout.

Caspar's eyes filled with fire, even though she was joking. 'I could never forget about you.' He ran his nose down hers. 'You will wake up, and when you do, I won't leave your side.'

Amari smiled, tracing his cheekbone with her thumb.

'But you have to promise me something too.'

Amari frowned. 'How can I? I can't make a promise for someone else.'

'You can make a promise for the part of Raina that's you,' said Caspar.

She gave him a skeptical look, but said, 'Go on.'

'Come with me, after you wake. Come with me when I have to travel to the far-flung places of the world.'

Wariness prickled in Amari's mind. 'Will you come with me to the places I need to go?'

'Yes.'

'What if our needs conflict?'

'Then we'll work it out together. We'll talk. We'll compromise.'

'Will you, really?'

'I promise I will.'

'Will Raina?'

Caspar stopped short, then said quietly, 'That's up to you.'

Chapter 14

Caspar and Amari whiled away the afternoon, drinking beer, joining in with dressing the maypole, kissing, and frolicking, and becoming ever more wild.

Spit-roast pigs were wheeled out, along with another enormous banquet, and as the sun began to set, the bonfires and torches were lit. Everyone crowded around the stone circle, buzzing with excitement.

Caspar disappeared into the malt barn, returning moments later with a piece of jewelry Amari recognized.

'The headpiece?'

'It's yours. Made especially for Midsummer. It would be a tragedy if you didn't wear it.'

Amari pulled off her flower crown and let him place it on her head. It felt right as it settled on her brow.

'And these too,' said Caspar, pulling out a pair of long gold earrings with a half fan of hammered metal at the bottom. 'I had these in my office, where we were first attacked. I wanted to give them to you then.'

'They're beautiful,' she said, taking them from him, holding them up to get a good look.

'They're Egyptian, and they're … quite old.'

'Oh my God. How old?'

'Just put them on.'

Amari slotted them through her earlobes. 'I love them,' she said, feeling the weight of them. She shook her head a little, so they glimmered in the evening light.

'You look majestic,' he said, running a hand over her cheek, kissing her.

'Am I supposed to give you a Midsummer gift too?' asked Amari.

'Yes,' said Caspar, his lips twitching in amusement.

'Well, hopefully my being here is gift enough,' said Amari, wrapping her arms around him, 'because I don't have anything else.'

She tucked herself into Caspar's side, resting her head against his shoulder. Caspar breathed her in, kissing the top of her head.

They watched as Talli led a procession to the stone circle. Talli stepped inside, while everyone else fanned out around the edge. She looked dramatic, primal, as she knelt before the altar, placing a bouquet of summer flowers onto the stone.

Talli chanted words Amari didn't understand, and when she finished, prostrated herself on the ground, staying there until the final rays of light disappeared below the horizon.

Christa stepped into the circle of stones, moving gracefully to Talli, every step purposeful. She took Talli's hand, helping her to her feet, until they stood face to face in front of the altar. They kissed, and a drumbeat reverberated across the crowd. It sounded again, then again, other drums joining the first, slow, but building, electric tension thrumming through the crowd.

A pipe trilled above the drums, the sound sending a shiver shooting up Amari's spine. A stringed instrument joined the pipe, and Amari's hair stood on end. Other instruments joined until music poured around them, filling them.

The demons lining the circle danced, skipping and twirling, lighting fireballs on chains as they passed the burning element bowl.

Soon the whole place was writhing, frenzied, with fireballs twirling in the gloom. People whooped and thrilled and called to each other, cavorting, primeval in the flickering firelight.

It was different to the gentle swaying and dancing at the sunrise ceremony. The mood was darker, uninhibited, dangerous. Amari paused for less than a heartbeat to wonder if they'd all lost their minds, before her inhibitions too took flight.

Everywhere she looked people were coupling up: Talli and Christa, Gemma and Elliot, Jon and a man Amari didn't recognize. And then Caspar's mouth was on hers, and they were dancing, swirling, cavorting along with the rest.

Amari's body and mind gave in completely, letting go of any lingering reservations. She pushed herself flush against him. He slid his leg between hers, and they moved as one.

They danced, and kissed, and fondled. Amari slid her hands under Caspar's shirt, Caspar's hands skating across her behind.

He maneuvered them to the edge of the field, towards the darkness, then undid the laces fastening the front of her dress, gaining access to her bare breasts.

Amari gasped, recalling the memory from when she'd first worn the headpiece. It had been so like this; it all made sense now.

Caspar pushed her against a tree, pinning her with his hips, pressing against her. She clawed at his backside, her hands against his bare skin, inside his clothes.

He dipped his head to her breasts, Amari's hand going to his hair, holding him there. She moaned as he flicked her nipple with his tongue.

'Yurt,' breathed Caspar, 'before they're all taken.'

Amari had a number of questions about what he'd just said, but none of them mattered. She followed him, their fingers linked as they danced towards the yurts.

Caspar pulled her in front of him, kissing her neck from behind, his hands wrapped across her as he moved them inside the nearest open door. Caspar closed the flaps behind them, wasting no time before prowling towards her, sliding her dress off her shoulders. He let it drop to the floor, revealing her naked body beneath.

Caspar dropped to his knees, holding her hips as he kissed her, licked her, sucked her. Amari shivered, crying out at the first contact, grabbing his hair, pressing him to her until she could take no more.

She crouched, resting her weight on his legs. She grabbed at his shirt, tearing it off, then unfastened his trousers. She pulled them down around his knees, then climbed on top of him, guiding him inside her.

They both moaned as she sank onto him, Caspar's hands gliding over her backside. They moved together, fast and hard, nothing like it had been before.

Caspar picked her up, and Amari wrapped her legs around him. He lowered them back onto a pile of sheepskins, eyes locked as he moved inside her.

She rolled them over, straddling him, throwing her head back as the pressure built. She wound tighter, tighter, until Caspar slid his fingers between them, and suddenly, she was free. Caspar drew out her pleasure until he could take it no more, his body stiffening as he, too, found release.

Amari woke the following morning and nuzzled into Caspar's naked body, under a sheepskin he must have pulled over them at some point during the night. He stirred, tracing leisurely lines up and down her side, dipping in and out of her curves.

'Mmmm,' she purred, 'that's nice.'

'How about this?' he said into her hair, slipping his fingers between her legs.

She bucked against the shock of his touch. 'That's something I'd like to find out more about, once we get out of this field,' she said, lifting her head to look into his eyes.

'You didn't care about that last night,' teased Caspar.

'Well, this is the morning, and there's no music and darkness and … whatever else was going on. Now there's only a field full of silence. People would hear us.'

'We could be quiet,' he said, squeezing her nipple.

She arched into his touch, feeling her resolve weaken as his mouth found her other breast.

'Caspar!' shouted a female voice from somewhere close by. 'Caspar, wherever you are, Rose wants you, now! Don't make me search every tent in this God-damned field! I'm counting to three … one …'

Voices shouted in protest.

'He's not in here!' said a cross-sounding man.

'Don't you dare come in here,' said a woman.

'Typical,' said Caspar, giving Amari one last kiss before casting around for his clothes. 'I'm coming!' he shouted.

He picked up the white fabric of Amari's dress, handed it to her with her jewelry, then put on his trousers and shirt.

Amari pulled her dress over her head, fastened it, and followed Caspar to the entrance, almost crashing into him as he stopped and turned back to face her.

'I … last night …' He searched in vain for words.

Amari looked up into his eyes. 'Me too,' she said, then kissed him.

They linked hands, Amari's heart swelling with love. But at the same time, it broke—for the person she'd been, who never would've cheated on her husband, and for everything else her life had been before.

Chapter 15

Rose watched as her council filtered into the kitchen at Maltings.

She wished endlessly that Raina would wake up; Raina's counsel was what Rose craved most.

This group were her chosen ones. They'd been with her, running the Pagan nation, for lifetimes. There were others too, between lives, or incarnated and asleep somewhere, but she was glad the group was so numerous and strong in this moment.

Not that that made it any easier to know how much to tell them ... The whole truth was rarely the best option when it came to demons. The promise of reincarnation led to a certain disregard for the value of life. They could be unpredictable, rash, and damn the consequences, even if they'd lived enough lives to know better. But tell them too little ... they'd grow suspicious, liable to act rashly then too.

She took in Caspar and Amari's linked hands, watched as they wrapped their arms around each other, whispered together, ignored everyone else in the room. Had she made the wrong decision? Letting Caspar be the one to try and wake her? Letting him bring her here, where Amari's emotions would be so muddled?

But these were no ordinary times. She'd done what she thought was best, as she always did. She just hoped the consequences weren't too severe, that Raina would understand …

Talli looked at Caspar and Amari too, then gave Rose a questioning glare, probably wondering why Rose wasn't stepping in to stop it. It was unusual for demons to take things this far before they were both awake. The power balance was tipped firmly in Caspar's favor, since Amari was unaware of all that had happened in the past.

Rose shook away the thought. Raina would be back soon, and she was old and experienced enough to look after herself. Rose needed Caspar on her side. If this was what it took, it was a compromise she was willing to make, for the good of them all.

Rose hadn't always been the leader. Raina, Caspar, Talli, and Christa had all had their turns, but none of them had wanted the job for long. Rose was the only one who'd stuck at it, finding it suited her skills. But then, she'd never fallen in love again, had never had to make the difficult choices the others had to face.

'Things are not looking good,' Rose started, without preamble. 'I told the Registerium about the attacks, along with the trade threats, the known trespassing, the disappearance of several Pagans. However, the Registerium doesn't consider this enough to justify war.'

'Rightly so,' said Talli.

'Yes. I don't disagree with their decision. The new Templar representative is a woman named Janet. She was all smiles and promises of friendship, but Malcolm, our representative, says Janet has been backchanneling whenever she gets a chance.

'She's promising the small nations the earth in return for their ongoing support. She's sweet-talking

Registerium officials, and she's intercepting messengers from other nations, gleaning as much information as she can about their visits. Malcolm says he thinks she's looking for something—or someone—but he doesn't have any proof.'

'Did he have anything else that was helpful?' asked Christa.

'Only that there's been increased Slayer activity. The Slayers are using social media to find new recruits, and they're utilizing technology to find us. They seem better organized and better funded than ever before.'

'Great,' said Jon. 'War with the Templars, no allies, and a whole load more maniacs who want to kill us for no reason.'

'You have *got* to get that melodrama under control,' said Talli. 'Who said we don't have allies?'

'Janet's bribing everyone!' said Jon, defensively.

'The smaller nations can be bought,' said Talli, 'but not the bigger ones. And there's no love lost between most of them and the Templars.'

'Didn't you guys say the smaller nations can tip the balance, though?' asked Amari, leaning back against Caspar's chest.

'Thank you,' said Jon.

'Yes, they can,' said Rose, 'which is why we're going to try and get to them. But Talli's also right, we have natural allies among the larger nations. Without them, we don't stand a chance.'

'We're going to build a coalition?' said Christa.

'Yes.'

'It's been a while since I traveled,' said Talli, with no hint of excitement, only resignation.

'Where to?' asked Elliot. He took hold of Gemma's hand and gave her a sad look.

'I'm still working out the details, but you'll need to go to the Aborigines, of course. Meredith should go to

196

the Wakan, then the Animists, Caspar and Amari to the Buddhists, and then the Vikings, Christa to the Aztecs, then the Russian Spirituals, Talli to the Egyptians, then the Persian Zoros. I'll see the Holy Star, and the Shindu Council.'

'What about me?' asked Jon.

'You and Gemma can hold down the fort in London. We can't leave the place abandoned,' said Rose.

'And you do have to keep the rest of us in food and clothing, remember?' said Talli.

Jon scowled at her.

'You can also work out an approach for the smaller nations,' said Rose. 'Go through the records and see which Pagans used to belong to the smaller nations. Especially from Asia, the island nations, the Canadian ones—they usually know something useful—and try to find out what's happening on the West Coast of America. I heard a rumor about a new nation, but haven't seen any evidence yet.'

'Will do,' said Gemma, visibly inching closer to Elliot.

Rose hated splitting them up, but what choice did she have?

'And if Raina wakes,' said Rose, 'you two fly back immediately, straight to the Registerium. I don't care what personal issues may be going on between the two of you. Put them to one side. All that matters is that Raina registers as Pagan, before anyone else can claim her as their own.'

Amari and Caspar went straight to their bedroom to pack. They would be driving back to London with

197

Meredith, Talli, and Christa as soon as everyone was ready.

'I'll book our flights,' said Caspar, pulling out his phone. 'Do you have your passport number? We can fly tonight.'

'Whoa, slow down,' said Amari, stopping midway through putting a handful of clothes in her bag. 'Dean's flying in from America this evening. I'm not going anywhere without seeing him first.'

'Amari, you can't be serious. It's too dangerous … for you and for him.'

'I've been ignoring his calls and messages for days. I've been cheating on him, sleeping with you, frolicking around the countryside like some kind of cult convert. The least I can do is talk to him, face to face.'

'Do you want to go back to him?'

Amari screwed up her face. 'How could you even ask me that? I just told you, I've been ignoring him … and everyone else I know. I turned my phone off because I know there's a barrage of abuse on there about how I'm treating Dean. Abuse I deserve.'

'He left you the day after your wedding. He's not blameless.'

'You don't believe that any more than I do. I knew who I was marrying. It's me who's changed, not him.'

'Do you wish none of this had happened?'

'Honestly? Yes, part of me does. But only so I wouldn't have to hurt Dean. What I had with him was special, among humans at least. We loved each other, deeply. We wanted the same things from life. But it's nothing compared to the way I feel about you.

'I can't remember the lifetimes, but some part of me can feel them. They hum through me, crisscrossing layers of antiquity, propelling me towards you. It's like I can't live without you.'

Caspar pulled her into his arms. 'It's the same for me.'

'But I know you did something to Raina. Something so bad that despite these feelings, despite the fact she would've had to rip out her own heart to do it, she stayed away. That terrifies me. The way I feel now, I never want to be without you, but …'

'Then don't be.' He buried his face in her neck. 'You've punished me long enough. You ripped out my heart too, and … I don't know if I can do it again. I'll do anything, anything you want, just forgive me.'

She pulled back. 'You know I can't promise that.'

He put a hand on her cheek. 'Just promise you'll remember how this feels. Remember us together. Remember everything I've ever done is because I love you.'

They got back to the city as the sun was going down. Amari was preoccupied with thoughts of Dean, even with Caspar's side pressed up against her, their fingers entwined.

She'd played scenarios over and over in her head, and still had no idea what to say to him. But before they even got close to Cloister Cottage, Meredith got a call. The male voice through the car's speakers told them to detour to rendezvous point five.

'What does that mean?' asked Amari.

'It means something's happened at Cloister Cottage,' said Meredith.

A few minutes later, Meredith pulled into an unassuming side street, coming to a halt in a loading bay. A stony-faced, plainly dressed man appeared out of the shadow of a tall office building, and Meredith rolled down the window. The man stepped close, speaking in tones so low the rest of them couldn't hear his words. Meredith nodded, rolled the window up, and drove on.

'Someone tried to break in earlier today,' said Meredith. 'Our guards called the police. Luckily, the police got to the cottage in time, so the guards didn't have to get involved. They watched the whole thing and played back the video footage. It was definitely demons.'

'Where are we going?' asked Amari.

'We can't stay at the cottage if it's been compromised. We'll go to one of our other houses,' said Talli.

'Will we ever be able to go back?' asked Amari, shocked. 'You've been there for generations ...'

'We might be able to,' said Christa. 'It's hard to say.'

'Whoever it was might only suspect the place belongs to us,' said Talli. 'They might not know for sure. It's lucky the guards didn't have to get involved. Often the main purpose of attacks like these is to gather intelligence.'

'But they're suspicious enough to test the place,' said Meredith, 'which isn't a good sign.'

'It's so much harder now with video cameras everywhere,' said Caspar. 'The cottage is protected with magic, but CCTV footage makes it impossible to stay hidden like we used to.'

'As soon as a demon's face is confirmed, all you have to do is infiltrate the right government department, and you can track them all over the place,' said Meredith.

'And as everything becomes more connected,' said Talli, 'it's getting worse.'

'They were confident enough to trespass to the center of our heartland,' said Meredith. 'Not good.'

'Although they did it at Midsummer,' said Caspar, 'so they're not so confident as to want to face us.'

'Not yet, anyway,' said Talli.

'But why do you need to stay hidden?' asked Amari.

'To avoid coordinated attacks on the leadership,' said Christa.

'The leadership?' said Amari.

'Us,' said Caspar. 'If the Templars—or anyone else for that matter—could take us all out at once, the Pagans would flounder.'

'We'd be ripe for a takeover,' said Talli.

'Most demons don't like war,' said Caspar. 'We've all seen too much of it.'

'Some Pagan demons would lobby for a new leader, rather than get involved in a war,' said Christa, 'or might even accept a takeover from another nation, if they thought it would avoid conflict.'

'That's part of the reason why events like Midsummer are so important,' said Talli. 'To show we leaders are still here, still strong, still a force to be reckoned with.'

'Hopefully, if they see us strong and united, they'll support the decisions we make,' said Caspar. 'Even if it means war.'

'We need to get out of London,' said Meredith, driving into an underground carpark somewhere near Waterloo Bridge. 'There are cameras everywhere … there's a chance we're being watched right now. We'll travel separately to the country house.'

The other demons agreed.

'Christa and I will take the underground, then get a train from Euston,' said Talli.

'We'll take one of the other cars,' said Caspar, 'and go a roundabout route.'

'Change cars a couple of times,' said Meredith. 'And meet one of the other demons somewhere. Get them to drive you, so you can hide in the back. I'll meet you all there.'

'Caspar,' said Amari, halting him with a hand on his arm. 'I'm not going anywhere until I've seen Dean. His flight landed two hours ago. He'll be back at the house by now.'

'No way,' said Talli. 'You can't be serious?'

'I've got to see him. To explain.'

'They found our headquarters,' said Meredith, as though she were stupid. 'They've already tried to kill you *twice*. They'll be waiting. You'll be walking into a trap.'

'I'll get Dean to meet me somewhere neutral, somewhere safe,' said Amari. 'But I'm not leaving London until I've seen him.'

Chapter 16

Amari messaged Dean, asking him to meet her by the river at Imperial Park, a small patch of grass with a fountain, not far from the house they'd shared in Chelsea. Meredith agreed, happy it was somewhere they could blend in, and that there were multiple ways out.

Talli and Christa left the underground carpark, heading for the country house—Amari still didn't know where that was. They'd offered to stay and help, but Meredith told them to leave, saying the risk was too high.

Meredith, Caspar, and Amari left the Range Rover and got into an unassuming Toyota Prius with tinted windows. They joined the evening traffic—light by London standards—and headed west, Amari and Caspar in the back.

Amari curled her arms around herself, bouncing her knees up and down. Guilt and dread and self-loathing swirled around inside her, their tide rising so violently she worried she might drown. And now, to cap everything off, there was the added weight of a potential attack. She might be putting Caspar and Meredith—and Dean—in danger.

Amari tried to distract herself by working out what to say. What could she possibly tell him that would sound plausible, yet not lay the blame at his door? This was on her, not Dean.

Should she tell him she'd met someone else? Or that the time alone had made her realize she wasn't ready to settle down? Or that she didn't think she could make him happy? She could tell him she'd been diagnosed with some illness ... no, he'd ask to see evidence. It had to be something emotional, something he couldn't refute with logic ... she had to tell him about Caspar.

The best lies deviated from the truth as little as possible, that's what endless TV shows had told her. But her feelings for Caspar weren't even a lie ... at least that was something.

Caspar got out of the car first, walking to the far end of the park, where the river ran by, conducting a sweep of the area.

Plenty of people were out enjoying the warm summer evening, but nothing prickled his honed, ancient senses. There were CCTV cameras however, and Caspar's face had been seen by the men who'd attacked Amari. He wore a scarf around his neck, the kind favored by hipster types, obscuring as much of his face as he could without drawing attention.

The chance of someone looking at the right CCTV footage at the right time, and of it being of a high enough quality to recognize him, was slim. He repeated that thought again and again, telling himself it would be okay, offering the words up as a prayer. But there was a chance they'd already been spotted. It didn't matter how small. There was a chance, and that was horrifying.

They were giving their enemies an opportunity to find them, an *invitation* to find them. This was madness.

Meredith moved the car, parking at the end of the street opposite the park. 'I'll wait here, ready to go,' she said, 'but the river's a fair distance. There's not much I'll be able to do if this goes wrong.'

'I know,' said Amari. 'Hopefully it won't come to that.'

'I wish we'd had more time to plan. I wish we had backup.'

'We don't have any more time,' said Amari. 'We just have to hope we weren't followed.'

'And that Dean wasn't,' said Meredith.

Amari hadn't thought of that … well, too late now. She got out of the car and entered the park. She'd made it to the grey fountain in the middle before a voice behind her said, 'Amari,' halting her in her tracks.

Of course. He was always early … She spun around. 'Dean.'

Dean walked slowly towards her. He pulled her into a hesitant hug, raised his hand to her cheek, then leaned in to kiss her. She turned her head away, her hands gently pushing him back, her head suddenly pounding with pain.

'What's going on?' he said. 'You've got everyone worried. Are you okay?'

He tried to take her hands. She didn't let him. Tears filled Amari's eyes … why did he have to be so nice?

'I'm fine,' she said, reaching into her pocket, pulling out her engagement and wedding rings. 'But I need to give these back.'

Dean looked at her outstretched hand for a long moment, as though he didn't understand, was racking his brain for some plausible explanation that didn't mean she was ending their relationship.

'Amari? What's going on?' He had tears in his eyes now too.

Amari looked away. *Coward.* She forced herself to meet his gaze, to show him she meant the horrible, piercing, poisonous words she was about to say; she owed him that much.

'I've met someone else.'

Dean shook his head in disbelief. 'I've been gone two weeks.'

'I know, it seems strange … impossible even. But I love him.'

'You love me!' said Dean. 'And I love you.'

He shook his head again, as though if he did it enough, her words would shake around and land differently, or, better yet, not land at all.

Something dawned in his eyes, something that caused a spark of hope.

'What's really going on? Are you in some kind of trouble? Amari, whatever it is, we can face it together. I'm a lawyer, for Christ's sake.'

Tears spilled down Amari's cheeks. 'I know this is hard. It breaks my heart, because I love you, and I didn't mean for any of this to happen. But what I feel for him is … different. It's unlike anything I've ever felt. It's over, Dean, and I'm seeking an annulment.'

'An annulment?'

'We've only been married for two weeks, and the marriage was never consummated.'

'What the hell?' Dean ran his hands through his hair, disbelief and hurt turning to anger. 'How long has this been going on? Who is it?'

'It's hard to explain, but I promise I've only known him for two weeks.'

The best lies are mostly truth.

Dean laughed. 'You've got to be kidding me. You're throwing away everything we have for some guy you've just met? Who is he? The one who came to the house ... the one Leila saw you with? Was Jade right? Is it him?'

'I wasn't having an affair when I saw Jade, but yes, it's him. And I ... I feel like I've known him for lifetimes. It's hard to explain, but if I stayed with you, we'd be living a lie. It wouldn't be fair to either of us.'

Dean laughed again, then turned serious. He took a step towards her, placing his hands on her arms, looking into her eyes.

'Please, Amari, we can work this out. I know it feels like this guy is the love of your life right now, but new relationships are like that. In a couple of months, you won't feel like this. We've stood the test of time. We're right for each other; I've never been so sure of anything.'

'Dean,' she said. She took a step back, out of his grasp. 'It's not like that. This isn't just some fling. If it was, it never would've happened.'

'So that's it? There's no hope? No part of you that wants to stay with me? To *try*?'

He threw the words like javelins. Each hit its mark, wounding her, tearing her apart.

Tears poured down Amari's cheeks. 'Of course there's a part of me that wants to stay with you; we were going to have the most perfect life together. I'll mourn the loss of what we had, but ... no. I'm sorry, there's no hope for us.'

Dean took a staggering step backward, tears spilling down his cheeks now too.

'If I'd stayed. If we'd gone on our honeymoon like we were supposed to. Would it be different?'

'No,' said Amari. 'This would have happened either way. If you'd stayed, it just would have taken longer.'

Dean's features hardened. 'Goodbye, Amari,' he said. And then he walked away.

Amari curled into a ball and cried. Caspar wasn't sure whether to comfort her or give her space. He'd had to deal with most things over the course of his many lives, but this was a new one.

'Take us to Heathrow Airport,' said Caspar.

'Why?' asked Meredith.

'Something doesn't feel right. Can you ask one of the guards to pack some stuff for us, and bring our passports?'

'Where are you going?'

'We'll get a local flight to somewhere in Europe, and then hire a jet to Asia.'

'Okay,' Meredith said with a shrug.

By the time they reached the airport, Amari had stopped crying. She sat up straight, staring out of the window. Caspar reached for her hand and she let him take it, although she didn't turn her head to face him, nor did she return the pressure.

Meredith dropped them off, then left, wishing them luck. It was dark now, and they headed straight inside, Caspar checking the departures board for suitable flights. He should've found flights on his phone in the car, but he hadn't been able to tear his eyes from Amari.

'Rome,' he said. 'Eight PM. That'll do nicely.'

Amari followed him to the desk, where he bought two tickets.

Caspar's phone buzzed and he picked up the call. 'We're coming now,' he said.

Amari followed him back out through the entrance. A tall, broad man approached, carrying two bags. He handed one to each of them, then walked away.

They joined the line leading to security, their luggage small enough to carry on. Caspar pulled Amari in for a hug as they shuffled along with the other travelers.

'Are you okay?' he said into her hair.

'No,' she said, her hands closing tightly around him.

'Is there anything I can do?'

Silence. Caspar told himself to be patient, to give her time. He had to fight the urge to press her, to force her to say something. He practically shook with the effort, so lost inside his head that he was surprised when she said, 'I've seen him brush people off, the way he did earlier, when he walked away. And every time he did it, I felt smug, because I knew he would never do it to me. I knew that no matter what, he would always have time for me, would want to be near me … turns out I was wrong.'

'Amari, you could never have foreseen this.'

'I know. The logical part of me at least … if any of this can be called logical. But it still hurts. Maybe I'm vain … but I'm sad he was capable of doing that to me.'

'I mean … you've always been a little vain.'

Amari half-laughed. 'Thanks, that's wonderful news.'

'Just being honest,' he said, shrugging. He tipped her head back, his hands stroking away her hair. 'But I love you for it. Always have.'

She looked up at him. 'You have a strange sense of humor, but I guess that's part of what I love about you too.'

They landed in Rome after an uncomfortably full flight; thank goodness it was only a couple of hours. They didn't even leave the airport, getting straight onto a private jet Caspar had made appear. A male flight attendant greeted them with a broad smile and a request for their drinks order.

'This isn't terrible,' said Amari, walking up and down the sizeable jet.

'There's a bedroom too,' he said, raising an eyebrow.

'Of course there is.'

'There's something we need to talk about,' said Caspar, becoming serious.

'What is it?'

'Your marriage to Dean ...'

'We need to get it annulled.'

Caspar let out a breath, looking relieved. 'Do you want me to take care of it?'

'Yes,' she said, with a resigned nod. 'No point in prolonging it.'

Caspar pulled out his phone and typed for a few seconds before putting it away again.

The flight attendant returned, placing two espresso martinis on a table. *Good.* She needed a stiff drink.

'Here,' said Caspar. He pulled a passport out of his pocket and handed it to her. 'We're changing names, so we can't be so easily tracked. Rose had a few passports made when we found you.'

Amari raised an eyebrow. She flicked through the blank pages, not asking how the Pagans managed to get their hands on so many fake passports.

'And here's your new phone,' he said, opening a box that had been waiting for them.

Caspar had made her destroy her old phone at Heathrow, which had hurt more than she cared to admit.

'Where are we going?' she asked, as Caspar took a seat in front of a martini.

'Tibet. We're flying into Ngari Gunsa Airport, where the Buddhist demon nation will meet us. They'll take our phones, blindfold us, and drive us to their current headquarters. They usually pick somewhere on a lake. It's generally very beautiful.'

'You've been to see them a lot over your lifetimes?'

'Yes. I spent some of my early lives in Asia. I was with the Buddhist nation for a while. But the leader of the Pagans—then a man named Albert—came on a diplomatic mission. Rose was with him. Their philosophy resonated with me—it felt more of a fit than the Buddhist life, so I decided to go with them.'

'How did you end up in Asia? I thought you were born in France?'

'I was, but my experiences there weren't enjoyable. I awake at an uncommonly young age … have done in every life. In my early lives, I didn't know I'd reincarnated … I didn't know anything about demons. I would start speaking very young, in an unusually clear voice, and would rant about my previous lives. It led to a series of unfortunate deaths, usually preceded by exorcisms.'

'Oh my God. That's horrible,' said Amari.

The plane started moving, so she buckled into the seat next to Caspar, tasting her cocktail. It was glorious, just what she needed. She took another big gulp.

'I caught on eventually and kept my secret to myself, and then a hunter found me. He was going to take me straight to the Druids, but I was in such a state—screaming that I didn't want to go to the people who'd caused me so much pain—that he decided the Buddhists would be a better home for me. It was a trek, but they pay well.'

'Druids?' asked Amari.

'The nations have undergone numerous mergers and name changes over the years. The Pagans are an amalgamation of a number of groups, including the Wiccan and the Druids.

'There used to be many small nations, but over the years, people sought safety in numbers. Small nations were easy targets for empire builders, so they grouped together to defend themselves.'

'Did you like being with the Buddhists?'

'I loved it, especially at the start. They gave me a purpose, and structure, and a safe home. They made me feel like I belonged, taught me their way of seeing the world, and to think about my place in it. They're a good nation with strong morals.'

The female voice of the captain told them they were ready for takeoff. They threw back what remained of their cocktails.

Moments later, the force of takeoff pinned them to their seats. The plane lifted off and Amari twisted, bringing her legs up and resting them across Caspar's lap.

'And what exactly are we going to do when we get there?' she asked.

'We're going to give them our account of what's going on, and ask for their support.'

The flight attendant returned once they'd reached cruising altitude. 'Everything looks good for the flight,' he said. 'We should be in Tibet in time for breakfast. Can I offer you some food? Another drink?'

'Yes, please,' said Caspar.

Now food had been mentioned, Amari found she was ravenously hungry. When had they last eaten?

'I have a ramen broth, roast chicken salad with new potatoes, or antipasti. I also have fresh fruit and smoothies.'

'All of it,' said Amari. She cracked a smile at the attendant's expression.

'Of course,' he said, then hurried off.

'And two more espresso martinis, please,' she called after him.

Caspar laughed. 'Good to see you haven't lost your appetite,' he said, running a hand up her leg.

'Never.'

Their food came, they ate, and then they moved to the luxurious bedroom at the back of the plane.

The bed linen was white and soft and fluffy; it called to her. It had been a long and eventful day, and her head was fuzzy from the drinks. Had they really been in Somerset only this morning?

They stripped off, Amari donning the silk pajamas that had been laid out for her, Caspar not bothering. They fell into bed and curled up together. Seconds later, they were fast asleep.

The flight attendant woke them thirty minutes before landing. They'd slept like the dead, but woke feeling refreshed.

'Sleeping in a bed on a plane feels a lot like sleeping on a boat,' said Amari. 'I like it.'

'I like it too,' he said, burying his head in her neck.

He kissed and nipped her, his hand going to her backside. She enjoyed it for a while, then batted him away. 'We don't have time for both sex and breakfast, and I know which I want right now.'

'Sex, obviously.'

Caspar made a grab for her, but she evaded him.

'Who knows what these Buddhists eat, and who knows how long we'll be here.'

'The Buddhists have great food, actually. No meat, for the most part, but their food is delicious.'

Amari stood, and Caspar stroked his fingers up and down her leg, gliding higher with each pass. She bent to kiss him, then pulled away.

'Breakfast,' she said.

She found clean clothes in her bag and put them on.

'Spoilsport.'

Breakfast was sausage sandwiches with red onion chutney, fruit, croissants, and coffee. It was delicious. The flight attendant had pre-empted Amari's request for everything on the menu, and it was all laid out by the time they appeared. Amari smiled; this was certainly the way to travel.

'We need to plant some trees,' she said, between mouthfuls.

'Huh?'

'For carbon-offsetting purposes.'

'Oh, yeah, the Pagans have an impressive negative carbon footprint. We don't use jets often, only when there's a pressing need, and we believe in living in harmony with the earth.'

'Oh, good.'

They ate in silence for a few moments.

'What did Rose mean yesterday? When she said someone else might try to claim me?'

Caspar stilled, looking at her over his latte. 'She meant that someone like the Templars might try to take advantage of the recent discord between you and I, and convince you to join their ranks.'

'Why would they?'

'Once you've registered as part of a nation, it's tricky to get out. In every new lifetime, you can choose which nation you want to be in, but as soon as you've chosen, you have obligations. Some nations take those more seriously than others.

'The Buddhists let people come and go freely, and so do the Pagans ... mostly anyway. But the Templars view their demons as assets to be deployed in whatever way their leadership sees fit.'

Amari swallowed a mouthful of croissant. 'What happens if a demon goes against Templar orders?'

'They're tortured, or killed ... or worse.' Caspar's eyes went dark.

'Worse?'

'Their loved ones are tortured and killed. Or they're killed permanently, never to be reincarnated again. The Templars don't believe in mercy.'

'Why would the Templars want me?'

She played with a strawberry, her appetite waning.

'Endless reasons. You're an incredible strategist with lifetimes of experience. You have extensive knowledge of the Pagan nation, and others. They know it would hurt the Pagan leadership to see you go ... Rose relies on you. We all do. And they know what you and I are to each other.'

'You think Raina might choose to register as a Templar?' *A sadistic, merciless nation—really?* This was what she'd left her happy human life for?

'Honestly, I don't know. Their leader—Jamie—and you ... have a past. And it sounds like something happened between you two, during the time we were apart.' Caspar looked at his hands. 'So I guess there's a chance you'll choose them.'

'The guy on the beach? In the memory? He's the Templar leader?' He'd seemed like a puppy dog ...

'Yes. Horrible, slimy little piece of work. You wouldn't have given him the time of day under ordinary circumstances.' Caspar's fists clenched.

'Then what happened?'

His eyes flicked up to hers. 'That's what I want to know. What the hell happened?'

Chapter 17

Amari and Caspar sat in the back of a Toyota pickup, blindfolded, hot and uncomfortable, bouncing down a dirt road towards a destination unknown.

'Are we nearly there yet?' asked Amari, for the tenth time.

Her words were, once again, met with silence. They'd been on the road for several hours, at least.

She sat in the middle seat, Caspar next to her, his hand on her leg. He seemed relaxed, resigned to whatever length of journey they would have to endure, but Amari wasn't wired that way.

'Seriously? You've got nothing? Doesn't this bother you?'

'Was that a question for me?' asked Caspar.

'It's for anyone who'd like to chip in.'

'We can't do anything about it,' said Caspar, squeezing her leg. 'I'm sure it won't be too much further.'

Sometime later—Amari wasn't at all sure how much—the pickup came to a sedate stop, and they were told they could remove their blindfolds. They had to turn away from the assault of the light, waiting for their eyes to adjust.

Amari was stunned by the beauty. The dazzling sun reflected off a beautiful, crystal-clear, deep blue lake, with snowcapped mountains in the distance. Lush green trees lined the banks, and behind them, a beautiful temple butted up against the cliffs ... no, was built *into* the cliffs. Amari couldn't help but stare.

'The water in the lake comes from a glacier,' said Caspar. 'It's perfectly pure.'

Amari's eyes were alight, taking in as much as she could. She couldn't believe how flawless everything was.

They walked towards the temple, through a wooden pagoda, into an open area with an engraved stone column at its center. It must have been fifteen meters tall, towering above them, topped by an elaborately carved circle with eight spokes.

They walked past the column and up a set of stairs cut into the stone. At the top was a set of stone pillars carved with flowers and animals and symbols, most of which Amari recognized as Buddhist iconography.

The pillars had been cut out of the cliff itself, making for a strange transition at the tops. The carefully carved stone starkly contrasted with the rugged natural stone above. In the middle of the pillars stood an open archway. Amari and Caspar stepped inside, following the Buddhist demon escorting them.

They found themselves in a colossal stone cave. Amari's mouth dropped open at the hall full of stone structures and intricate carvings. In some ways it reminded her of a Christian cathedral, but instead of being built from the ground up, brick by brick, it had been carved, thousands of years before, out of the solid stone of the cliffs.

The hall must have been forty metres long, fifteen high and wide, with stone arches supporting the roof. How ancient humans had managed such a miraculous feat, Amari couldn't fathom.

Ornate pillars ran the length of the hall on either side, space behind them for a walkway. At the far end stood a domed structure. A pillar with three horizontal rings protruded from the top, and it, too, had space behind it, separating it from the wall.

The walls were like nothing Amari had ever seen, polished yet highly elaborate, featuring carvings of people, animals, and plants, symbols and patterns. Amari couldn't even begin to comprehend the amount of time, the number of people, the level of devotion that must have gone into the hall's construction. Lifetime upon lifetime's worth of sweat and determination and fervor, an endless string of people painstakingly chipping away.

Caspar put his hands together and performed a little bow, pointed toward the far end of the hall. Amari copied him.

'It's quite something, isn't it?' said Caspar.

'That's the most obnoxious understatement of all time,' she replied, not looking at him, her eyes hungry to take in every detail.

'The dome at the end contains holy scriptures and relics. They're buried inside, and the dome was built on top.'

'This hall's used for worship?'

'Meditation, yes. There are more rooms through those doors,' he said, indicating toward the doors on each side of the hall, near to where they stood.

'More?'

Caspar laughed. 'Yes. There's an assembly hall, a dining hall, a garden, and accommodations.'

'All carved into the rock like this?'

'Most of it.'

'How long did it take to build?'

'Hundreds of years. Thousands, if you count the ongoing work.'

'Did you … were you here? When they built it?'

'Some of it, although I came in at the later end, and was only suitable for grunt work; I lacked the finesse of the master carvers. I only dedicated one lifetime to this particular cause.'

'A whole lifetime?'

'Yes. These caves aren't the only ones. There are a number of examples across Asia.'

'It's crazy what people achieved, with only their bare hands.'

'It is,' agreed Caspar.

'This way,' said the Buddhist, who'd stood patiently while they marveled.

He led them through the left-hand door, along a corridor with windows overlooking the lake. They entered another hall, this one squarer than the first. It had a flat ceiling with a lotus flower carving protruding from the centre, and more pillars around the outside. It was lighter than the meditation hall, due to the windows cut all along one wall.

They continued down the corridor, until they entered a garden chamber at the very end. It too had windows all along the lake-side wall, but also had a hole at the back of the chamber, where part of the ceiling had collapsed, allowing sunlight to pour in.

Plants had been cultivated here, and there was running water, sprouting up from a split in the rock floor. It trickled along the length of the room, flowing out through a hole under the windows.

On the far side of the garden sat a small, unassuming monk dressed in maroon robes, meditating on the unforgiving rock.

The Buddhist who'd escorted them left the room, and Caspar went to sit opposite the meditating monk, sinking down to sit cross-legged too.

Amari sat next to him. 'What are you doing?' she whispered.

'Meditating,' he replied, with a smirk.

'Okay …' said Amari. 'How do I meditate?'

'Just close your eyes, relax your body, and pay attention to your breathing. If you notice your mind wandering, bring it back to your breathing. In and out.'

'That's it?'

'That's it.'

'Seems simple enough.'

Caspar gave her a look and huffed out a laugh. 'If you say so.'

They meditated for a time, although, seeing as their phones had been confiscated, it was impossible to tell exactly how long. Amari lost concentration easily at the beginning, her mind wandering to the lake, the monk, the caves, when they would have their next meal, what the food would be … But after a while, she got the hang of it, catching her mind before letting it scurry away. She was wholly consumed by the time Caspar took hold of her hand, pulling her back to the world.

Caspar put his hands together and bowed to the monk. The monk did the same. Amari, feeling a little foolish, copied them, and the monk returned the gesture.

'Caspar,' said the monk.

'Tsering,' said Caspar.

'Who is this you have brought me …? It is Raina's great power, but … muted, is it not?'

'This is Amari. Raina is yet to awake.'

Tsering slapped his leg and let out a shout of laughter. 'Ha! That old sack! So stubborn. More stubborn in old age, I think.'

Amari scowled.

Caspar laughed. 'I can't say you're wrong.'

Amari resisted the urge to hit him, fairly sure such behavior would be frowned upon in present company.

'You come about the Templars?' said Tsering.

Caspar nodded. 'How much do you know?'

'Only what my envoy at the Registerium has told me. Rose visited the Registerium to report hostile behaviors, saying the Templars want war.'

'And, understandably, the Registerium don't want to act. Not yet anyway,' said Caspar.

'So you're here to butter me up, in case it comes to side picking.'

'You know as well as I do how this goes,' said Caspar.

'When will you have had enough? Warmongering? Killing? Lying? Stealing? Ending lives, needlessly. And for what? Eh? Lust. Lust of the body. Lusting after possessions. Clinging to impermanent things. You people will never find peace, enlightenment.'

'My philosophy is the same as yours, ever since you taught it to me,' said Caspar. 'Right views, right speech, right action. I don't want war. I want ...'

'... you want *her*,' said Tsering, pointing at Amari. 'And she is a corrupter, a warmonger. Suffering will follow wherever she goes. Suffering we must leave behind on the path to enlightenment.'

Amari recoiled at the quiet ferocity of his words.

'Love is its own kind of enlightenment,' said Caspar.

'Love of this kind is suffering, embracing impermanence.'

'We can't all be celibate,' said Caspar.

'No. Only those of us who want to be happy.'

'I would have thought, with all the time you've spent working towards enlightenment, you'd have reached nirvana by now, and would no longer be with us. Maybe your teachings aren't quite as perfect as you like to believe,' said Caspar, with a little smile.

'I'll reach enlightenment when it is right for me to do so. Until then, I can but follow the eight-fold path. You are ignorant, so much bad karma.'

'I hope to buy some good karma with the gifts we've brought you,' said Caspar. The Pagans made a point of being generous with their allies, and Tsering knew it.

'Charity is enlightened. I thank you for your gifts, whatever they are. Now tell me, what else do you have to say about the Templars?'

Caspar relayed everything he knew.

Tsering spent several minutes pondering Caspar's words, then said, 'I will think on this further.'

'May we stay until you've done so?' asked Caspar.

'Of course; it is our pleasure to host the Pagan nation. You shall be in separate accommodations, in the dormitories. And everybody here contributes, as you know.'

'Thank you,' said Caspar. 'We're honored to help in any way we can.'

'Well, that was a delight,' said Amari, as she and Caspar walked back to the meditation hall alone.

Caspar laughed. 'Tsering never liked you. He thought I would rejoin the Buddhists eventually, but then I fell in love with you, and he knew all hope was lost. And he's right, you're not a natural Buddhist.'

'Would you have gone back to the Buddhists, if not for Raina?'

'No. I've told him that, but I can't make him believe me.'

Another monk greeted them in the meditation hall. 'This way to your accommodations,' he said. 'Your bags are already there.'

They followed the monk across the meditation hall and out the other side, into another large hall. A number of doors led off it, at the back and along the far wall. Thick mats lined the near wall, and Amari spotted Caspar's bag towards the middle.

'This is where you will sleep,' the monk said to Caspar.

'Thank you,' said Caspar.

'And you will be through here,' said the monk, leading them through a door that led out into the sunshine.

They walked fifty metres down a compacted dirt path to a wooden building with beautiful carvings around the top. The men waited outside while Amari looked around her sleeping quarters.

The setup was much like Caspar's, with a series of small rooms off a large central area. She peeked into one of the side rooms, and found it, like the main room, contained little aside from mats on the floor, although it did have the luxury of a window.

At least, she reasoned, she'd have a wooden floor to sleep on, whereas Caspar would be sleeping on stone.

Outside, she found Caspar alone. 'We've got time to wash and change before dinner,' he said.

'The sleeping arrangements are dreamy,' she said, voice dripping with sarcasm.

'Just think how much you'll appreciate the bed in the jet on the way back home.'

'Mmmm,' she purred, 'it's going to be glorious. So, where do we wash?'

Caspar laughed. 'You'll see.'

Caspar led Amari down another dirt path, and through the trees, to the edge of the lake. A little hut stood on the bank, containing a shelf full of thin, worn towels, and a couple of benches.

'Are you serious?' asked Amari.

Caspar just looked at her and smiled. He went into the hut and began to take off his clothes.

'Are men and women supposed to be in here together?' she asked. 'Because that's not the vibe I've been getting.'

Caspar laughed. 'No. Generally, any fraternization with the opposite sex is frowned upon. So, no PDA while anyone can see us. Men and women are supposed to wash at different times.'

'Well, seeing as I've already been labelled a corrupting influence ...' said Amari, stripping off too.

They grabbed towels, wrapping themselves up for the short walk to the edge of the lake. Caspar discarded his towel and jumped straight in, but Amari had to psych herself up first. She knew just how cold these glacial waters would be. She inched down the stone steps, still clutching her towel around her for warmth.

'Come on,' called Caspar, splashing around. 'It's invigorating.'

'It's flipping freezing, and you know it.'

Amari took one last deep breath, threw aside her towel, and launched herself into the water.

It made the stream pool near Maltings seem positively balmy. Amari took staccato breaths, trying to get over the shock.

'Oh my God. Oh my God. Oh my God,' she said, without conscious thought.

Caspar laughed. 'You'll be fine in a second.'

'Jesus. Shit. Jesus. This is so ... ' She didn't have the words to describe what this was. Her brain was shutting down.

Caspar didn't stop laughing.

Amari's body eventually acclimatized, her shoulders relaxing enough for her to move. They splashed around, Caspar dunking his head, trying to convince Amari to do it too. She refrained. Once was quite enough for her.

It was invigorating, but neither of them wanted to linger. Amari's lips turned blue with surprising speed, and her teeth chattered as she climbed out and grabbed her towel. She quickly wrapped it around her freezing, shaking body, sad they couldn't use each other's body heat.

'We can walk back up wearing our towels,' said Caspar, following her out, 'and change into fresh clothes in our sleeping quarters.'

They made it halfway back through the trees before Caspar pulled her off the path, pushing her behind a tree. He dropped his clothes, discarding hers too, then kissed her with urgent lips.

'I hate not being able to touch you,' he said.

Amari drew open her towel and pulled him flush against her, the heat of his naked torso delicious against her freezing skin. She pressed her face to him, seeking any patch of warmth.

'We've been here less than two hours,' she said.

Caspar's hands roamed over her skin. 'But there's nowhere private, and Tsering doesn't like you. He's probably concocting a plan to keep us apart.'

'We're only going to be here a couple of days ...'

Caspar wrapped his arms around her, and Amari hummed, appreciating his heat.

'Going to be a long couple of days,' he said.

He pulled away, rewrapped her towel, and gave her one last resigned kiss.

By the time Amari and Caspar made it to dinner—now dressed in monks' robes—they were exhausted. They'd been enlisted to help as soon as they'd entered their respective dormitories. Amari had been put on cooking duty with a group of five nuns. Caspar had been given a hammer and chisel and told to work on a new room they were carving from the stone. His hands weren't used to physical labor, and his palms were blistered and bleeding.

The men and women were separated during the meal, each sitting on their own side of the room. However, Tsering, Caspar, Amari, and several of Tsering's senior monks sat together in the center of the room. They'd eaten a meal of vegetable curry and steamed bread, sitting in near silence the entire time. Amari wondered if this was normal, although she enjoyed the uninterrupted opportunity to observe everyone as she ate.

Once they'd emptied their food bowls, had cleared them away, and had collected a warm cup of something called yak butter tea, Tsering finally got down to business.

'I have thought on your words,' he said. 'We Buddhists do not believe in killing. We avoid war at all costs. However, we also believe that you should not take what has not been given, as it would appear the Templars are trying to do.

'We will send an envoy to the Templars. We will try to broker an agreement between the Templars and the Pagans. We will make it clear that, although we do not want war, our utmost goal is to end suffering. If war will cause the least suffering—is most in accordance with the eight-fold path—we will support the Pagans. Of course, we ourselves will never fight.'

'Thank you,' said Caspar, 'although, as you know, the Templars have been known to lie. We appreciate your assistance, but would ask, even if a deal is brokered, that you remain vigilant. Their war is not only with us, but with everyone.'

Tsering nodded. 'Naturally.'

'Thank you,' said Caspar again. 'In which case, I believe our business is concluded. I'd be most grateful if you could make arrangements to take us back to the airport in the morning.'

'Of course, if that is what you wish. But I had hoped that you would stay a few days. An envoy from the Shindu Council is due to visit. It would be prudent to stay and speak with them.'

'We would be honored to stay with you. Thank you,' said Caspar, as though nothing would give him more pleasure.

Amari's heart sank. She was going to have to sleep on the floor for multiple days, in a hut full of women whose language she didn't understand, separated from Caspar. She took a deep breath. People paid a fortune for authentic *back to nature* retreats such as this ... she would do her best to embrace it.

Amari and Caspar barely saw each other over the next few days. They caught only glimpses as they went about their duties, exercised, washed, listened to Buddhist teachings, and meditated. They sat next to each other at mealtimes, but Tsering was always there, either inflicting silence, or dominating the conversation with Buddhist philosophy.

Tsering barely spoke to Amari, focusing all his attention on Caspar, who answered politely but refused to bite on anything contentious.

Caspar and Amari managed to snatch moments together on three separate occasions. Once behind a pillar in the meditation room, once in the garden, and once behind the nuns' sleeping accommodations. But Tsering had seen to it that for the most part, they were apart, or surrounded by others.

The first night on the floor had been uncomfortable, although one of the nuns had given Amari a warm blanket, so at least she hadn't been cold. By the fourth night, she'd got used to it. In fact, the whole experience had her feeling pretty zen.

'How are you faring?' Caspar asked, during one of their rare private encounters.

'Surprisingly, I'm having a wonderful time,' she said. 'I feel great, and life is so straightforward here. Although I wish the nuns could speak English; there are so many things I want to ask them.'

Caspar laughed.

'What?' she demanded.

'They're demons. Every single one of them speaks perfect English.'

Amari pulled away, blushing. 'Are you serious?'

'Have you asked any of them a direct question?'

'Only things about cooking, or where dirty towels go … I've always had props to show them what I need.'

'Ask them something that needs a spoken answer, and you'll see.'

It had taken Amari a further half day to pluck up the courage to speak to a nun directly. When she did, she found Caspar was, of course, right.

'What do all the carvings mean?' she asked a firecracker of a nun as they walked past a particularly beautiful section at the back of the assembly hall. The nun was short, old, and round, but had boundless energy and sparkling eyes.

The nun smiled broadly at the question, as though someone had cracked a hilarious joke, then answered in flawless English.

'Some are decorative: the patterns, some of the flowers and plants, and some of the animals. A lot of them are symbols of our faith: the eight-fold path, the Bo tree, the lotus flower, lions, deer, the endless knot, and later, the Buddha himself.'

'And what are they building down there?' Amari asked, pointing down a new section of corridor. She knew Caspar spent most days chipping away at the rock, but hadn't had a chance to ask him about it.

The nun's face lit up. 'Let me show you,' she said, bounding down the corridor, towards the ceaseless sound of chiseling.

They emerged into a new cave, more modestly sized than the rest, and with no windows at all. It was lit only by burning torches set at intervals along the wall.

'We're building a stupa here, a place to hold our sacred relics. This will be a most holy place for us to pray. The square base represents the earth, the steps: water, the bell: fire, the spire: air, and the crown at the top,' she paused, looking at Amari with delight, '*wisdom*. This is a nirvana stupa. It represents the Buddha's death and transition to nirvana. It reminds us of our purpose.'

'Earth, air, fire, and water?' asked Amari. 'Like the Pagans?'

'There are similarities,' said the nun. 'But the Pagans don't put much stock in wisdom …'

The following day, Eka, a middle-aged woman from the Shindu Council, arrived. She and Tsering spent the day shut away in the garden cave, but Amari and Caspar were invited to join them for a private meal at the end of the day.

They arrived, bowed respectfully, then sat cross-legged on the floor, accepting bowls filled with noodle soup, given to them by another monk.

They made polite small talk for a few moments, then Tsering got to the point.

'We have had very interesting conversations today,' he said. 'Eka brings news that you will not like.'

Caspar's insides gave an involuntary lurch, but he and Amari sat in silence, waiting for Tsering to share.

Tsering drew out the silence. 'The Shindu Council have received word that the Pagans are antagonizing the Templars. The Templars say they are only responding to the Pagan's warlike actions. They strongly refute the notion that they are the instigators of discord.'

Silence settled while Amari and Caspar let the words sink in.

'And what is your view on this matter?' Caspar asked Eka. 'Is it the Pagans or the Templars whose words are untrue?'

'The Templars were convincing,' said Eka.

'You've told Eka all that we told you?' Caspar asked Tsering. He nodded. 'And you don't find our account convincing? Especially in light of their historic actions? The Pagans want the same things as the Buddhists, and Shindus. We don't believe in expanding our empire, or manipulating stock markets, or involving ourselves in politics. We want only to establish and maintain peace, prosperity, and fairness, for everyone.'

'At whatever cost?' asked Eka.

'We don't want war, but if it comes to that, to protect us all—to protect our beliefs—then yes,' said Caspar.

'And what about kidnapping?' said Eka. 'Is that an appropriate cost?'

'What do you mean?' said Caspar, taken aback. 'We would never condone that.'

Eka turned sharply to Amari. 'This is the demon Raina, is it not?'

'Asleep, but yes,' said Caspar.

'The Templars have accused the Pagans of kidnapping her, holding her hostage, and feeding her lies. The Templars have been attempting to recover her,' said Eka.

'What?' said Caspar, a million thoughts running through his head. 'We would never do that.'

'Where was she when she died last? Who was she with? What was she doing?' asked Eka.

'I … I don't know,' said Caspar. 'But Raina would never have joined the Templars. She's a Pagan, and will be until her dying breath.'

'Is she?' said Eka. 'A lot can change in a lifetime or two, and I hear that's how long you two have been estranged.'

'What benefit could we possibly obtain from kidnapping Raina?' he said. 'She's asleep now, but she will awaken, and when she does, she'll be free to go anywhere she likes.'

'We can but wait and see,' said Eka.

Caspar prickled. Who was this woman to accuse him of kidnapping? 'I know Raina; she won't go to the Templars. This is another of their lies and manipulations.'

'The Shindu Council have no natural affinity with the Templars,' said Eka. 'Indeed, we've been friends to the Pagans, happily so, for hundreds of years. But if there is truth in the Templars' story, then we have no choice but to stand with them. Kidnapping is a serious offence.'

'And you'd be right to do so,' said Caspar. 'But seeing as we have not kidnapped Raina—a fact she will confirm as soon as she wakes—I am certain our friendship will endure.'

'Of course,' said Eka, '*if* that is the case.'

'I have known Caspar a long time,' said Tsering. 'I will send my envoy still. We will see if there is light we can shine.'

Caspar breathed a sigh of relief. At least Tsering was standing with him. 'Thank you,' he said.

Tsering's expression shifted. 'Don't misunderstand me. I have no love for the Templars, but that woman, Raina, has always been trouble. I cannot entirely discount the idea that you would do something stupid in pursuit of her.'

Amari left the meeting having not uttered a single word. She didn't know what to think, let alone say. Caspar was right behind her. He grabbed her hand, pulled her to his chest, heedless of who might come along the corridor.

'I'm sorry,' he said into her hair. 'I promise we didn't kidnap you. We need to speak to Rose ... maybe she knows something more.'

Amari clung to him. He was the only stability she had in the bizarre, turbulent world she'd somehow landed in.

'I don't know what to think,' she said, 'but those men who came after us, if they only wanted to retrieve me, then why did they throw knives at me?'

'The Templars are trying to turn our allies against us. They're trying to weaken us. I don't know why they're coming after you ...' He pushed away. 'I don't know what happened in your last life ...'

Amari sat on the nearest window ledge, her eyes scanning the lake.

'Part of me wishes I would just wake up, and part of me is terrified to.'

'I know,' said Caspar, moving in front of her.

Amari rested her cheek against his stomach. Caspar's hands stroked her hair.

'I feel the same,' he said. 'We'll leave for the Vikings tomorrow, and call Rose from the plane.'

Chapter 18

Caspar and Amari were back on the plane by dinnertime the following day. Amari was less vocal on the return car journey, her mind going over and over what Eka had said, along with everything else she'd learned since finding out she was a sleeping demon. Those words still seemed absurd.

Amari boarded the plane and threw her phone down on the table, not even bothering to switch it on. It wasn't like there was anyone she could speak to ... Did anyone even have her new number?

Amari paced, barely realizing her feet were moving, frustration building.

Caspar was already on his phone, first calling the Vikings to make arrangements for their visit, and then trying to get hold of Rose. Rose didn't answer, so Caspar called round everyone else. Most of their phones went straight to voicemail, the rest rang out, except Talli's.

'Have you heard from Rose?' Caspar demanded.

'No,' said Talli, the phone on speaker so Amari could hear too.

'You know the Templars are saying we kidnapped Raina? They've got to the Shindu Council. The Shindus are half-convinced.'

'That would explain what the Egyptians were alluding to,' said Talli.

'Do you know why they're saying it? Anything from Raina's last life?' asked Caspar.

'No,' said Talli. 'You need to ask Rose.'

'I've tried; she's not answering. Has anyone else put their reports up yet?' asked Caspar.

'Nothing helpful,' said Talli. 'A few meeting write-ups. Most nations are on the fence.'

'Okay. We're heading to the Vikings now. If you hear from Rose, tell her we need to talk.'

'Okay. Good luck.'

'You too.'

Caspar hung up, then pulled a laptop out of a compartment under his seat. He began a furious assault on the keyboard.

'What are you doing?' asked Amari.

'Writing up my report. We upload them to a central system so the rest of the leadership can see what we've learned. We can't always speak on the phone, and we're spread across time zones, so this way, everyone can stay up to date. And the write-ups provide a record we can go back and look at later; it's very useful.'

'Do I need to do one too?'

'Yes. There's another laptop here,' he said, leaning under the next seat and pulling one out. He handed it to Amari. 'Your fingerprint should unlock it. Double-click on the cloud archive icon, and it's self-explanatory from there.'

This was good. Something to take Amari's mind off her potential kidnaping.

The plane took off and they worked on their reports for the next two hours. Caspar said every detail could be important, so she created a blow-by-blow account of their time with the Buddhists, along with an executive summary containing the pertinent bits.

The flight attendant had spent his time in Tibet testing out the local restaurants, sourcing food for the return flight. He'd done well. Once their reports were finished, they ate Sichuan beef, lamb skewers, naan bread, and Tibetan yoghurt. They washed the meal down with Tibetan barley wine, and although it wouldn't be Amari's future beverage of choice, it was surprisingly pleasant.

Caspar and Amari ate appreciatively, enjoying the plush leather seats and the luxury of having someone to clean up after them.

Amari peppered Caspar with the questions she hadn't had a chance to ask him while they'd been with the Buddhists: Had he been chiseling every day? *Yes.* Were any of the Buddhist nation allowed to have romantic relationships? *Only if they were happy to be lay people, which meant they were never* in the know*, and were looked down on by everyone else.* Why did Tsering hate Raina so much? *Because he thought Raina was the reason Caspar had never returned to the Buddhists.* Was that really the only reason? *Raina had caused her fair share of wars. Buddhists frowned upon this kind of behavior.* Had he been tempted to stay this time? *Not even for a second.*

'Why not?' Amari asked.

'Because I want you, and because I'm Pagan. I believe in what the Pagans teach.'

'They're kind of similar though,' said Amari. 'Earth, air, fire, water, living with nature, doing the right thing.'

'A lot of religions have similarities, it doesn't mean they're the same.'

'I know. It just … surprised me.'

'Enough with the questions. We've only got a few hours until we land in Norway, and I plan to spend every one of them in that wonderful bed,' said Caspar, standing. 'I'm hoping you'll keep me company.'

Amari and Caspar landed in Norway, in Honningsvåg, where two women with long, blonde, plaited hair waited for them. They were greeted with warm handshakes that turned into backslaps, ushered to a white Volvo, and asked about their journey.

The women gave them mead, encouraged them to take pictures of the beautiful landscape on their phones, and openly informed them that they were going to Skarsvåg.

'You don't keep the location of your headquarters secret?' asked Amari.

Maja, who was driving, laughed. 'No! We don't care if the whole world knows. If anyone wants to come and kill us in our beds, good luck to them!'

Not one single thing about this was comparable to their visit to the Buddhists, and Amari's head was spinning—probably the jetlag. They'd followed the day around the world, landing in Norway around the same time they'd taken off in Tibet.

Twenty minutes later, they drove past a sign announcing they'd reached Skarsvåg, a small fishing village. Amari was surprised to find their destination was a hall right in the centre.

'Is the whole village Viking?' she asked Thea, the other woman.

'Most, not all,' Thea replied. 'Those who are not Viking see only what they want to. They don't know we're here.'

'How's that possible?'

Thea laughed, as though this were obvious. 'Magic.'

Amari was totally unprepared for the scene that greeted them when they entered the hall of the Vikings. In the centre sat a fire pit, roaring and cracking, even

238

though it was the middle of summer. To each side of the fire there were long banquet tables with benches. A raised dais with two thrones dominated the far end, its two occupants observing all that took place below.

The hall was bursting with people eating, drinking, and conversing in loud voices. Caspar and Amari stepped over the threshold, and silence rippled through the room, a sea of expectant faces turning to greet them.

'King Henrik, Queen Sofie,' said Caspar, 'we, of the Pagans, thank you for your hospitality.' Caspar bowed and Amari followed suit.

'Cas-par,' boomed Henrik. He leaped up from his throne, jumped off the dais, and hurtled towards where Caspar and Amari stood.

Henrik wrapped Caspar in a hug so fearsome that Amari worried Caspar's ribs would break. Henrik was a bear of a man, with long, dark, shaggy hair and beard. He looked to be in his late twenties or early thirties.

'And ... Raina?'

'Amari,' she said, 'although maybe one day I'll be Raina.'

Henrik pulled her into a bear hug too. 'Why always so stubborn? Heh? You'd think, after all this time, you'd give in.'

Amari had no idea what to say to this.

'You're calling *her* stubborn?' said Caspar, raising an eyebrow.

A laugh came from behind and hands clapped together. 'Yes! If anyone could give lessons on being a stubborn, pig-headed old oaf, then surely it would be this one,' said Queen Sofie, joining them at the door.

She pulled Caspar into a hug, then Amari. Then she took Amari's arm and led her towards the thrones. 'Come with me, before my husband keeps you standing on the threshold another minute.'

Sofie, who, up close, Amari was surprised to see looked to be in her late forties, had long auburn hair, full of small plaits that cascaded down her back. She led them to the area of banquet table closest to the thrones, the inhabitants of the benches hastily clearing out.

Henrik and Sofie sat on one side, Caspar and Amari on the other. Henrik called for food and mead to be brought for their guests.

Amari wasn't particularly hungry, having finished off the Tibetan yoghurt with some fruit not long before landing, but she got the feeling that to refuse the Vikings' hospitality would be unwise.

They were offered spit-roasted pork straight from the hearth, flatbread, butter, salads foraged from the surrounding land, thin slices of raw salmon, cheeses, and an array of berries, honey, and skyr—a yoghurt-like Nordic specialty.

'You are, as always, most generous,' said Caspar, helping himself to a little of it all.

Amari helped herself too. The meat was juicy and delicious, complemented perfectly by the tart lemony flavor of the dock leaf salad. 'Oh my God, this tastes amazing,' she said. 'Caspar, you've got to try this.'

Once they'd eaten more than their fill, Sofie turned to business. 'You're here because of the Templars,' she said, looking shrewdly at Caspar, then Amari.

'Yes,' said Caspar. He told them of the Templar's antagonistic behavior, and the lies about the Pagans kidnapping Raina.

'They are a troublesome nation,' said Sofie, 'there is no doubt about that. And I don't believe these kidnapping charges for a second. But the Templars expanding their territories is not something we Vikings are overly concerned with.'

'It would make life more interesting if more nations took chances, eh?' said Henrik, laughing loudly.

'We're not scared of a fight,' said Sofie. 'In fact, I'd like one. The Gods know it's been too long, but then, fights now are so absurd. There's no fun in all the cloak-and-dagger bullshit. Manipulating stock markets, and influencing politicians, and spreading rumors.'

'Assassins came after us,' said Amari. 'It didn't feel very cloak and dagger to me.'

'But that's all a war can ever be now,' said Sofie, waving her hands. 'We could send our men and women into your nation to help protect you. And we could send them to America, to target the Templars, killing as assassins, quietly, with no honor. And all the while, Templars would attempt to do the same to us. Where's the fun? The thrill of lining up opposite your enemy on the battlefield? The war cries? The bloodlust? The euphoria of victory?'

'And what's in it for us?' asked Henrik.

'I'm assuming you have something in mind?' said Caspar.

'Now you mention it,' said Henrik, 'a member of our war council is in need of a wife. He's suggested Meredith would be a most suitable option.'

Amari nearly spat out her mead. Caspar smirked at her expression.

'I'm afraid you'll need to take that up with Meredith directly,' said Caspar.

'Not with Rose?' said Henrik.

'It's been a long time since any Pagan has been forced into a marriage; we don't sell our people. If Meredith wants to marry this Viking, and to live as Viking, the Pagans would support it, regardless of the significant loss to our nation. Equally, if she refuses the marriage, we won't force her.'

'Fucking moralistic creatures,' said Henrik, slamming down his mead. 'You'd turn down this alliance?'

'If we go to war and the Templars defeat the Pagans, who do you think will be next?' said Caspar, unfazed by Henrik's sudden aggression.

'They could go in any number of directions,' said Henrik.

'And leave a formidable force such as the Vikings at their backs?' said Caspar. 'I think not.'

Henrik made a noncommittal gesture with his head.

'The Pagans have no love of war,' Caspar went on, 'but if they continue to attack us, we'll have no choice. Your support could mean the difference between a swift, early victory, and a long, drawn-out disaster for us all.

'The Vikings are a warrior nation. Knowing you're on our side will sway many nations our way, especially the smaller ones. And there will come a time, if the Templars persist, where you'll have no choice but to pick a side. Will it be the Templars?'

Henrik growled.

'We will think on it,' said Sofie, placing a hand on Henrik's arm. 'Pagans and Vikings have been allies for many lifetimes. We despise the Templars. We will speak with our war council.'

'And I will speak with Meredith,' said Caspar. 'But I warn you, she isn't usually the marrying kind.'

Chapter 19

Henrik stood, downed his drink, and called for music. All eyes were upon him, the energy in the hall picking up, anticipation hanging in the air.

Henrik took Sofie by the hand, pulled her to her feet, then led her to the dance floor. They rampaged around the area in between the two banquet tables, cheered on by the whole room. Other couples joined in, until the space was one big mass of moving bodies. Henrik and Sofie eventually returned to where Amari and Caspar sat, though not, as Amari had assumed, to take a break, but to pull them up onto the dance floor too.

'Pagans don't sit idly by when there's dancing to be had!' boomed Henrik.

He twirled Amari so fast she lost all sense of direction. She couldn't help but laugh, filled with exhilaration; this was just what she needed after so long with the Buddhists.

They hurtled around the hall, narrowly missing other dancers as they looped and jumped. Henrik ignored her shrieks to put her down as he lifted and spun her.

By the time Caspar intervened, having to pry her away from Henrik, Amari was covered in sweat and breathing hard.

'This is a welcome change!' she shouted, as Caspar led her across the floor with gusto to match Henrik's.

'The Vikings are a more exuberant people than the Buddhists,' laughed Caspar. 'They've got a lot in common with us, given their ancestors followed pagan religions too.'

'Different ones, though?' asked Amari, pulling Caspar to the side so she could take a breather and have a drink.

'Yes. Our Pagan nation is a fusion of beliefs from many different groups. The ancient people of Scandinavia were similar—they had many small groups with varying beliefs.

'Eventually, the Vikings dominated with their Gods: Odin, Thor, and the rest, but that was an evolution, and even then, they didn't have a total monopoly. The Sami, for example, remained separate.'

'Sami?'

'The people indigenous to this area,' Caspar said. 'A few hundred years ago, the Vikings and the Scandinavian Sami demons merged into a single demon nation. So the nation we call Viking is, in fact, more than that.

'Under the Viking umbrella, there are different groups of demons practicing different religions. It's the same with most demon nations; we're mongrels. It's only the new ones, like the Templars, who are pure.'

'Does it cause problems, when people join together? What if the Vikings want to support a war, but the Sami don't?'

'It could cause problems, although nations don't generally air their dirty laundry, so it's hard to tell. Civil wars inside nations do sometimes pull alliances apart.'

'It's so complicated,' said Amari.

'Anything involving people is complicated,' said Caspar.

'Don't make me come over there and steal Amari again,' roared Henrik, swooping past with Sofie in his arms.

'Don't you dare,' cried Caspar. He drew Amari to him, then led her back into the melee.

They danced and drank and laughed for hours, until the revelers were thoroughly drunk and wildly raucous.

Caspar pulled Amari to him, kissing her. Her mind was foggy from all the mead, her instincts taking over, so she pressed up against him, kissing him back, not even thinking about where they were or who was watching.

All around them, couples were doing the same, some against the wooden struts supporting the hall, some sitting at the banquet tables, some on the dance floor.

'Let's get out of here,' whispered Caspar.

Sofie appeared at their side. Evidently she and Henrik had had the same idea.

'See you at breakfast, my friends,' said Sofie. 'You're in the same hut as last time. Your bags are already there.'

'Thank you,' said Caspar.

Henrik and Sofie disappeared though a door behind their thrones. Caspar and Amari exited through the main door at the opposite end of the hall.

They emerged to find it as bright as day outside, although overcast. This far north, at this time of year, it didn't get dark at all. It was surreal.

Caspar wrapped an arm around Amari, pulling her tightly to his side, leading her along the meandering route to their small wooden hut down by the water.

It wasn't much to look at, and it wasn't much inside either, just one big open room with a small bathroom attached. But it had an enormous, inviting, fur-covered bed, with a pile of blankets folded at the base.

'Heaven,' said Amari, taking it all in. After sleeping alone on the floor, this was absolute luxury.

Caspar had barely shut the door before Amari hauled him to her, locking their mouths, tearing off his clothes. As soon as they were naked, she pushed him back onto the bed and straddled him, guiding him inside her, rocking against him.

He growled, his hands on her backside, grasping her skin, urging her faster. It was frantic, and frenzied, and they climaxed together, Amari collapsing forward, Caspar enveloping her in his arms.

Amari and Caspar woke to bright sunlight streaming in through the window. Their naked bodies were intertwined, Amari's head on Caspar's chest, legs wrapped together.

Amari pulled her head back, looking up at Caspar to see if he was awake. She found his sleepy eyes on hers.

'Hey,' he said. His gravelly tone made her stomach go tight.

'Hey,' she replied, running a hand over his toned torso, tracing each ridge. She tipped her head back, seeking Caspar's lips, and he lowered them to hers.

She let out a hum of pleasure; this was how she wished to wake up every morning. Caspar's kisses were deep but gentle, unhurried, as though they had all the time in the world. He rolled her onto her back, covering her with his body, and Amari arched to meet him.

'We've died and gone to heaven,' said Amari. She relished the feel of his skin, and weight, and kisses.

'That as may be,' he said, pulling back, 'but I've got something to show you, before everyone else is up and it gets crowded.'

Amari gave a pout of disappointment. 'What is it?'

He kissed her jaw, then stood. 'You'll see. Put on something you can run in; we can get some exercise on the way.'

They threw on their clothes and left the hut. Caspar set off at a jog along the road that hugged the waterfront. They soon reached the end, but kept going along an old, worn track, Amari marveling at the ocean on both sides as they ran along the headland.

They jogged across the tricky terrain, almost until they ran out of land. Caspar stopped and pulled her to a halt. 'This way,' he said, and headed down a tiny path over the side of the cliff.

'Okay,' said Amari, 'but seems a tad suicidal.'

'Trust me, it's worth it,' he said. 'Just watch your footing.'

They descended a few metres onto a ledge that led into a cave, hollowed out over the course of thousands of years by the wind and rain and sea. It was deep enough that Caspar had to pull out a small torch to illuminate the way.

The walls were covered with etchings that had been chiseled into the rock, then filled in with reddish paint. The etchings near the entrance had been destroyed by the weather, but the images at the back made Amari's jaw drop.

'Oh my goodness,' she said, her hand tracing a four-legged animal that looked kind of like a deer. 'This is ... this is so exciting!'

Caspar watched as she took in the animals, people, boats, and symbols that adorned the walls. 'Petroglyphs going back hundreds of years,' he said.

'What's this one?' asked Amari, tracing a symbol with eight spokes, a series of smaller lines dissecting each spoke.

'That one's the Helm of Awe,' he said, cryptically. 'It's magical.'

'How so?'

'It provides protection and brings victory.'

She gave him a skeptical look.

'If invoked correctly. But most demons don't know how to wield magic anymore. The knowledge is being forgotten, made all but irrelevant by technology. Most of us can only manage small magics these days.'

'Seems strange,' said Amari, 'that people would forget something so … well … magical.'

'Magic, like everything, comes with a cost. Most aren't willing to pay it.'

'Can *you* do more than small magics?' asked Amari.

Caspar smirked. 'I can barely even manage that.'

'Could you once?'

'No. I was never interested in magic.'

'Why not?'

'It takes lifetimes to get anywhere, so most proficients will only agree to train someone if they're willing to dedicate at least three hundred years. And magic can be helpful, but it's not straightforward. A protection spell, for example, cast by a proficient, could halt the rain of arrows in a battle. But a protection spell cast by a neophyte—a beginner—might only direct the arrows away from the eyes of those being attacked.'

'The eyes?'

'Eyes are a window to the soul, and it's the soul that reincarnates. The way to kill a demon, so they never come back, involves destroying their eyes prior to death.'

'So directing arrows away from the eyes might still result in the demons dying, but it would protect them from final death?'

'Exactly. But in a battle, magic that causes arrows to move unpredictably can be more dangerous than no magic at all.'

'I see.'

'All magic is unpredictable, sometimes even for proficients … and adepts, although I don't know if any adepts still exist.

'Technology's often a better, more reliable option, so magic isn't as important anymore. Why communicate with someone via magic, when you can call them on a phone?'

'Do any demons still study magic?'

'Yes. I'd imagine every nation has some kind of magical contingent.'

'Did Raina have an interest in magic?'

'Not really. I think you dabbled in some lives before we met.'

'Is Talli a proficient? She was using magic at Midsummer, right?'

'She was using magic, but she's a long way from being a proficient. The Pagans only have two proficients currently, and they live together in Wales. They have a few neophytes training with them.'

'Anyone I've met?'

'They keep to themselves.'

'What about Rose? Does she use magic?'

'Rose was never inclined that way. Magic isn't just about learning; you need natural ability, and Rose has none.'

'It feels … different in here,' said Amari, 'from the way it felt outside.'

'There's a concentration of magic here. We're on a ley line, and the magic is particularly potent ... maybe because demons have been performing rituals here for so long.'

'It's such a strange feeling,' she said, running her hand over the image of a long boat, the stone cool against her fingers.

Amari's eyes scanned the petroglyphs. They landed on the image of a man and a woman holding hands. A convulsion racked her body, and it became difficult to breathe.

'What is that?' she choked, pointing at the image.

Concern washed across Caspar's face. He followed the direction of her finger. 'That's us, after our Viking wedding,' he said, stepping to her side, putting a hand on her arm. 'What's happening?'

'Our Viking wedding?'

Something clicked in her mind; the same feeling she got when the pieces of a particularly difficult puzzle finally made sense.

'We've had a wedding in virtually every lifetime. Seven or maybe eight lifetimes ago, we got married in this very spot.'

'Here?'

The pressure in her chest eased. She took a deep, cool breath. The tension that had held her rigid blew away on the salty sea breeze.

He nodded, relaxing. 'Our next wedding—the one we have in this lifetime—should be somewhere awe-inspiring. Somewhere with magic. Somewhere as far from a hotel ballroom as it is possible to be.'

She scowled and shoved him. 'It was a very nice hotel, I'll have you know.'

Caspar grabbed her hand. 'It was still a hotel.'

She gave him an indulgent eye roll, then kissed him, electricity sparking through her veins.

'Hang on, was that a marriage proposal?' she said, pulling back. 'You know we've been dating for about two minutes, right? That's kinda desperate.'

'Oh really? Desperate?'

Amari laughed, pecking him on the lips. 'Tragic, actually.'

'That hurt.'

'Ludicrous.'

'Now you're just plain mean.'

'But I suppose it's loveable.'

'You love me?'

'You know ...' She paused, as though thinking hard. 'I think I do.'

They kissed again, slow and contented. 'I love you too,' he said, his hands on either side of her face.

Amari smiled. She covered one of his hands with hers, caressing his skin with her thumb.

'We should get back. We don't want to miss breakfast,' he said, kissing her one last time.

'You're right. I'm starving.'

Caspar broke away, heading for the entrance.

Amari reached out and placed her fingers on the petroglyph of the man and woman, of Raina and Caspar. And in that instant, the moment her skin touched the unforgiving stone, her whole world changed.

PART 2

Chapter 20

Amari dropped to the floor, her head hot, as though all the thoughts rubbing against her consciousness were causing friction burn. Endless images flashed before her eyes, endless thoughts filled her, endless songs, words, languages, faces, endless conflicting ideas and opinions.

In an instant, she knew how to play countless instruments, how to cook innumerable recipes, how to sew, and weave, and make pottery, and forge iron, and play politics, and she felt … different.

She felt powerful.

'Amari?' Caspar rushed to her side. 'Are you okay?'

He clasped her arm, but she pushed him away, with more strength than she knew she possessed. Caspar stumbled backwards, landing hard on the floor. 'Amari?'

She lifted her head, hair wild around her face, poised like a deadly animal, crouched, ready to attack or run. She flicked her gaze to Casper, pinning him with fearsome, aged, furious eyes.

Understanding dawned on his face. And with a voice filled with startling, ancient power, she flung three deadly words at his ears. 'Amari is dead.'

'Raina,' said Caspar, reverently.

'Caspar.'

They stayed there—on the floor—for several moments, each considering their new circumstances. They launched to their feet at the same moment, Raina heading for the cave's entrance, Caspar leaping on her. He brought her to the ground before she could escape.

'No,' he said, trying to pin her arms, but before he could, she'd already flipped them.

Caspar landed on his back, forced to release her, and Raina was up and running before he could blink.

Raina flew up the cliff face, racing across the rough terrain, back towards the Vikings. She didn't look back, so she didn't see Caspar closing the distance.

Amari hadn't been unfit, but her physical condition certainly wasn't anything to write home about. Even with Raina's superior mental ability, there was only so much this body could do. Even so, they were only five hundred metres from the Viking hall by the time Caspar caught her.

He grabbed her arm, and they tumbled to the ground together, rolling, narrowly missing a boulder.

This time, he managed to pin her face down, arms twisted awkwardly so she couldn't throw him off.

'We need to talk,' said Caspar, when she finally stilled.

'I have nothing to say.'

'You ignored me for an entire lifetime; it's been long enough.'

Raina said nothing, lying limp beneath him.

'Raina?'

Still nothing.

'Raina, I know you're fucking with me.' But his voice contained an edge of panic.

He stood, leaning down to turn her over, but before he could, she moved, rolling, taking his legs out from under him. Caspar went down hard, Raina over him in an instant, and then, his world went black.

Raina reached the hut she and Caspar had slept in, and packed her things. She grabbed Caspar's phone and dialed Rose's number. Rose picked up almost immediately.

'Caspar,' said Rose. 'I read your report ...'

'Rose, it's Raina,' she said, cutting her off.

'Oh, thank the Gods,' said Rose, 'any and all of them. Please tell me I'm not dreaming.'

'It's me. I'm with the Vikings. I'm going to the Registerium.'

'Caspar?'

'He'll come round in a while; I'll be gone by then.'

'You knocked him out?'

'He pinned me to the ground. He had it coming.'

'He pinned you to the ground?'

'It's mortifying, I know. Amari was seriously out of shape.'

'Don't tell anyone you're you. If Jamie knows you're awake, he'll have an army waiting.'

'I won't.'

'I'll send Meredith and Gemma, but it'll be easier to pretend you're still Amari if you take Caspar with you.'

'I'll be there as soon as I can, but I'm going alone.'

Raina took one last look around, picked up her bag, and headed for the carport. All of the vehicles were open, most of them with the keys still in the ignition; crime wasn't exactly a problem here. She took the same Volvo they'd been picked up in, and drove out of the village, her pace sedate. Nobody gave her a second glance.

The plane was ready to go by the time she arrived, the flight attendant surprised to find Raina alone.

'Caspar's staying another few days,' said Raina, with a shy smile. Is that what Amari would've done? Amari was still a part of her, despite what she'd said to Caspar, but already, it was difficult to distinguish her from the myriad lifetimes in her head.

'Of course,' said the flight attendant. 'Can I get you some breakfast? I don't have much, given the short notice, but I have tea and pastries?'

'Sounds wonderful,' said Raina, strapping herself in.

Minutes later, they were in the sky. Raina took out a laptop and read the reports everyone else had submitted. No one had learned anything much. The Templars had visited a few of the other nations, but most of them were on the fence. No one wanted war.

She put away the laptop, ate her breakfast, then stared out of the window, turning over memories in her mind.

She hated waking up, the jarring, roiling feel of it. It was the same every time: immense pressure, a pounding headache, and more memories than she could possibly process.

She buzzed with knowledge and power, but also dread, knowing what was to come. Because now she knew what she'd been doing with Rose during the course of her last two lives. She knew why Jamie wanted her. She knew why he was happy to risk war, and it was all based on a horrible, terrible lie.

The plane journey was short, but Meredith was already waiting when Raina's plane arrived in Inverness. They embraced, Raina glad to see her, even more so now she remembered all they'd been through together.

'It's good to have you back,' said Meredith, throwing Raina's bag in the back of the waiting Range Rover. 'Gemma's been delayed in London, but she should be here in the morning.'

'How were the Wakan? And the Animists?' asked Raina.

They headed out into the Scottish countryside, covered in heather at this time of year.

'On the fence,' said Meredith. 'The Wakan are worried about antagonizing the Templars, especially given their close proximity. And the Animists talk in riddles; I have no idea if they'll back us or not. They're both concerned about the increase in Slayer activity though. From what I could glean, both nations have had losses.'

'Are they random, or is there a pattern?'

'They're targeting the oldest, most powerful, and most capable. We've been getting similar messages from the other nations too,' said Meredith.

'The Buddhists and Vikings didn't mention anything about losses,' said Raina. '*Although* ... the Vikings did say we could have a firm and lasting allegiance on one single condition.'

'What?'

Raina couldn't keep the chuckle in. 'That you marry one of their generals. Apparently, he's smitten.'

Meredith rolled her eyes, although the corners of her mouth twitched upwards.

'Who do they want me to marry?'

'Would you consider it?'

'Probably not. But who?'

'I don't know. All I know is it's someone senior. Henrik and Sofie were very keen on the idea.'

'Great, just what I need ... pressure to marry a Viking.'

'No one's going to pressure you.'

'Not overtly,' said Meredith, 'but it'll be there, hanging in the air between me and every other Pagan: *the Vikings are strong allies, and nothing brings allies closer than a marriage ...*'

'Who are you and what've you done with Meredith? She's not usually this whiny.'

Meredith punched Raina's arm.

'Ow.'

'Now who's whiny?'

Raina barked out a laugh. 'Oh, it's good to be back.'

Meredith drove them deep into the countryside, encountering little in the way of traffic and a great deal in the way of stunning scenery. Raina had seen the world, but these landscapes were some of her absolute favorite.

Around lunchtime, they pulled off the main road, through an imposing gateway, then along the mile-long drive to the modestly sized castle that housed the Registerium.

'And here we are again,' said Raina, looking up at the battlements. 'At least they're doing a good job of keeping the old place going.'

'If nothing else,' said Meredith.

Instead of entering the castle, they skirted around the side. They got almost to the back, then dropped down a set of stone steps that delivered them to a single standing stone. Raina walked straight to the stone and placed her hand upon it.

'Wait!' shrieked a female voice from the top of the steps. The voice was accompanied by the sound of racing feet.

'I pledge my allegiance to the Pagan nation, from now until the end of this life,' said Raina, rushing.

A small, electric buzz pinged the centre of her hand, and she breathed a sigh of relief. She turned to see Meredith and a small, slight, dark-skinned woman fighting.

'It's done,' she said. 'Now we can hear what's so urgent.'

Meredith and the woman pulled apart, and the woman's features contorted with rage. 'I told you to wait,' she said.

'Oh, I'm sorry, I didn't realize you were my master,' said Raina.

'You had no idea what I was going to say.'

'No, but lucky for me, I'm old enough to know when to ignore people.'

'You've ruined it.'

'Ruined what?'

'You should've heard me out.'

'You know in films,' said Raina, 'when someone has a gun to the bad guy's head, but they stand around chatting instead of pulling the trigger?'

'Or when someone needs to cut a wire to a bomb,' said Meredith, 'but the main characters have to say something meaningful to each other, so they wait until the last second?'

Raina looked expectantly at the woman, giving her time to respond. The woman stayed silent.

'I've learned, over the course of many hundreds of years, that if I've got something I need to do, I do it—without delay—and worry about everything else later.'

The woman shook with rage. She stormed back up the steps without another word.

Raina and Meredith couldn't help but laugh.

'Who the hell is she?' asked Raina.

'I have no idea, but welcome to the Pagan nation,' said Meredith, embracing Raina. 'It's a relief to have you back.'

Raina and Meredith walked back up the steps, round to the front door, and entered the castle. They stepped into a lofty entrance hall with a flagstone floor, solid wooden furniture, and tapestries adorning the walls. A tall, spindly man was there waiting for them.

'Registrar,' said Raina, shaking his hand. 'I would like to have it entered into the official record that I have just sworn my allegiance in this life to the Pagan nation.'

'Indeed,' said the Registrar. His tone was frosty, but he was always that way. Not to mention, he liked at least a little pomp and ceremony to accompany a nation pledge, especially when it concerned very old or very young demons. Raina had snatched that out from under him.

'Right away, please,' said Raina, not waiting for the Registrar before she set off in the direction of the record room.

Meredith followed her. The Registrar did not.

'This doesn't feel right,' said Meredith, her voice low.

'I know,' said Raina. 'The quicker we get out of here, the better.'

They walked through an inner reception hall with a sweeping staircase, a large dining room through a door on one side, and a drawing room on the other.

They climbed the stairs, coming out onto a spacious landing, turning to the right, heading down a long corridor lined with ancient portraits, tapestries, and other treasures. The room right at the end, with windows giving a good view of the drive, was the record room.

Although it was called the record room, most of the records were actually kept in the dungeons. This room was sparsely furnished, with only a formal seating area, a couple of large desks—devoid of any adornment, as you would find in a library—and a few racks of books and scrolls.

It was sterile and perfunctory, its only redeeming feature that it was flooded with light, three vast windows punched in each of the two outer walls.

An animated conversation was taking place within the sun-soaked room. The woman from outside gesticulated wildly at a balding, bespectacled man. The man did not look impressed.

'Ah, Raina, I believe that's you?' said the man, getting up to greet them.

'Pablo Picacho?' said Raina. 'Is that you?'

'One and the same,' he said, although he looked nothing like the Spanish Pablo she'd once known. This man was white as snow, short, and wrinkled. They embraced warmly.

'I would like to record my pledge to the Pagan nation, which I just completed at the stone outside,' said Raina.

'Any witnesses?' asked Pablo, pulling out a smartphone. It looked strange here; Raina was so used to ink and parchment during registrations.

'Meredith, and whoever this is,' said Raina, pointing to the brooding figure in the corner.

'Janet,' said Pablo, 'of the Templar nation.'

Raina raised an eyebrow.

'Jamie wants to see you,' said Janet. 'He has news he knows you'll want to hear. It would be best for you if you heard it before making this registration official.'

Raina let out a half laugh. 'You're obviously young, because otherwise you'd know my registration's already official; it's been sealed by magic. What we're doing now is merely making it public.'

Janet faltered, unsure for a beat, then drew herself up, squaring her shoulders. 'If you don't go to see Jamie, there will be war. The lives of countless demons are resting on your shoulders.'

'Why me?' asked Raina, although, of course, she already knew.

'That's between you and Jamie. What he sees in *you*, I have absolutely no idea.'

Janet left the room, closing the door behind her with a loud, echoing bang.

'She seems charming,' said Meredith.

'Don't get me started,' said Pablo. 'She's in here every bleeding day, scouring the records, watching to see if anyone comes up the drive, asking endless questions. She's trying to glean every little secret out of all and any source she can get her hands on.'

'What's she looking for?' asked Raina.

'I have no idea,' said Pablo. 'She's backed off in the last week or so; maybe she's finally run out of questions …'

'Yet she didn't know it's the magic from the standing stone that makes a registration official?' said Raina.

'Oh, she doesn't care about magic, or protocol, or anything that's actually important. All she cares about are the demons themselves. If this were the seventeenth century, I'd suspect she was trying to find herself a husband.'

Raina laughed. 'I guess dating apps make that more straightforward these days.'

'There isn't one for demons,' said Meredith. 'Maybe the Registerium should branch out ...'

'Don't fret, Meredith, all you need to do is visit the Vikings,' said Raina, smiling broadly.

Meredith scowled.

'Here we are,' said Pablo, pulling up Raina's record. 'Everything's been digitized. Took years. We've still got all the original records, of course, but this is so much more convenient.

'Now, if you could just check your record and confirm I've got the right one.' He handed over the phone. 'Not that *you* could ever be mistaken for another ...'

Raina scrolled through her history, right back to her birth in the Middle East. Not all demons had agreed to make their previous lives public, but the Pagans were an open people. Although, even Pagans had been known to omit one or two of their lives from the official record, for varying, usually embarrassing reasons.

Not that it mattered; the magic couldn't be altered. A proficient could determine a demon's history with only some biological matter and access to one of the many connected standing stones around the world.

Stones had been used for centuries by demons, to register in a nation, as well as for other magical purposes. Of course, that had all but died out now, and what a shame that was. Most standing stones weren't even maintained any longer; some had deteriorated so far as to have lost their attachment to the web of magic that spun beneath the surface of the world. So most demons registered here. At least the Registerium's stone was reliable.

The Registerium hadn't even existed for many of Raina's lives. And it had been simpler before technology, when demons had relied on magic alone. But these days, with so much connection, and international travel, it was helpful to have a verified, searchable public record of who belonged to whom. The alternative was to rely on a proficient, and not only were proficients in short supply, but their rituals took time—usually longer than it took the Registerium to conduct a simple search of their database.

'That's me,' said Raina, handing back the phone.

'You're getting on a bit, you know,' said Pablo.

'Alright, no need to remind me,' said Raina, 'but, need I point out, so are you.'

Pablo shrugged. 'Are we a little touchy in our old age?'

'In old age?' said Meredith. 'She's always been this way!'

'Hey!' said Raina.

'Don't pretend it isn't true,' said Meredith.

'You're no spring chicken yourself, Miss Soon-To-Be-A-Viking,' said Raina.

Pablo turned an inquisitive eye towards Meredith. 'Do I need to prepare a transfer of nation?'

Meredith fixed Pablo with a particularly fearsome stare.

'Should I take that as a yes? Or a no?' he said, innocently.

Meredith shook her head in disbelief.

Raina walked to a desk, on which sat an enormous old ledger entitled *Inter-Nation Marriages*.

'Oh look,' said Raina. 'It's fate.'

'You two are ridiculous,' said Meredith, walking over to look at the book anyway. 'When's this one from? See anyone we know?'

'Janet requested that. It covers the last five hundred years or so,' said Pablo.

'All that work,' said Raina, placing a hand on the volume, 'interviewing every demon, and painstakingly writing it all down.'

'It must have taken an age to input everything in databases ...' said Meredith.

'It brought back a number of fond memories,' said Pablo, 'and we had a small army dedicated to the task. Now, give me your hand and look into this retina scanner.'

'You can have my hand, but there's no way I'm letting you scan my eyeball,' said Raina.

'Oh, for heaven's sake ... why not?' said Pablo.

'You know very well why not. I have no desire for my unique demon eye to be recorded in your database of questionable security. Privacy's important.'

'I don't get this crap from the young ones,' said Pablo, electricity cracking between their hands as he took hold of her.

'Ow! No need to injure me,' said Raina.

'Okay, Raina Halabi, it's really you and you're officially registered to the Pagan nation.' Pablo made a series of taps on the tablet. 'Please sign here, unless you're against that now too.'

Raina rolled her eyes, took the pen, and signed.

Chapter 21

Raina and Meredith went downstairs, into the castle's main hall, where lunch was being served. The hall had banquet-style tables, food laid out in the middle of each, thirty or so demons milling around.

They chose a secluded spot near the door, watching others come and go as they munched their beef and horseradish sandwiches.

Janet entered, this time flanked by two other demons, one a young guy, the other an old woman. She made a beeline for the Registrar, who was holding court across the hall.

Janet bent low and said something in the Registrar's ear. The Registrar looked over at Raina and Meredith, then flicked his eyes back to Janet. He shrugged. Janet said something else into his ear—something that made him uncomfortable, judging by the way he shifted in his seat. The Registrar said something back, and Janet left, her two cronies still in tow.

'How old do you think she is?' asked Raina. Janet was brash; probably very young.

'Who knows,' said Meredith, 'but she's done something to impress Jamie. Otherwise she wouldn't be here … not with the threat of war.'

'Maybe,' said Raina, 'although with Jamie, it's not usually that simple.'

'I guess you'd know,' said Meredith.

Raina threw her a dark look.

'What are you going to do about Caspar?'

Raina took a deep breath. 'Maybe I'm misjudging Janet … turns out old demons can be brash too.'

'Haven't you punished him for long enough?'

'No.'

'He forgave you when you had an affair. Is what he did any worse than the things you've done to him?'

Raina was about to say yes, but in truth, Caspar's actions hadn't been worse; only the outcome had been.

'Caspar's honest, and dependable, and exceptional, and he loves you … will love you until the end of time. I know you love him too.'

'It's complicated,' said Raina, averting her gaze, balling her napkin ferociously in her hand.

'Is it? Really? '

'Raina, Meredith,' said a man's voice from behind them, making them jump. A portly, middle-aged Indian man with a mustache and glasses looked down at them.

'Malcolm!' said Meredith, standing to hug the Pagan's representative at the Registerium.

Raina stood and hugged him too. 'It's great to see you.'

'Likewise,' he said, and sat. 'You've ruffled Janet's feathers already, I hear.'

'I registered as a Pagan,' said Raina. 'She tried to stop me.'

'I take it you weren't deterred?'

'Of course not,' said Raina, 'but apparently, if I don't go and see Jamie, he's going to start a war.'

'Bloody Templars,' said Malcolm. 'Do you think they're bluffing?'

'No,' said Raina. 'They want war; any excuse will do.'

'Will you go?' asked Malcolm.

'Probably,' said Raina. 'According to Janet, Jamie has information that will interest me.'

'He could be lying,' said Meredith.

'He could,' agreed Raina, 'but that isn't his usual style.'

Raina and Meredith left the hall and followed Malcolm out of the castle. They drove a short distance past the castle, to an estate cottage Malcolm had booked for their use.

It was a sweet, cozy little stone house with tartan furnishings and fresh flowers. It smelled of whiskey and woodsmoke, and felt wonderful. A pang of disappointment rushed through Raina that she'd have to leave so soon.

After Malcolm left, Raina and Meredith spent the rest of the afternoon training in the garden. Raina was determined to get her body in shape, especially given all the talk of war.

They trained until they could take no more, collapsing onto the grass, sweaty, wobbly-legged, and full of endorphins.

'I'm going to hurt tomorrow,' said Raina, massaging her shoulder while looking at the pretty planted borders.

'That's the whole point,' said Meredith, 'but did you really have to kick me in the face?'

'Sorry. Just wanted to see if my leg would go up that high. Turns out I'm quite flexible.'

'I'm happy for you.'

A twig cracked behind them. They were on their feet in a second, turning to face the threat. But it wasn't a threat, it was Caspar.

'I'm going to have a shower,' said Meredith, 'and then join Malcolm at the castle.'

Neither Caspar nor Raina paid any attention as Meredith disappeared. They stood staring at each other, endless aching seconds ticking by, neither keen to make the first move.

'What are you doing here?' Raina eventually managed.

'Sofie and Henrik found me on the floor. They wish me to convey their gratitude. Apparently, it was the funniest thing they'd seen in some time.'

Raina couldn't help but crack a smile; Caspar would be teased for lifetimes.

'They also had a good laugh about you taking off in the plane without me.'

'How did you get here?'

'The Vikings lent me a plane.'

'That was nice of them.'

'They said it was the least they could do in return for such entertainment.'

'Why are you here?'

Caspar gave her an incredulous look. 'All the things I said before, when you were Amari, it was all true.'

'That you love me?' said Raina.

'I love you. I would do anything for you. All that matters to me, in this life—in any life—is you.'

'Love was never the problem. And you lie; something did matter more than me.'

Devastation contorted Caspar's face. 'I'm sorry for what happened, but … it wasn't all my fault.'

Raina turned away, rage filling her. She balled her fists. She wanted to scream, and kick, and hit, mostly because … he was right.

It wasn't only Caspar she was angry with—she was just as angry at herself. It was easier to project her hatred and loathing and despair onto someone else … onto Caspar.

'You had an affair,' said Caspar, pressing her without mercy. 'You promised me you would never do that again.'

'My child was murdered,' Raina countered, not turning around.

'It was my child too.'

'If you'd come with me when I asked, we would've been safe, hidden. We would've had our child.'

'I know,' said Caspar, his voice softening. 'I know.'

'The stuff with Jamie wasn't real. Rose and I were infiltrating the Templars. We knew they were up to something, and we wanted to find out what. You were away all the time, with the Buddhists, or the Shindus, or the Russian Spirituals … anywhere but with me.'

'I wanted you to come with me.'

Raina whirled around. 'Following you around the world like a lost puppy? I don't think so. I wanted a family, stability. I'd had enough of playing politics.'

'I was doing important work.'

'Really?' laughed Raina. 'Did any of it bear fruit? Are the Russians now firm allies? Or the Buddhists? Or anyone else for that matter?'

'We're closer than before,' Caspar said. 'And turns out *you* hadn't had your fill of politics either. So much so, you had another affair … with *Jamie*.'

'I was trying to find out what he was doing. I was trying to prevent a war. I hated every second of it. I hated lying to you. I hated his hands on me, his smug self-satisfaction. I was a possession—a powerful woman he'd conquered. I put an end to it as soon as I could.'

'Have you got any idea what that felt like?' said Caspar. 'Sitting in a meeting with the Holy Star, hearing that Jamie was bragging my wife was his? That my baby was his?'

'It was our baby,' said Raina, harshly. 'Yours and mine.' Tears filled her eyes, then spilled over. 'I was going to tell you … I never wanted you to find out that way.'

Caspar hesitated. He watched her for a beat, two, then strode towards her, wrapping his arms around her.

She didn't fight him. She clung to him, breathing him in, feeling whole for the first time in a hundred years, shattered by the knowledge she would have to leave him again so soon.

The time she'd spent with him as Amari was all her brain would let her see. The hatred and hurt and disappointment of the past was all buried under an ocean of love.

'I'm sorry,' she choked.

'I'm sorry too,' said Caspar, squeezing her tighter. 'I shouldn't have let you run away when I confronted you about the affair. I should've gone after you. But I thought you needed time to cool off … I thought chasing you would make it worse. And then I felt your anguish, like a stab in my gut, and I ran, cold from fear. I'd never felt a magic call like it.'

'It was too late the minute I stepped outside,' said Raina. 'Slayers. They were waiting for me. I barely managed to pull out my knife … there was only one thing I could do.'

'They were panicking when I got there,' said Caspar. 'Shouting at each other, saying it wasn't supposed to go like it did, trying to move your body. They ran when they saw me.'

Raina pulled back to look into his eyes. 'But I was already dead ... the eternal death ritual wouldn't have worked. Why did they want my body?'

'I don't know. I moved you inside and called Rose. She said she'd felt something was wrong and was already on her way. By the time she got to us, I was dead too.'

'They came back and killed you?'

'I had a heart attack.'

'Gods, no.' She pressed her head to his chest, and they stood in silence, clinging to each other.

Raina knew she had to tell him the rest, but there was nothing she wanted to do less. Dread mounted. She started shaking, and grabbed handfuls of his shirt to steady herself.

'What is it?' asked Caspar, making her look at him.

'There's something else.'

Caspar sucked in a breath, visibly bracing for impact.

There was no way to soften the blow, so she just came out with it. 'In my last life, Rose and I continued our work infiltrating the Templars. I was ... with Jamie. He thinks I love him, and I ... I never denied that the baby was his.'

Caspar went rigid, pulling away. He looked at her as though she'd stabbed him in the heart.

'For a whole lifetime, you refused to so much as look at me. I was falling apart ... desolate ... and all that time, you were sleeping with *him*?'

'Caspar ... I was playing a part.'

'You think that makes it okay?'

'If it prevented war ... and ... Caspar ...' she looked imploringly at him, knowing, from hard-won experience, it was best to rip off the band aid. 'I have to go back. Janet—Jamie's envoy here—says if I don't, he's going to start a war.'

'So you're going to run back to his side? Still not done playing politics ...? Or maybe there's more to it than that ...'

'No! Caspar ...'

He shook his head, yanked free of her grasp, and walked away.

Raina went inside, sank into a tartan-covered armchair, and cried. In her last life, she hadn't shed so much as a tear over the deaths of herself and her baby. She'd awoken uncharacteristically early—at eighteen— and had been so, so angry. She'd wanted revenge, to assign blame, to kill those responsible.

A hunter in Rose's employ had found her. Rose had convinced Raina to continue their work ... to find out what the Templars were up to.

Rose had pushed Raina to give herself space from Caspar, had said they both needed time to cool off. In truth, Rose had wanted Caspar out of the way, so Raina would be free to seduce Jamie. So she could play on the notion that Jamie had lost a baby too, so they could grieve together.

Raina wasn't an idiot, she'd known this was Rose's motive. But that hadn't stopped her from grabbing hold with both hands. She'd taken the easy path, instead of confronting her own part in her baby's death, instead of grieving honestly, with Caspar. Not only that, but she'd blamed him.

Raina had told herself she was doing the right thing, for the greater good, trying to prevent war. But really, she was a coward. A coward unable to face her own feelings. A coward who'd let another man have her—had willingly given herself to him—just to try and numb the pain.

She'd refused to see Caspar, because she couldn't face him, or the pain. She would most likely never have another child ... children to demons were so rare. Their actions, hers and Caspar's, had killed their one and only baby.

She buried her head in her hands. Tears poured from her eyes, great racking sobs shaking her body, her lungs gasping for air.

She played the moments of her death over and over in her mind. If only she'd stormed upstairs. If only she'd fought longer with Caspar. If only she'd never had an affair with Jamie in the first place. If only she'd been paying more attention when she'd opened the front door. Centuries of training negated by hateful, rageful thoughts. Raina: the formidable force. What a joke. She couldn't even protect her own baby.

At some point, Meredith came back. She did her best to offer comfort, but there was no comfort that would help. She took Raina to one of the small but immaculately decorated bedrooms, pulled back the crisp white covers of the twin bed, and tucked her in. She asked if there was anything Raina needed.

Raina shook her head. *A time machine ... that's what she needed.*

Memories and destructive thoughts plagued her, and eventually, when she fell asleep, she found nothing but hateful, feverish dreams.

The following morning, Rose, Gemma, Malcolm, and Caspar arrived on Meredith and Raina's doorstep.

Rose and Gemma had taken the overnight sleeper train from London, and Caspar had slept on Malcolm's sofa.

Raina tried to catch Caspar's arm as he walked in, but he shrugged her off. By the looks of him, he hadn't slept much either.

Rose placed a hand on Raina's arm. 'I can't tell you how good it is to have you back. To say I've missed you would be a terrible understatement.' Rose pulled her into an embrace, something she rarely did.

'It's good to see you,' said Raina. But her eyes were on Caspar, watching his every move.

Seeing him yesterday had broken something in her, had demolished the dam holding her emotions. She loved him. She had always loved him. Their demon lives spun around each other, their souls, like magnets, pulled back together in every lifetime. She couldn't go to America with things like this between them. Not even if it meant war.

Rose began to talk, but Raina missed chunks of what she said. Her conscious mind had no room for anything but Caspar. She watched him from across the sitting room, taking in his tired eyes, disheveled hair, drawn features, and stubble. She wanted to kiss every inch of his face, hold him, run her hands through his hair, chase away his pain.

'It's suspicious,' said Rose. 'The Registerium and the Templars are too close. Janet has privileges the rest of us are denied … access to records and such.'

Raina watched Caspar's hands ball into fists and then straighten, again and again. She longed for those fingers to entwine with hers.

'They seem to be searching for something,' said Rose.

'Or at least they were,' added Malcolm. 'Janet's less frantic of late.'

Raina scrutinized Caspar's eyes, which were fixed on Rose. His eyes were like home; they had been for lifetimes. Her single constant in a world of shifting sands.

'And from what the Holy Star told me,' said Rose, 'the Slayers' stronghold is right under the noses of the Templars. It's too much to believe that's a coincidence.'

'Wait,' said Meredith, 'you think the Templars are working with the Slayers? The Slayers want to kill demons … *all* demons, including Templars.'

'Unless they've come to some arrangement,' said Rose.

'Do you think that's possible?' said Meredith.

'You've lived long enough to know we can't rule anything out,' said Rose.

Raina watched as Caspar's face scrunched in annoyance—he'd always hated the Templars.

She wished he'd look at her. Then he did, his eyes meeting hers: two pools of deepest brown, with gold flecks visible, even from across the room, at least to her.

He held her gaze, and she saw nothing there but devastation. Not only had she treated him in the worst of all possible ways, but she'd told him she needed to do it again. Their marriage—their eternal vows—lay in tatters between them, and it was all down to her.

'If Raina doesn't meet Jamie, war is guaranteed,' said Rose. 'I don't like it, not at all, but I like the alternative less.'

'Jamie's slippery,' said Meredith. 'He always has a hidden plan, an ulterior motive. Raina could be walking into a trap.'

Neither Raina nor Caspar looked away from each other. Raina hoped he could see her regret, her own anguish. She hoped he knew that she loved him, had never stopped, never would.

Eyes are a window to the soul, everyone knows that, but souls are old and complex things. Raina caught a glimpse of Caspar's ravaged, tattered soul, and a wave of nausea hit her. She'd been the one to do that ... the one he trusted most. She prayed he could see inside her, could see her depths were shredded too.

'What if the Templars are working with the Slayers, and they hand Raina over?' said Gemma, silent until now.

'In that case,' said Rose, 'Raina would almost certainly wind up dead. The final kind.'

It was only then that the room turned their attention to Raina and Caspar, who were still looking at each other, their eyes locked.

The others said nothing as they left, Raina and Caspar barely noticing. They stood there, neither moving, seconds ticking by. It had been over a hundred years since they'd been like this, together, neither racing for the exit.

'I never loved him,' said Raina eventually. 'I've never loved anyone except you. And what I was doing, in my last two lives, it had nothing to do with love, or attraction, or anything other than trying to find out what the Templars were doing. I was trying to protect us all. That doesn't make it right, but it's something I know you understand. Your sense of duty and mine, it drives our actions ... it's what put us here.'

'I've never made someone believe I loved them— or had sex with someone—out of a sense of duty.'

Raina looked away. Every time Jamie had kissed her, touched her, licked her, pressed her down, pushed inside her, a little part of her had splintered. Jamie had never forced anything on her; she'd been a willing participant. She'd even taken pleasure from it, the carnal, physical kind. But she'd hated herself too, felt violated, wished there was another way.

'I know,' she said, 'you never would … couldn't. You wear your love for me like a badge, and I love that you do. But I'm different … closed. I lock away my love, so people wonder.'

'I wonder,' whispered Caspar.

Raina's heart broke. Her eyes filled with tears. 'I will love you for all time.'

'A throwaway, frivolous love, to be tossed into the background when excitement beckons. A backup, reserve love.'

'Caspar,' she sobbed, moving carefully towards him, tears running down her cheeks, 'that is precisely the opposite of what you are.'

He turned his head away.

'Caspar.' She took his hand. He neither snatched it away, nor gripped her fingers. She held it in both of hers. 'I've never known how to tell you. Despite hundreds of years, I've never learned how to make you understand what you are to me. You are everything to me that I am to you. We are matched. In everything. Including our love.'

Caspar pulled his hand back, turned away, walked to the window.

'I want to believe you,' he said, staring at the garden, 'but this isn't the first time.'

Raina choked on his words. 'How can I show you?'

'Don't go. Stay here, with me. Find another way.' He still refused to look at her.

'And cause a war?'

'Jamie's bluffing.'

'You know as well as I do, he's not.'

Caspar ran a hand over his face, grasped hold of his hair, threw his arm away, spun towards her.

'Then yes, let him declare war. That's on him, not you. He's going to do it either way.'

'We don't know that. We don't know what he's going to say.'

'And if his price is you? For all time, as his wife? What then?'

'I'll find a way back to you.'

'If he puts you in chains? Or hands you over to the Slayers?'

'He won't.'

Caspar exploded towards her. 'You don't know that. You haven't seen him in decades ... maybe he's not in love with you anymore. Maybe he was *pretending*, like you were. Maybe he knew it would weaken the Pagans if he could steal you away. Maybe you're playing right into his hands.'

His words were cruel, but she held his gaze. He was close enough that she could smell his scent, feel his body heat. She looked up into his eyes, swayed towards him, put her hands on his chest.

'Raina ...' he choked. He placed his hands on top of hers, bowed his head. 'I can't lose you again.'

'You won't,' she whispered.

He pulled her into him. They wrapped their arms around each other, Raina's silent tears soaking his shirt.

'You never cry,' he said into her ear, stroking her hair.

Raina laughed, squeezing him tighter.

They stood like that, minutes ticking by. The world finally felt right, like all their puzzle pieces had lined up at last.

'Don't go,' said Caspar, 'Jamie ...'

Raina looked up into his eyes. 'We are matched, in everything, including our sense of duty. I promise you I'll do everything I can to keep Jamie away from me. But if the choice is between war or personal sacrifice, we both know what I have to do.'

Chapter 22

Raina arrived in New York with little fanfare. A limo waited for her at JFK, whisking her to an achingly cool warehouse apartment in Chelsea. She could think of little but Caspar as they battled through the Manhattan traffic.

He'd held her for such a long time, silently mulling over the options, and had come to the only conclusion available: Raina had to see Jamie. For the good of not only the Pagan nation, but of everyone who'd be caught up in a war.

Caspar had kissed her, told her he loved her, told her not to die. He'd pulled her down onto the sofa, onto his lap, had run his hands through her hair, and clasped her to him. She'd buried her head in his chest, holding on as though, if she did it hard enough, she could stay with him. But Janet had shown up at the cottage, demanding that Raina make a decision.

'Tell Jamie I'll meet him,' Raina had said. She'd wanted to get rid of Janet before she saw Caspar.

'Good,' said Janet, primly.

Raina had wanted to punch her in the face.

'The jet's ready. The car will be here in fifteen minutes.'

Thankfully, Janet didn't accompany her; she'd stayed at the Registerium, to continue her work ... whatever that was.

Raina had hastily packed her bag, Caspar helping, so they could spend their last precious minutes pressed together. They'd heard the car pull up outside, kissed one final time, then ripped themselves apart.

'This way, please,' said a Black man of around sixty. He was formal, curt. 'Jamie has assigned you this loft. I'll be here whenever you need me. Jamie's hosting a dinner tonight, in your honor. It's black tie, and he's taken the liberty of providing a dress for you. It's in the closet.'

Raina's mind raced to take in all the details. 'Where will this dinner be held?' she asked.

'In the opposite warehouse: Jamie's private residence.'

Of course. Her loft's enormous windows meant Jamie could spy on her whenever he saw fit. 'What time am I expected?'

'Seven o'clock,' he said. 'I'll escort you.'

The man left, giving her a few hours before she had to get ready. It had already been a long day, and she'd barely slept the night before. She lay on the chic king-size bed, not bothering to look at the dress she would have to wear, and fell asleep.

Raina woke to the insistent sound of knocking at her bedroom door.

'Come in,' she called sleepily, refusing to take her head off the pillow.

'You're going to be late,' said the man from earlier. 'Please get ready; I'll be in the kitchen if you need anything.'

Raina suppressed her anger. She pried herself out of bed and walked to the adjoining bathroom to shower. She didn't have time to wash her hair, nor did she want to give Jamie the satisfaction of looking like she'd made a big effort, but she needed to shower.

She closed her eyes as the curtain of steaming water hit her, relishing its soothing impact.

She eventually forced herself to turn off the water. She wrapped herself in a towel, applied a light covering of makeup, tied her hair back into a severe bun, and went to the closet to see what costume she'd have to wear.

She threw open the doors and rolled her eyes. Of course, Jamie was never one to miss an opportunity to make a statement.

Raina stepped into the vast open space of Jamie's loft. The kitchen, dining, and seating areas were one big open-plan space, and the furniture had been pushed back to allow room for dancing. The guests—about forty of them—were mingling, sipping champagne, several of them huddling conspiratorially together.

A hush fell over the room as they noticed Raina. Her tight, floor-length, backless gown of gold shimmered in the soft light. Raina surveyed them, taking a moment to study each and every one, trying in vain to identify them.

Her eyes settled on a tall, well-built man with olive skin and a perfect sweep of dark, floppy hair. A blonde woman in a tight maroon dress stood before him, her back to Raina. There was something familiar about the woman, but Raina could only see her back as she leant into Jamie, whispering in his ear. Jamie's hand rested casually on her waist, but his eyes, stormy and grey, found and then fixed on Raina.

The woman left, but Jamie barely seemed to notice, his lips spreading into a broad, confident smile. It was the smile of a spoilt rich kid, who knew he'd got his way again.

'Darling, Raina,' said Jamie, walking towards her, arms outstretched. 'My God, I've missed you.'

Raina's heart raced. She willed it to still, but biology worked in mysterious ways. Just seeing him made her feel as though a live wire had been touched to her skin; there had always been something raw, feral between them. He reached her, placed his hands on her arms, and gooseflesh spread out from his touch. Her hair stood on end. He kissed her cheek, sparks of desire pooling low in her belly.

But when his eyes held hers, her blood ran cold. He was a snake, a force of destruction, driven by lust, treachery, and power. He was exciting, that was for sure, in the way of a ticking timebomb, set to explode. A drug with the most unbelievable high, followed by a low that would last lifetimes.

'It must have been terrible,' said Jamie, 'for you to have been kidnapped as you were.'

His hand moved to her back, lingering there.

'And I'm led to believe Caspar started a relationship with you while you were asleep ... most uncouth.' He projected his voice, giving his audience a show.

'I was never kidnapped,' said Raina, with equal volume, 'as you well know.'

'But you threw him out on his ass as soon as you awoke. Not surprising, after what he caused.'

Raina's insides lurched. 'Your spy network is admirable.'

'Indeed, it is. Let me get you a drink,' he said, offering her his arm.

She took it, hating that she had to, hating even more that her body liked the proximity.

They walked to the bar, most guests openly gaping, the rest watching from behind a thin pretense.

Jamie handed Raina a glass of champagne, took one for himself, then led her to a seating area. He sat on a vulgar red velvet loveseat and pulled her down beside him.

Raina sat at as much of an angle as she was able, but even so, their legs were firmly pressed together. He placed a hand on her thigh, tracing circles with his fingers. She had to fight the temptation to break every bone in his hand.

Her eyes flicked to the leather cuff on his wrist—every Templar wore one—and her mind conjured images of her attackers. She wondered if any of them were here, in this room; that was the kind of thing Jamie would do.

'Now, my love, tell me about this lifetime.'

'It's been dull,' said Raina, 'and yours?'

'I awoke quite early, at the age of ten. I contacted my caretaker leader, she came to get me, and everything's been wonderful ever since. I've achieved a lot. Funny how some lives are so much better than others, don't you think?'

Raina gave a half nod.

'I missed you,' he said, leaning close, so no one else could hear.

He was so close she could feel his breath on her ear. He bit her neck, not hard enough to leave a mark, but hard enough to send a warning: *You are mine, and at my mercy*.

Raina's hand went to his neck. 'I missed you too,' she breathed, dragging her fingernails down his delicate skin. *I might be at your mercy, but don't forget who I am.*

Jamie huffed a laugh into her ear. 'My God, I love you. I'd forgotten how much.'

'You forgot me?' She pressed her fingernails harder.

Jamie growled. 'We belong together. We always have.'

'Who knew you were such a romantic?'

He kissed her jaw. 'You know it's true.'

'Do I?'

He kissed her hard on the lips. She bit him, just enough to cause pain. He pushed her roughly away, laughed, brought his lips to her ear, ran his nose along it. 'I want nothing more than to fuck you right here, in front of everyone.'

'No, thank you.'

'Shame. Later then.' He pecked her on the cheek then pulled back, casting his eyes around the room, forcing their fascinated audience to avert their gaze. 'I want you to join me ... to join the Templar nation. I'll drop all grievances against the Pagans.'

'What grievances are those?'

'Stealing you away from me.'

Raina laughed. 'Go on.'

'Badmouthing the Templars to the Registerium, and other nations. Poking their noses into my affairs. Accusing me of playing human politics, of manipulating stock markets.'

'Which of course, you would *never* do.'

'If I had, surely the Registerium would have imposed fines and sanctions. Have any such measures been taken?'

'Well then, you must be entirely innocent.'

He cocked an eyebrow. 'Not necessarily the word I would've chosen.'

'No?' She looked up at him from under her lashes.

'We could rule this world together.'

'This world?'

'It's right there, for the taking.'

'And the other nations? What of them?'

Jamie sniggered. 'As though the great Raina Halabi cares about them. Every war has casualties, but many—the wise ones at least—will come to our side.'

A shiver ran down Raina's spine. This was a trap ... even if she was yet to figure out its exact nature. Jamie would never have told her these things if he had even the slightest worry she would leave. The question was whether he was planning to physically detain her, or if he had some other method of assuring compliance, aside from their supposed love.

'You have the numbers?' Raina asked. She had to find out as much as she could.

A strange smile pulled at Jamie's lips. '*We* do.'

'How? Even with the most persistent of recruitment drives, the other nations are strong, especially if they unite, which they surely will.'

'We have allies.'

'Who?'

'All in good time, my love. First, I have a surprise for you.'

Jamie nodded to someone by the door.

Raina felt sick. She was being ambushed, and there was nothing she could do about it.

The door swung open, and, to her horror, Dean walked in. Dean, her ex-husband. Dean, the good, kind, honest man who she'd loved—at least the part of her who was Amari. He looked disoriented, confused, angry.

'Jade,' he said to the girl beside him—his sister—the girl in the maroon dress. 'What's going on?'

Raina knew she'd recognized her ... not a gangly gazelle any longer ... Her blood rushed in her ears. She had to get ahead of whatever the hell was going on, but she'd been asleep, she had no idea what Jamie was playing at, what he wanted ...

Dean locked eyes with Raina, whose brow was furrowed.

She shook her head, little movements back and forth, showing him she was in the dark too. She fought the urge to act, to do something rash; Jamie obviously wanted a reaction.

Raina looked back at Jamie, whose eyes were tracing the slit of Jade's dress, a slit that extended almost all the way to the apex of her thighs. Was Jamie sleeping with Jade? Was this some bizarre love square? If so, what was Jamie's purpose?

Jamie stood, walking to the centre of the room. 'Dean, you are most welcome,' he said.

Dean whirled around, looking at the exit, but his way was blocked by two burly demons.

'What the hell is going on here?' Dean said loudly, turning back to where Jamie stood. Jade was now on Jamie's arm. 'Jade?'

Jade looked adoringly up at Jamie, her eyes the eyes of a demon. Jade was a demon? How long had she been awake?

Raina schooled her face into neutrality; Jamie was watching her now.

'Surprise!' he said.

'Jamie, what the fuck is going on?' said Raina.

'I brought you a present. You can thank me any time.'

'Dean? He's my present?'

'Yes. He ran off straight after your marriage. His disappearance allowed the Pagans to sweep in and claim you. Unfortunately, Tamsin awoke too late. Of course, you know her as Jade. Such a strange coincidence, don't you think? That a Templar demon should have been lying dormant right alongside you? Maybe your demon souls recognized each other, even if your conscious minds did not.'

It was too strange for words. 'I suppose that's possible,' said Raina, at a loss for anything more articulate.

'But you must be angry,' said Jamie.

'Angry?'

'Yes. Angry at Dean. After all, if he hadn't left you on your wedding night, you would have gone on your honeymoon. Tamsin would have awoken in time to bring you straight to me. The Pagans never would've got hold of you.'

'Dean had no idea about any of that. He was just doing his job,' said Raina.

She was pleased to find she no longer felt anything but fondness for Dean, even if he was looking at her with hatred in his eyes.

'Nevertheless, you could keep him as a plaything.'

'No, thank you,' said Raina.

'But playthings offer such stress relief,' said Jamie, running his hand down Tamsin's back.

'Take your hands off her,' said Dean, moving towards them.

His way was once again blocked by Jamie's cronies.

'Jade, what are you doing? Why's he calling you Tamsin?'

'Oh, big brother, I'm not so young and innocent as you might think,' she said.

'You're eighteen!'

'If only that were true,' Tamsin laughed, running a hand down Jamie's arm. She was all hyena these days.

'What?' said Dean. He looked to Raina for an explanation.

There was nothing Raina could say that would sound in the least bit sane, so she said nothing. What was Jamie's goal? What did he want? She cast around for clues.

'We should really cut him some slack,' said Jamie. 'Dean's been very useful to us.'

Raina didn't ask how. If Jamie wanted to tell her, let him come to her.

'Let us dance in his honor. And who better to dance with Dean than his former wife?'

The music changed from calming, classical tones to upbeat jazz. Jamie pulled Tamsin to him, dipping her back over his arm, her bare leg extending skyward.

Dean looked appalled. Raina stayed in her seat.

'Come on,' said Jamie, 'I'd hate to have to compel you; it would really ruin the mood.'

They both stayed where they were.

Two demons went to Dean and two to Raina, grabbing their arms, maneuvering them to the dance floor. Dean went, swearing extensively, demanding they take their hands off him. But Raina refused to be manhandled by babies.

She had her two on the ground in one swift movement, her muscles protesting after the heavy workout with Meredith the day before. She left them on the floor, her warning glare keeping them down.

Jamie laughed loudly.

Raina walked to Dean, but they didn't dance.

'What the fuck is going on?' Dean asked, his tone low.

'Jamie's a ... dangerous man. And your sister's been working with him for ... some time.'

'She's eighteen.'

'Age is meaningless,' countered Raina. 'There are five-year-olds in Africa who have to fend entirely for themselves and their siblings. She's eighteen; you'd be unwise to underestimate her.'

'Why did he call you Raina? And what was he talking about? Pagans? Templars? Demons?'

'You wouldn't believe me if I told you. All you need to know is that you're in danger.'

'Then so is Jade.'

'Jade isn't who you think she is.'

'What's happened to you?' he asked. 'You're … different, somehow.'

'My demon self awoke.'

'What the fuck?'

'Exactly. We need to get you out of here, and you need to forget the notion that Tamsin—Jade—is going to come with you. She's the one who got you into this mess.'

Jamie left Tamsin and strode towards them. 'No dancing?' he said.

'No,' said Raina.

Jamie held out his hand to Raina, puffed up with the belief she would take it. Of course, she had little choice, so she went to him, the air between them taut.

Her survival almost certainly relied on keeping Jamie sweet, and he was testing her. So she danced, not holding back, holding his gaze, following his lead, letting him believe she was enjoying every minute of it.

'I thought you'd be happy with my gift,' said Jamie.

Raina raised an eyebrow. 'He's human. He'll live one single life. What fun could someone like that provide *me*?'

'What would you have me do with him then?'

'Send him away,' said Raina, sensing the trap, 'and forget all about him. He's not worth the time of day.

And that fact will cause him more distress than anything we could ever do.'

Jamie stopped dancing. 'You still have feelings for him ... I would never have believed it.'

Raina gave him a look. 'You're missing the point,' she said, mocking him. 'I have no feelings either way. I don't love him, I don't hate him, I'm not annoyed at the way he treated me. I couldn't care less about him. Do I like your gift? No, I don't. How's he a gift for me? I'd got rid of him, and now you've brought him back to me, making an issue of him, wasting my time. If anything, he's a gift for you.'

'For me?'

'You're jealous. You've driven yourself crazy thinking about his hands on me, his lips on mine, his eyes on my naked flesh. *You* want revenge. I couldn't care less.'

'Maybe part of me's jealous, but not of some human.'

Raina laughed, cruelly. 'Caspar? Your own sources told you I threw him out.'

'You left me for him once before.'

'He killed my baby,' she said, letting him see the tears in her eyes.

A look of triumph flashed across Jamie's features. It disappeared again in an instant. 'Then why did you register as a Pagan?'

'Because I am a Pagan; I almost always have been.'

'What about us?'

'What about us? You seem to be entertaining yourself with others,' she said, throwing a look at Tamsin.

'Who's jealous now?' he laughed, taking hold of her face, moving in to kiss her.

Raina pulled back, swiping his hand away. 'You think it's going to be so easy?'

Jamie laughed. 'Oh, my dear Raina, I have missed you. What will it take?' he asked.

But something in his manner worried her. Something that suggested he already had her, whether she liked it or not.

'For starters, I need to be the only one.'

'For starters?' he mocked.

'Why do I get the feeling you're not taking me seriously?'

'Come on, my dear, let's dance. Everything will become clear in just a short while.'

Raina's stomach dropped. He had a trump card, and she had no idea what it was.

Chapter 23

Caspar and the rest of the Pagan leadership sat around the kitchen table at Cloister Cottage.

'You let her go?' said Jon, indignant. 'Without a fight?'

'Believe me,' said Caspar, 'it wasn't without a fight. But she was right, there was no other way to avoid war.'

'So you just ... let her go?' said Jon.

'Evidently,' said Caspar, scowling.

'Like he could have stopped her anyway,' said Meredith.

'I guess that's true,' said Jon.

'So, what now?' asked Elliot, looking to Rose.

'Now, we wait,' said Rose. 'Raina made it to the States. She's in Manhattan. We can't do much but wait for her to make contact.'

'Like lemmings,' said Elliot.

'Raina's done this kind of work before,' said Rose. 'We have to trust her. Any action we take could compromise her cover.'

'Do you know what Jamie wants?' asked Gemma.

Rose took a deep, laborious breath. 'Honestly, I don't. Although he's always been single-minded when it comes to Raina.'

Meredith laughed. 'He's infatuated with her.'

Caspar flinched.

'Sorry, but it's true.'

'We don't know if that's still the case,' said Rose, firmly.

'Do you really think it's that simple?' asked Gemma.

'People have gone to war for less,' said Rose, 'but with everything going on with the Templars, it's hard to believe there isn't more to it.'

'Raina's been the architect of many wars,' said Meredith. 'Maybe he wants her as his general.'

'I think that's an option,' said Rose.

'But for that, he'd have to be sure of her loyalty,' said Caspar, giving Rose an appraising look. 'It's one thing to summon her to him, when she thinks she's preventing a war. It's entirely another to keep her there as his ally. Raina's a loyal Pagan … he must have something making him believe otherwise …'

'Caspar, I'm keeping nothing from you,' said Rose, a warning in her tone.

Caspar banged his fist against the table. 'Could he have leverage over her?' He ran his hand through his hair, stood abruptly, paced to the fire. 'Does he have leverage?'

'There is no leverage, as far as I know,' said Rose. 'But Raina spent time with Jamie in her last life, and the one before. They grew close. Raina assured me she was acting only for the Pagans, that she was loyal to us. She said her relationship with Jamie was a cross she had to bear for the greater good.'

'Did you believe her?' asked Jon.

'Yes, I truly did,' said Rose. 'She gave me no reason to suspect otherwise.'

'Do you think it's as simple as Jamie being in love with her?' said Jon. 'I mean, there's a chance *she* could be …'

Caspar whirled around, glaring at Jon. 'She is not in love with him.'

'I didn't say she was,' he said. 'But there's a chance she could be lying to us, and Jamie might *believe* that she is, even if she's not.'

'I've had enough. I'm going,' said Caspar, striding for the exit.

The remaining demons looked at each other, sitting in silence until he'd gone.

'Did she love Jamie?' Elliot asked Rose.

Rose shook her head. 'I don't think she did. There was chemistry between them, to be sure. Raina enjoyed the thrill after so many lifetimes with Caspar. But Raina would choose Caspar over any other, in any lifetime.'

'Even after what happened, with the baby ...?' asked Jon.

Every one of them scowled at him.

'What? I'm only being thorough.'

'Even then,' said Rose. 'Raina needed time to come to terms with what happened, that's all. She's loyal to us. Raina's been our mole inside the Templars for the last hundred years, but right now, she's as clueless as we are. The fact is, we have no idea what Jamie has up his sleeve. We can do nothing but wait. And Meredith, for Gods' sake go and get Caspar, before he does something stupid.'

Caspar stormed through the great hall, threw open the front door, and stepped onto the small, cobbled street outside. He slammed the door behind him with considerable force, then put his head down, fuming as he headed out into the city.

Does Raina love Jamie? Will Raina join the Templars? What's Jamie's plan? What can I do? The thoughts repeated, again and again.

Caspar turned onto another side street, barely noticing the man standing to one side, chatting on his phone, nor did he see the second man, standing in the shadows opposite the first. It was late, and dark.

It was lifetimes of training that made him react, without thinking, when he sensed a presence too close. He ducked, then spun around, racing back the way he'd come.

Idiot. He knew the cottage was compromised, should've been more careful.

A weight crashed into Caspar's back. He went flying to the floor, a blinding, stabbing pain coming from his shoulder. He was disorientated, didn't know what had happened, didn't see his attacker pull the knife from his shoulder and try to thrust it down towards his ribs.

The second man caught the arm of the first. 'We need him alive, remember?'

The one with the knife grunted, shifting his weight.

Caspar's mind frantically calculated his options, desperately trying to figure out an escape.

'Get the cuffs.'

'Here.'

Caspar felt cool metal slip around his wrists, which had been pulled behind his back. *Shit. Shit. Shit.* How could he have been so stupid?

'Let him go,' said a bored female voice.

Meredith. Thank the Gods; he was saved.

The men looked at her and laughed. 'One of you, two of us,' said the man with the knife.

'I know, it's unfair on you, but you did pick the fight,' said Meredith, walking towards them.

The first man threw his knife at Meredith. She sidestepped, pulled out her own blade, and threw, all in one fluid motion. Her attacker went down hard. He was already dead.

'Knife-throwing's one thing,' said the second man, 'but hand-to-hand combat, with a man? You really think you can win?'

Caspar rolled over, blinding pain making him cry out. The man was young, cocky, but even so, no demon would make such a ludicrous statement. Caspar could see his eyes, was close enough to feel his presence. This was a human, and an uneducated one at that.

Meredith approached him with light, even steps. 'Come over here and we'll see, shall we?'

The man took a couple of halting steps in Meredith's direction, then thought better of it, turning to run.

Meredith was on him in a second. 'Oh no you don't,' she said, pulling him to the ground. 'You're going to talk.'

Meredith tied the man to a chair in the great hall for his interrogation. She started in a pleasant fashion, wishing for a simple business transaction.

'Look,' she said, 'if you tell me everything I need to know, we'll let you go. If you don't, I'll have to use other, less amiable means, and you probably won't leave here alive.'

'I'll never tell you a thing. If I did, they'd kill me anyway.'

'Then the only option you have is to defect to us,' said Meredith, with an easy smile. 'Problem solved.'

'You people are an abomination,' the man spat. 'God put you here as a trial for his loyal servants. I was put on this earth to kill you.'

'Is that so?' said Meredith. 'Then why are you working with the Templars?'

'Templars are the closest of your kind to our God.'

Idiot. That was too easy.

'Your God seems a little cutthroat. What happened to loving thy neighbor?' said Meredith.

'You're demons, sent to test us. You're not my neighbor.'

'Well, much as I'd love to sit here all day, continuing this pointless theological discussion ...' she said, then slammed a dagger through his hand. It bit into the wooden arm of the chair beneath.

The man screamed, then started praying.

'What do you know about Jamie's plans?' asked Meredith. 'What does he want with Raina?'

The man eventually stopped screaming. He tipped back his head and looked Meredith in the eye, panting through the pain. He laughed a slow, vicious laugh. 'That bitch is putty in our hands.'

A crack sounded from the man's mouth. Meredith knew in an instant what it was. She rushed to him, tipped his head forward, propped his mouth open. But it was too late—the capsule hidden in his teeth had broken. The poison would do its work.

Chapter 24

Jamie finally stopped dancing. He pulled Raina off the dance floor and back to the loveseat. Tamsin and Dean sat opposite, Tamsin looking every inch the seductress, her bare legs on display as she lounged.

Dean looked furious, although his rage was tempered by fear. Tamsin ignored him, her eyes tracking Jamie's every move.

'Darling Tamsin, come here,' said Jamie, reaching for her, pulling her onto his lap. Raina made to get up, but Jamie stopped her with a hand on her arm. 'I think you should stay, my dear.'

This was all so very wrong. Jamie would never have treated her this way in their past lives. He'd been too worried she would walk away, back to Caspar. She looked directly at him, her eyes flashing with rage.

Jamie was delighted. 'Jealous?' he said.

'Jamie, what's going on?' said Raina, as Jamie ran his hand over Tamsin's bare leg.

Raina flicked her gaze to Dean, who was watching, his fists balled in fury.

'I'm just having some fun before the evening's main event,' said Jamie, burying his face in Tamsin's neck.

Raina longed to get up—both Jamie and Tamsin had body parts pressed against her. It made her nauseated.

'You can join us, if you'd like,' said Jamie.

'Not really my thing,' said Raina, looking away.

Tamsin giggled at whatever Jamie did next, one of her feet flying past Raina's head.

Raina turned to scowl at them, but found Jamie kissing his way down Tamsin's décolletage, every kiss taking him further down the v of her dress, towards her breasts, which were pushed-up and mostly exposed. Tamsin arched her back, encouraging him. Jamie plunged his face into her cleavage, and Tamsin's leg flew once more past Raina's nose.

Dean sat bolt upright, rigid, pale.

'Jade,' he said, standing up. 'What the hell are you doing? And you, pervert. Get your hands off my eighteen-year-old sister.'

Jamie didn't so much as look up.

Tamsin giggled, her hand in Jamie's hair. 'If only I were eighteen. And my name's Tamsin.'

'What the fuck?' said Dean. 'Has he drugged you? Brainwashed you? Is this a cult?'

Dean grabbed Tamsin and pulled her off Jamie, but she was up and attacking him in the blink of an eye. Dean dropped to the floor, clutching his now-bleeding nose.

'Touch me again, and I'll kill you,' Tamsin said, sitting back down.

Jamie resumed.

Dean laughed, the way anyone would laugh if their naïve younger sister threatened to kill them.

Raina winced.

Tamsin stood, drawing a dagger from a holster on her leg. 'I know you're a stupid human,' she said, putting the knife to his throat, 'but I'm a *demon*. If I say I'll kill you, you should know that I mean it.'

Dean was horrified. He looked to Raina.

Raina shrugged. What solace could she offer him? Maybe Jamie hoped Raina would come to Dean's defense ... that there would be a fight between Tamsin and Raina. Or maybe he hoped Raina would kick Tamsin's arse for sitting on Jamie's lap; he loved a jealous woman. But Raina was neither jealous nor prepared to give him the satisfaction. She might be in Jamie's power, but that didn't mean she had to play his games.

'Okay,' said Dean, holding up his hands in defeat, 'I believe you. But why am I here? What do you want with me?'

Jamie stood and clapped his hands. '*Excellent* question. You're right, the preamble has gone on for long enough; time for the main event. Bring in our guest,' he said to the two demons by the door.

They disappeared.

Dread clawed at Raina's stomach. Who did he have? Caspar? Rose? Her human mother?

But when the demons returned, it was none of them; it was so much worse. Raina stood, took a pace forward, stopped. *Fuck*. This couldn't be ... even Jamie wouldn't sink this low. Her head spun. She grabbed the back of the nearest seat for support, swallowed down the bile rising in her throat. She was living a nightmare.

Caspar sat in the kitchen, nursing a whiskey. It was late, or, more accurately, early. He played the Slayer's last words over and over in his mind. *That bitch is putty in our hands.*

The Slayers and the Templars were working together, and they did have something on Raina. She'd walked into a trap, one she might never walk out of …

That bitch is putty in our hands.

He slammed his fist on the table. One of the dogs ran away. The other came to sit beside him, resting his head on Caspar's leg. Caspar let out a breath and stroked the dog's ears, grateful for the uncomplicated company.

Later, the same thoughts still circling, the door from the great hall crashed open. Gemma hauled in a familiar figure, that of a hunter.

'What's happened?' said Caspar.

'This piece of shit sold you out,' she said, slamming the man's face down onto the table, forcing him to bend at the waist. 'He's been playing us off against the Templars.'

'It was you who told the Templars we'd found Raina?' said Caspar. 'That's why they came after us?'

The hunter said nothing.

'That's not the worst bit,' said Gemma. 'And not how I found out.'

'What then?' said Caspar, perplexed. He hadn't had any other leads from the hunter for some time. Although … 'The commission? What did you find?'

'Tell him,' said Gemma, slamming the man's head against the table again.

'She's awake,' he said, through gritted teeth.

'And?' said Caspar. 'Is she someone we know? Someone important? Someone Jamie wants?'

The hunter gave a half laugh. 'She's Raina's daughter. And, so Jamie claims, his daughter too.'

Caspar went very still, his mind whirling, trying to make sense of the man's words. Could it be possible? Raina's daughter … *his* daughter … alive?

Gemma slammed the man's head so hard that he fell, unconscious, to the ground.

Time stopped for Raina as she took in the scared little girl who'd been shepherded in. The girl looked wildly around, first at the elegantly dressed people, then searching for a place to hide, or a way to run.

There was no familiar leg to hide behind, no comfort. She seemed to shrink, as if by making herself small she'd be forgotten. The girl started to cry.

Raina's heart thundered. She couldn't believe this was happening. She couldn't believe Jamie would do this. Raina ran across the room, calling out her name.

The guards moved to block her. She floored them without effort, dropping to her knees when she reached the terrified little girl.

'Callie,' she said, pulling her in. The adorable little girl who'd lived next door. Her flower girl. The only child with whom she'd ever felt a connection. Raina held her close, and Callie's arms closed, vicelike, around her.

Raina gently pulled back, looking into her eyes, which were … 'Are you …?'

'Demon,' Callie whispered, tears streaming down her face.

'Have they hurt you?'

Callie shook her head. 'No. But they won't let me leave my room. I want Nana.'

Raina pulled her in for another hug. 'It's okay. I'm here now,' she said, stroking Callie's hair.

Jamie was suddenly behind them. 'The most perfect reunion, don't you think? Mother and long-lost child, together at last.'

'What?' whispered Raina.

'Our baby was almost at term when you died. She was a demon. Demons reincarnate. So here we all are: one big happy family.'

Shock hit Raina like a wave, suffocating her. Her daughter?

Emotions flooded her: rage, regret, longing, love. She felt like someone had reached into her chest and taken hold of her heart.

She took a breath, blinking away tears, feeling the gaze of every person in the room upon her. Her heart raced, urging her to grab Callie and run, to fight their way out. But her head knew that was folly; there were too many Templars, and Callie didn't know how to fight.

'How many lifetimes have you had?' asked Raina, stroking Callie's back.

'This is my third,' whispered Callie, still clutching Raina. 'The first was okay, but I died of a disease when I was ten. I was the eighth child of a family with twelve kids, and we all had to work in a factory.

'The second life was horrible. I was four when I woke up. I kept talking about my previous life and everyone thought I was mad. They gave me electric shocks. I'm not sure what happened, but somehow, I died.'

Tears rolled down her cheeks. Raina brushed them away.

'And now I'm here. These people keep saying I'm a demon, but I don't really understand. I just want to go home.' Callie burrowed into Raina's shoulder, her body shaking.

They'd been together, for one brief moment, Caspar and Callie and Raina. How could the world be so cruel? How had they not realized ... how had Caspar not recognized what Callie was ...?

'When did she wake?' asked Raina.

'A week or so ago,' said Jamie. 'A friendly hunter sold us the lead. He thought this one would be of particular interest, given that she has your eyes.'

Raina gasped ... it was true.

'It seems as though Caspar put the hunter onto her,' Jamie went on, 'so I guess we should thank him. And Dean helped too; he made the introduction. It's poetic, don't you think? All the men in your life working together to make you happy.'

Chapter 25

Rose sat at her desk, poring over every intelligence report they had on Jamie, going back lifetimes. It didn't make sense. He'd always put Raina on a pedestal, had worshiped the ground she'd walked on, had professed his love for her. Why the sudden, hostile, demanding shift?

Caspar came hurtling in, not bothering to knock. 'I know what Jamie has on Raina.'

Rose's heart gave a leap; knowledge was power, after all.

'He has our daughter.'

'What?' Rose stared at him, blank-faced. 'How?'

'That little girl we put a hunter on ... the one I met at Amari and Dean's house? It's her.'

Dread dripped through Rose's veins. There was no move they could make. No wonder Jamie had been so bold.

'Then he has her. Hook, line, and sinker,' said Rose, rubbing a hand across her face. 'There's nothing we can do; she's not coming back.'

'We have to get them out.'

Rose gave a small laugh. 'You're suggesting we go into the heart of Templar territory, and steal Jamie's most prized possessions? One of whom is a little girl?'

'Then we lure them out.'

'Jamie would never be so stupid as to bring them out in the open, especially not together. Certainly nowhere we could get to them.'

'Then what do we do?'

'We sit and wait,' said Rose, folding her hands on the desk. 'You know as well as I do, the only viable path is to do nothing. Raina will find a way to communicate with us eventually. She's behind enemy lines. She's the one who must gather intelligence, identify their weaknesses, and come up with a plan to escape.'

Caspar buried his face in his hands. 'I've got to *do* something.'

Rose's features set hard. If there was one thing she couldn't stand, it was old demons acting like kids.

'Then help me scour the intelligence reports. Help me recruit informants. Help me map out Templar movements and hold meetings with other nations. Help me by spreading what we know about the Slayers and Templars working together. Help me find out what Janet's doing at the Registerium. There's no shortage of work.'

Caspar sat, then immediately stood, wincing at the pain from the dagger wound. 'Fine, you're right. But I need to punch something first.'

'Might I suggest sparing with Jon? He could do with being punched.'

Rose's words pierced a tiny hole in his frustration. He gave a small, knowing smile. 'Teenagers ...' he said.

'Be careful of that shoulder. And Caspar,' said Rose, as he walked to the door. 'Remember Raina's the very best we have. If anyone can find a way out, it's her.'

Raina cradled Callie in her lap. Callie clung to her like a limpet.

'They brought another girl to play with me, but she didn't want to play. She was mean.'

'She's a little older than you, that's all,' said Jamie.

Raina scowled at Jamie, but didn't say anything. Trying to get an old demon, who happened to be inside a kid's body, to play with someone who'd never made it past the age of ten, was ludicrous.

'Jamie, she's scared.'

'I'm not very good with kids,' he said, shrugging. 'Not like I've had any experience.'

A statement true of most demons.

Raina had told Jamie to send his guests home. She'd said they had no right to witness their reunion as a family. Jamie had perked up at the word *family*, obviously assuming he was included too.

Now only the three of them remained, along with a couple of demons by the door, out of earshot. Raina and Callie sat on the loveseat, while Jamie paced nearby.

'What's your plan?' Raina asked Jamie, stroking Callie's hair. 'How do you see this working?'

'You'll both stay here with me, of course. We'll be a proper family, the likes of which most demons never are.'

'Here? In this apartment?' said Raina.

'Yes. This is my home.'

'She'll need space for toys, and to learn.'

'Of course. We can change one of the bedrooms into a playroom.'

'What about school?'

Jamie laughed. 'She's not going to school; it's too dangerous. But we can find a tutor to come and teach here.'

'What about friends? People her own age?'

'She doesn't need them,' said Jamie. 'She's got her family. That's all she needs.'

'No,' said Raina, firmly. 'Our daughter needs friends. She needs people she can run around with and make forts with. She needs to be a kid.'

'But she's not a kid! She's had two lives already.'

'Short, gruesome lives, where she experienced nothing but hardship and torture. She's still a child.'

'Okay, fine. What do you suggest?'

'I don't know. Maybe there are afterschool activities she could join. Or classes for homeschooled kids we could take her to.'

'I guess that could work,' said Jamie. 'But no play dates here, or at other people's houses. It would be too easy for our enemies to target you. She can only go to neutral, third-party sites. And our security team have to check them out first.'

'Okay,' said Raina. 'She's going to need demon education as well. We need the best tutors—in everything—even if we have to travel.'

'Out of the question. It's too dangerous.'

'Jamie, we are going to provide our daughter with the best possible education. If that means we have to travel, find a way. I will not keep her cooped up in New York for all time.'

Jamie looked fondly at Raina. 'Okay, if you insist. We can work out what she needs and go from there.'

'Thank you,' said Raina.

'And, of course, you'll need to change nations. Our daughter must have a proper Templar family. Callie's already been registered.'

'I didn't see a public notice for anyone called Callie,' said Raina, confused. 'What's your demon name?'

'I don't like my other names. I want to be called Callie.'

'The Registerium agreed to hold off on the announcement until I'd delivered the news to you in person,' said Jamie.

'That's unprecedented,' said Raina.

'So is our situation,' Jamie said with a smile.

It wasn't, but no good would come from arguing.

Raina put Callie to bed in the huge double bedroom Jamie had given her, right next to his room. There were virtually no toys, only antiques and beautiful fabrics. That would need to change.

Callie's head was in Raina's lap. Her hands clutched the fabric of Raina's dress, her knuckles white.

'It's all going to be okay,' said Raina, running her hand across Callie's back in soothing strokes.

'They … they …' Callie broke down. Her tears soaked Raina's dress.

'Shhh,' said Raina, 'it's going to be okay now. I'm here.'

'They killed my Nana,' Callie choked.

Raina went still. 'What makes you think that?'

Callie lifted her head and looked Raina straight in the eye, tears streaming down her face. 'I saw it. They came to our house and took me. Nana tried to stop them … they … they had a knife …'

Raina pulled Callie onto her lap. Callie rested her head on Raina's shoulder, her little body shaking with grief.

'It's all going to be okay. No one will hurt you now.'

Rage boiled white hot in Raina's gut. She might have to bide her time, to gather allies, to plan. But that was her forte: strategy. Jamie had won the first battle, but Raina knew how to win wars.

Callie finally slept. Raina stroked her hair, even after Callie's breathing became light and even. She still couldn't believe her little girl was right here ... after everything she and Caspar had gone through.

She eventually pulled herself away, going back to the living room, now occupied by Jamie, Tamsin, and Dean. She curled up inside.

'Ah, darling,' said Jamie, beckoning her to him, putting his hand on her back.

Raina fought the urge to shrug him off, but caught the daggers Tamsin threw her way; it made the contact a little easier to bear.

'We were just discussing what to do with Dean.'

'What do you mean?' said Raina. 'He's nobody. Throw him out on the street and never think of him again.'

'He knows too much for that,' said Jamie, rubbing circles on her back.

'He knows nothing,' said Raina. 'Look at him; he's scared half to death.'

'He's my brother,' said Tamsin. 'I should decide.'

Dean looked relieved, until Tamsin pulled out a knife.

'Jade,' Dean said, 'what are you doing?'

Tamsin advanced towards him.

'Jade, stop joking around. I'm not going to say anything to anyone. I don't even understand what's going on.'

'You've always been a patronizing pain in my ass. I'm tired of it,' said Tamsin.

'You're going to let her do this?' Raina asked Jamie.

He didn't reply, watching Tamsin instead.

'Oh, please,' Tamsin said to her. 'I'd be doing Jamie a favor. My brother obviously still has feelings for you. And if I'm not much mistaken, you have feelings for him too.'

'I've heard enough,' said Dean, puffing himself up to his full height. 'Jade, I don't know what the hell is going on here … what Amari's got you into … but I will come back for you.' He turned and strode for the exit.

They let him get all the way to the steps, let his confidence in escape grow, before one of Jamie's guards appeared. With a small incline of Jamie's head, the guard stepped into Dean's path.

Dean laughed, still not comprehending the danger he was in. 'I'm going to sue you people for everything you've got. When I'm done with you …'

The guard sprang forward, and a loud, sickening crack reverberated around the room. Dean went down, clutching the arm now hanging limp by his side.

'Bring him here,' said Tamsin, the picture of calm.

The guard immediately obeyed, forcing Dean to his knees in front of Tamsin.

'I think we've all had enough of you, *brother.*'

'Oh, I see,' said Raina, smiling a wicked smile.

She stepped toward Tamsin, out of Jamie's grasp. She no longer loved Dean, but she had, as Amari. She owed it to him to at least try …

'You think by eliminating Dean, Jamie's going to see what you're made of, and choose you over me? Or maybe you're jealous, and want to take your anger at me out on your brother. You know you can't fight me and win, so you're going to kill an innocent human instead.'

Tamsin turned slowly to face Raina. 'You are irrelevant to me,' she said.

'Young demons are so disappointingly transparent, don't you think, Jamie?' said Raina.

Jamie smirked. 'That they are, my dear. But sometimes they're diverting.'

'You find this *diverting*?' said Raina. 'You haven't seen enough pointless executions for them all to blend together into a tedious mass?'

'Execution?' Dean rasped.

The word finally woke him to the gravity of his situation. He cast wildly around for an escape, but the guard's grip was firm.

Tamsin chuckled. 'There's the reaction I wanted to see.'

'Some stand out,' said Jamie. 'I think this'll be one of them.'

Bitter cold swept through Raina; there was nothing she could do. Callie was her priority, and trying to save Dean would not only result in failure, but jeopardize her chances of escape.

She looked at Dean one final time, then flicked her gaze to Jamie, her eyes full of scorn. 'Do what you want, but I'm bored; I'm going to bed.'

She made it five paces before she heard the knife go in, the suction as it came out, the thud of something heavy hitting the floor. She halted, closed her eyes, then resumed, making a point of not looking back. She couldn't show weakness; Callie was all that mattered now.

Caspar lay in Raina's bed in Cloister Cottage. The sheets had long since been changed, all trace of her gone, but he could still see her next to him if he closed his eyes.

The first rays of sunlight punctured the room, casting in shadow the towering London skyscrapers beyond. It was the middle of the night in New York. Was Raina asleep? Had she seen their daughter? Was she in bed with Jamie ...?

Caspar had unwittingly led the Templars right to Callie ... his daughter. Did Raina know that? Did she hate him for it?

A sudden impact hit Caspar in the chest, winding him, panic crashing over him. *What the hell?*

He was being crushed, the pressure intensifying, the air and his life being squeezed from his lungs. And then, a surge of ... something else, pulling the pressure wave that pinned him back to sea. A voice followed—Raina's voice—inside his head.

I'm okay. I'm with our daughter. I love you.

The words repeated, again and again, growing louder, then gradually fading away.

Caspar tried to hold onto the sound, willed it to come back. He concentrated on listening as hard as he could. He tried to send magic after it, to let Raina know he'd received her message, that he loved her too. But his grasp of magic was a pathetic thing, useless and inadequate.

He hoped that somehow, she knew.

Two days later, Raina sat in a park near Jamie's house, watching Callie play. She couldn't help but smile as her daughter chased the other kids, and was chased in return. This was all she'd wanted, for lifetimes. She had to remind herself of that as she mourned her loss of Caspar.

At least the sending had worked. Her magic was rusty at best, and even that small use had left her drained, but it had worked.

Jamie sat beside her, handing her a coffee.

'There are things we should discuss,' he said.

'Like what?' asked Raina, her tone neutral, conveying none of the hate she felt towards him.

'Like how we solidify our family by your joining the Templars. You never know ... maybe we could have more kids.'

Raina nearly threw her coffee at him. The thought made her skin crawl.

'What about Tamsin?'

Jamie laughed. 'She's a natural Templar; awoke just in time. So strange, the Powers That Be, putting you all together.'

'What could possibly make you think I'd have a relationship with you, while you're screwing her, and who knows who else? And *if* I become a Templar ...'

'... *when* you become a Templar,' said Jamie.

'You'll promise not to go to war?'

'For the time being.'

'I'm a Pagan. I always have been. Forcing my hand isn't an act of love.'

'It's an act of love from you, for our family.' He turned to face her, agitated, his façade finally coming down, casting light on the vulnerable man beneath. 'Are you loyal to me? You told me, in the last life, that you loved me ... wanted me. That you just needed time to move on from Caspar.'

'Do you love me?' said Raina. 'From the way you draped Tamsin across your lap, it would seem not. I thought we had something meaningful, exclusive. And now, what am I supposed to think? That you want me to be one of many women?'

'I wanted you to join in,' he said, with a smirk.

'Jamie.'

'Okay,' he said, facing forward, his eyes tracking Callie. 'No other women, unless you tell me I can.'

Raina huffed out a disbelieving breath. 'You think it's going to be that easy? I need proof before anything happens between us.'

Jamie laughed. 'You can't prove a negative.'

'I need to know where you are and who you're with at all times. I need to know you're not alone with another woman.'

'You're growing paranoid, and dare I say needy, in your old age.'

'Don't insult me. I'd be stupid not to be cautious,' said Raina.

'And what about me? How do I know I can trust you?'

Raina turned to face Jamie. He met her gaze.

'Have I not been loyal to you for many lives? Fed you information? Sold out other nations? And anyway, my daughter's under your control. You know I'll never turn my back on blood.'

A week later, Raina and Jamie sat in a swanky steak restaurant. Raina wore a little black dress Jamie had picked out, with her hair swept off her face in an elegant arrangement.

This had been Raina's single romantic concession. In the time she'd been with the Templars, Jamie had taken her everywhere: to meetings, to the gym, shopping. He'd shown her every text message he'd sent or received, hadn't excluded her from a single conversation. That's not to say Raina liked everything Jamie was doing. He was manipulating everyone he could—humans and demons alike—but at least she knew about it.

Tamsin had been an endless thorn in Raina's side: forever present, forever flirting, forever trying to find an edge. Raina ignored her, but resisting the urge to knock her out was exhausting.

'Tamsin's been conspicuous in her absence today,' said Raina, sipping her blood-red wine.

'I sent her away, so her brooding presence would no longer bring us all down.'

Thank the Gods. 'Where did you send her?'

'To the West Coast, to meet with the new demon nation there. They're in territory we've been trying to secure for a while. The lands are registered to a secretive, seemingly independent demon. We've been trying to track him down, and then this new nation sprang up. They keep to themselves, but we need to know where they stand, for our security.'

'In case you go to war,' said Raina.

'War's an inevitability, you know that as well as the next demon. It never hurts to be prepared.'

'Do you think it'll happen in this lifetime?' asked Raina, swirling her wine.

'I should think so,' he said, cryptically.

'Why?'

'This isn't what I'd hoped we'd talk about tonight,' said Jamie, leaning across the table. He took her hand.

'What had you hoped to discuss?'

He linked their fingers. 'How long it's going to be before you join me in my bed.'

He looked in her eyes, his expression somehow both seductive and humorous. Despite herself, Raina felt the familiar electric spark of attraction between them. She looked down, paused, ran her eyes slowly up his torso, then flicked them up to meet his gaze. His pupils dilated.

'How many other women have there been, in this lifetime?' Raina asked.

Jamie sat back. 'I've slept with many, although usually only once or twice with each. Tamsin's been diverting for a few weeks; we had flings in previous lives, so she knows what I like. Aside from her, there was only one other longer-term arrangement. She's now dead.'

'And you think a single week of effort will land me in your bed?'

Jamie chuckled. 'A guy can hope.'

Raina shook her head. 'Not in this lifetime.'

The following morning, Raina came down to breakfast to find a group of unfamiliar demons sitting at the island in the kitchen.

'Raina,' said Jamie, 'come join us. We're going over the documents for your nation transfer.'

'My nation transfer?'

'You needed proof I'm loyal to you, and I've shown you I am. Now I need proof of my own. All you have to do is sign the paperwork,' said Jamie.

'Leaving the first part of that aside, a nation transfer requires me to visit the Registerium, to show I'm not under duress, to press my hand against the standing stone,' said Raina.

'Yes, well, the Registerium's willing to overlook those formalities this time. They're happy for you to put your hand on one of the stones in North America, and you can confirm it in Scotland at a future date.'

'That's not how the magic works,' said Raina, frowning.

'There'll be a video call where you can show you're not under duress,' said Jamie, 'and we'll email the paperwork.'

'I just told you, the magic doesn't work that way. If I put my hand on a stone here, nothing will happen. When the Registerium was founded, they added a condition that nation transfers could only take place through the stone at the castle.'

'Then we'll do the magic mumbo-jumbo later. The Registerium agreed to this approach. We have all we need to go ahead,' said Jamie.

'Magic mumbo-jumbo?'

'Magic's been outdated for at least a century.'

Raina's magic kindled. Did he really know so little?

'The Registerium's happy with this? It's against every rule in their book,' she said.

'They agreed, given the circumstances, that special dispensation should be granted.'

'Without a vote of nation representatives?'

'They were happy to make the decision autonomously in this case. A new era's dawning; the Registerium recognizes that fact.'

'Will you ever complete my transfer through the Scottish stone? Assuming I agree to transfer at all, of course.'

'Oh, probably, just so nobody can dispute your belonging to the Templar nation. But only when it's convenient, and when it's safe. And we both know, you'll agree to the transfer.'

'Do we?'

'If you don't transfer, you'll never see your daughter again. Not in this lifetime, at least, and in no future lifetime if I have anything to do with it.'

'Why's this so important to you?' asked Raina, holding back her emotions, not letting her face betray her hatred. Nobody got away with treating her this way.

'Because you and I together are unstoppable. Your brain, experience, and reputation, coupled with my resources. We'll be the most formidable partnership in history. You've made king after king, queen after queen. If you say I'm the rightful leader of the demon world, people will believe it.'

'I've never made a demon king.'

'You've made nation leaders.'

'Yes, but only when there was a need. What claim do you have to be king of all demons? All nations?'

Jamie smiled. 'Don't worry about that for now. Just sign the paperwork and make the call. And, Raina …' his tone turned cruel, 'don't ever doubt I mean what I say.'

Caspar, Rose, Talli, and Christa were in the great hall, completing a cleansing ritual. There had, after all, been a great deal of negativity in the cottage, with first the Slayer, and then the hunter.

Talli had placed only a single foot inside before demanding to know what had happened, saying she could feel the disturbance. She'd run for the sage plant, had smudged as an immediate fix, then began an elaborate ritual to properly sort the place out.

'Ahhhh, that feels so much better,' said Talli, lying back against the cold stone floor. 'Can you feel the positivity all around us? It's like a tonic to the soul.'

'It does feel calmer,' said Caspar, sitting with his back to the wall. The past few days had taken it out of him; he felt as though he could sleep for a lifetime.

Rose's phone vibrated and she pulled it out.

'Rose, what have I told you about mobile phones in here?' said Talli. 'You're ruining the balance.'

Rose ignored her, taking time to read, deep lines appearing on her forehead.

'Oh Gods,' said Caspar, sitting upright. 'What's happened?'

He hadn't had a sending of distress from Raina, but that didn't mean she wasn't in any.

'Raina's switched to the Templar nation,' said Rose.

'In Scotland?' asked Christa.

'No. The Registerium has approved the application without the transfer having been sealed in magic,' said Rose.

'Then it doesn't count,' said Talli. 'She's not really a Templar.'

'According to the Registerium, she is,' said Rose. 'Malcolm's filed a complaint, although I'm not holding my breath. Apparently, the Templars are planning to complete the transfer in Scotland at a later date. Pablo—the record keeper—is furious, according to Malcolm.'

'We're supposed to be notified of the switching ceremony,' said Talli. 'We're supposed to be able to attend, to make sure there's no duress, to try and convince the switchee not to do it.'

'Raina may be under duress,' said Caspar, 'but she would've switched regardless. The Templars have our daughter. As long as that's the case, Raina will do whatever Jamie wants.'

'We have to find out when they're planning on making it official,' said Christa. 'Maybe they'll take Callie to Scotland too. Maybe we can get them both back.'

'They won't,' said Caspar. 'Jamie's not stupid.'

'And the Registerium's protected by powerful magic against such schemes,' said Talli. 'There can be no kidnapping of demons while on Registerium territory, nor while travelling to or from the Registerium. If you try, you die.'

'Does the magic still stand, given that the Registerium is so badly compromised?' asked Caspar.

'It's never that simple with magic,' said Talli. 'Intention's a big factor. Does the Registerium know they're acting in a corrupt manner, or do they believe they're fulfilling their mission? The political structure is supposed to keep them in check, but it appears that's been circumnavigated. So maybe everything the Registerium's doing is no longer protected by magic. Or maybe they've found a way to change the magic without needing the support of all nations.'

'How do we find out?' said Christa.

'We need a proficient, or better yet, an adept,' said Rose.

'Are there any adepts left?' asked Caspar.

'I think so,' said Talli, 'but they're secretive. It would take time to track them down ... maybe even lifetimes.'

'Then we should begin the search,' said Rose, 'and call in every magical Pagan we've got.'

'Even the neos?' asked Talli.

'Everyone,' said Rose. 'We need all the help we can get.'

I hope you enjoyed *Nation of the Sun* and, if you did, would really appreciate a rating or review on Amazon, Goodreads, Instagram, or any other place you can think of ... authors aren't fussy! Just a rating, a few words, or a line or two would be absolute perfection, and will help others find my books. Thank you for your support.

To be the first to hear all my latest news, get book recommendations, and find out about giveaways, sign up to my newsletter here:
https://www.subscribepage.com/r2a0n6_copy2

CONNECT WITH HR MOORE

Check out HR Moore's website, where you can also sign up to her newsletter:
http://www.hrmoore.com/

Find HR Moore on Instagram and Twitter:
@HR_Moore

Follow @authorhrmoore on TikTok

See what the world of *Nation of the Sun* looks like on Pinterest:
https://www.pinterest.com/authorhrmoore/nation-of-the-sun/

Like the HR Moore page on Facebook:
https://www.facebook.com/authorhrmoore

Follow HR Moore on Goodreads:
https://www.goodreads.com/author/show/7228761.H_R_Moore

ACKNOWLEDGEMENTS

Thank you SO SO much to everyone who's helped get this book out in the world. To my hard arse beta readers (and the softer ones too), thank you for your honest feedback and insights. To my editor, Jeff Deck, for making me a better writer. To my family, for putting up with me when I ignore them. To the whole FaRoFeb community, for being so utterly brilliant. And most of all, to my wonderful readers. Thank you so much for your support - it means the world.

TITLES BY HR MOORE

The Relic Trilogy:
Queen of Empire
Temple of Sand
Court of Crystal

In the Gleaming Light

The Ancient Souls Series:
Nation of the Sun

http://www.hrmoore.com